SWEPT INTO LOVE

THE RYDERS

LOVE IN BLOOM SERIES

MELISSA FOSTER

ISBN-10: 1-941480-67-5
ISBN-13: 978-1-941480-67-0

This is a work of fiction. The events and characters described herein are imaginary and are not intended to refer to specific places or living persons. The opinions expressed in this manuscript are solely the opinions of the author and do not represent the opinions or thoughts of the publisher. The author has represented and warranted full ownership and/or legal right to publish all the materials in this book.

SWEPT INTO LOVE

V1.0

Cover Design: Elizabeth Mackey Designs

WORLD LITERARY PRESS
PRINTED IN THE UNITED STATES OF AMERICA

A NOTE FROM MELISSA

The best way to stay up to date on my releases is to sign up for my newsletter:
www.MelissaFoster.com/News

If this is your first introduction to the Ryders, every book is written as a stand-alone, so jump right in and enjoy! For those who have read the entire Love in Bloom series, beginning with the Snow Sisters, you've waited a long time to read about Gage and Sally. Their love did not take me by surprise, but their story sure did. It's fun, emotional, and riddled with all the ups and downs you'd expect from a friends-to-lovers, second-chance, single-parent romance. I hope you enjoy their story as much as I do.

Be sure to read past the end of the book for a preview chapter of EMBRACING HER HEART, the first book in the Montgomery series! This new series is fun, sexy, and oh so sassy! I know you'll love it!

ABOUT THE RYDERS

The Ryders are a series of stand-alone romances that may be enjoyed in any order or as part of the larger Love in Bloom big-family romance collection (40+ awesome books). You can jump into the series anywhere. The characters from each family appear in other Love in Bloom subseries, so you never miss an engagement, wedding, or birth. For more information on the Love in Bloom series visit www.melissafoster.com/LIB

THE RYDERS

Seized by Love (Blue & Lizzie)

Claimed by Love (Duke & Gabriella)

Chased by Love (Trish & Boone)

Rescued by Love (Jake & Addy)

Swept into Love (Gage & Sally)

Download a FREE Love in Bloom series list:
www.MelissaFoster.com/SO
Download a FREE family tree and more here:
www.MelissaFoster.com/RG

Chapter One

SALLY TUFT AWOKE to a freight train running through her head and the worst cotton mouth she'd ever experienced. She lay on her back, eyes closed, trying to remember what happened last night after the conference she'd attended. Thank God what happened in Vegas stayed in Vegas, because she didn't need her boss finding out she got rip-roaring drunk. She rolled onto her side, coming face-to-face with hot whiskey breath. Her eyes flew open and she bolted upright, clutching the sheet to her chest. Her heart pounded wildly as she took in the gorgeous sandy-haired man lying next to her. *Oh shit! Shit, shit, shit!*

No. This can't be happening.

She slammed her eyes shut, trying to calm her mounting panic by breathing deeply, but that made her head hurt even worse.

Her eyes opened slowly, roving over Gage Ryder's scruffy jaw and the full lips she'd fantasized about so many times she should be arrested. This was bad. *Very bad.* Gage had been her best friend and co-worker since her husband was killed in a skiing accident several years ago. And worse, he was her son's confidant. The man whom Rusty went to with problems his father was no longer there to help him with.

Her gaze trailed over his broad shoulders and muscular chest as realization set in. She bit her lower lip, holding her breath as she lifted the sheet. *Please let me have something on. At least underwear.* The pit of her stomach twisted at the sight of her closer-to-forty-than-thirty, less-than-perky bare breasts, and stomach that had never quite regained its elasticity after having her now twenty-year-old son. *Oh God!*

Gage rolled onto his back, and her eyes were drawn to the formidable bulge lifting the sheets. *Look away. Look away.*

She couldn't look away. He'd made his feelings for her clear without ever actually spelling them out. Would *he* mind if she looked? *Oh God! I should mind!* She needed to force those desires back into Ignore mode. Closing her eyes and gritting her teeth, she tried to do just that. But the urge to look was too strong, and they popped open again, drinking in every hard inch of him.

His left arm stretched over his head, coming to rest on the pillow. The other reached beneath the sheet and adjusted himself. Her nipples prickled to tight points. Now was *not* the time to get turned on, but she couldn't stop staring as he sleepily pushed the sheet down his chest, revealing solid abs she'd seen a million times—but never once in *bed.* They were sexier than when he was playing basketball or chopping wood to heat his home. Oh God, she loved to watch him chop wood.

Her eyes moved to the *other* wood in sight. She heard a whimpering sound and realized it came from her. She snapped her mouth shut. She had to get out of there before he woke up and realized what they'd done.

What if *he* remembered what happened—*or didn't*—last night? She was never going to drink again. Not in this lifetime, and definitely not with Gage Ryder.

She clutched the sheet and slid to the edge of the bed, struggling to dredge up memories of last night from the muddled recesses of her mind, but her head was spinning. At least her hangover had taken a backseat to the reality of having slept with *Gage*. He rolled toward her as she stepped quietly from the bed. The sheet caught beneath him and pulled from around her. She gasped, her hands darting to cover all her private parts as Gage's amused blue eyes opened and followed her frantic hands. A slow smile crept across his gorgeous face. She needed more hands! She yanked the sheet from the bed and turned around.

"Don't look!" she yelled as she tried to wrap it around her. "Oh my God. *Gage*!"

"Sally…?"

"Don't say a word. *Wait*. Please tell me we didn't have sex. Just…" She shook her head and spun around, bringing Gage and all his naked glory into full view. For a second she was struck mute, her jaw hanging open. His thick arousal lay nestled between powerful thighs, on a manicured tuft of dirty-blond hair.

"See something you want?" Gage said with a chuckle, snapping her brain into gear.

"You're naked!" She spun around again, breathing so hard she feared she might pass out.

"You whipped the sheet off me," he said far too casually.

"*I'm* naked!"

"I see that, and I prefer you without the sheet."

"Gage!" She huffed. "Put a pillow over yourself! Cover that thing up."

He sighed loudly and she heard the rustling of the pillow.

"Okay, Salbird. I'm covered, but given that we're both naked, I'm pretty sure you got more than an eyeful last night."

Salbird. The first time he'd called her that they'd been at a party at Danica's house. Danica was Gage and Sally's boss at No

Limitz Youth Center. In addition to that, she and her husband, Blake, were two of Gage and Sally's closest friends. As everyone mingled around the party, Gage put a hand on her lower back and whispered, *Can I get you a drink, Salbird?* He'd flashed that boyish smile of his, and the endearment had stuck. Sometimes he just called her *bird.* It was a silly endearment, but it sounded magical coming off his lips. To this day it made her feel special in a way nothing else ever had, and though she'd wanted to know why a man she'd only recently met had likened her to a bird, she'd never asked. She didn't want to spoil the magic. But what if last night spoiled the magic?

She faced him again, tears stinging her eyes as she tried not to stare at his tempting body. "Did we…?"

"You don't remember?"

He sounded disappointed and confused, and it made her heart hurt for too many reasons. "I…um…Do *you*?"

He cocked a brow, his lips tipping up at the edges. It was the kind of answer a guy gave when he didn't want to commit one way or the other, and she knew him well enough to understand that he was playing it safe. If he didn't remember, he thought she'd be hurt. And if he did, she'd be humiliated.

She sank down to the bed, tears rolling down her cheeks. "Gage. How could we have done this? I'm so embarrassed." All these years she'd wondered what it would be like to kiss him, to be in his arms, to see him gazing deeply into her eyes as she made love to the only man besides her deceased husband she'd ever wanted—and the only one she shouldn't have. Between Rusty and their jobs, there was too much at risk. And now she'd blown it. Not only had they slept together, but she'd been so drunk, she couldn't even enjoy the memories of their only night together.

"I'm the last person you should be embarrassed with."

He touched her arm, something he'd done so many times she knew the feel of each of his fingers, but as he moved closer and his lips touched her shoulder, it felt different, sending heat and confusion cascading through her.

"*Shh*. Sal. It's okay." He brushed her hair over one shoulder. "You know how I feel about you."

He felt too good, sounded too reassuring. She pushed to her feet and paced to try to calm her racing heart. She knew exactly how he felt about her. He was always there when she needed him, even when she didn't realize she did.

They'd met months after she'd lost her husband, but the hurt had still been just beneath the surface. He'd been right there with her as she'd waded through the lingering devastation, and he'd helped Rusty deal with his anger toward his father for leaving behind a world of misunderstanding about a son—Chase, a half brother to Rusty—they hadn't known about. Gage had taken the brunt of Rusty's rage, and now he and Rusty were too close for her to jeopardize their relationship for her own happiness.

"This is anything *but* okay," she said adamantly. "The last thing I remember is having drinks and celebrating the new youth center. How did we get drunk enough to do *this*?" They'd come to Vegas for a youth management conference, as they had been tasked to open a new center in Oak Falls, Virginia, where they were due to arrive later today.

"Jesus, Sal." Irritation rose in his eyes. "You make it sound like sleeping with me is a horrible fate."

"That's not what I mean and you know it." She stared out the window and caught sight of her reflection in the glass. Her normally straight hair stood up in the kind of wild tangles that came from a man's hands during fits of passion.

From Gage's hands.

She swallowed hard, wishing she could remember the feel of them, see the heat in his eyes as he buried himself deep inside her. Great. Now she was thinking about having sex with him.

She looked at the clock. "We're going to miss our flight. I have to go to my room and get ready."

"Sally, wait. Let's talk."

"We've obviously *talked* enough."

Gage pushed to his feet, carrying the pillow in front of him as she ran around plucking her bra from a chair by the window and her dress from where it lay crumpled at the foot of the bed. *Evidence of our drunken fuckfest. A fuckfest I don't even remember.* Renewed panic shot through her. She wasn't on birth control. She spun around looking for her panties and trying not to completely freak out. She spotted her heels lying by the door and a condom wrapper beneath the edge of the bed. *Oh, thank God.* Memories of last night came back to her in stilted flashes, like an old movie reel. She remembered stumbling through the hotel room door as they kissed. She shuddered with the memory of her back hitting the wall and Gage's hard body pressed against her, and his mouth—*Lord, his hot, delicious mouth*—had trailed down her neck, her chest…

Gage bent down, fishing around in the bottom of the sheet draped around her, startling her from her erotic thoughts.

"Sweetheart, this is not the end of the world. So we had too many celebratory shots." He rose to his full height of six three or four, big and broad and so freaking hot her breath left her lungs. He lifted his hand and dangled her thong from his finger.

"Maybe not for you." She snagged the tiny strip of material, feeling her cheeks burn. She pulled on the thong beneath the sheet, trying not to think about his kisses, or how they had led to sex, which she desperately wished she could remember.

"Don't be ridiculous," he said with an annoyed expression. "We're adults, and we're totally into each other. This was meant to be."

"We're *friends*. It's not like that between us and you know it." It was partially true. They'd never crossed the line between friends and lovers before, even if she wanted to.

"But it *could* be." Gage stepped closer, heating up the temperature in the room by fifty degrees. "It *can* be." His arm circled her waist from behind, and he kissed her neck. "I *want* it to be."

She closed her eyes, fighting tears. "Gage," she whispered in a shaky voice. "Don't you get it? Rusty needs you more than we need each other."

"Why are you and I and he and I mutually exclusive?" He turned her toward him, his expression serious, his jaw tight. "You know I love you both. I have for years, Sally, and I know you feel the same for me."

Her heart reached out, capturing his confession, reveling in it, even if for only one painful moment. She knew she couldn't enjoy it, not at Rusty's expense, and she tucked Gage's words, and her feelings, away once again.

"What we feel doesn't matter," she insisted. "I'm not selfish enough to do that to my son."

Confusion—anger? hurt?—rose in his eyes. "What the hell does that even mean?"

"Rusty *lost* his father, Gage. He turns to you for everything. If you and I tried to be a couple and it didn't work, I'd be screwing him out of the best thing in his life, the one person who helped him find his footing again. I can't risk that."

"Bullshit, Sally." He tightened his hold on her arms. "Whether we're together or not, I'd never disappear from Rusty's life."

His eyes were trained on her, challenging and angry, and still, beneath it all, she saw the surety of his love and the friendship that had always been there, driving the pain of their situation even deeper.

She twisted from his grip and reached for her phone on the nightstand. "But it would never be the same. Not for him and not for us. I can't—" Her gaze caught on the papers beneath her phone. She lifted them with a shaky hand, scanning the marriage certificate and a receipt for something called an Elvis Hound Dog Wedding. "*Ohmygod.* What have we done?"

"What is it?" He peered over her shoulder, his hot breath momentarily distracting her from the papers. "Well, hot damn, Salbird. Looks like we're *married*."

"This doesn't mean…It's got to be a joke." She shifted the remaining papers on the dresser and gasped at the sight of a photograph of her and Gage kissing beside a heavyset man dressed in full Elvis garb, his arms outstretched, as if he were presenting them to the camera. Above them, a sign read VIVA LAS VEGAS WEDDING CHAPEL.

Gage lifted her left hand, revealing black marker circling her ring finger. They both glanced at his left hand. A matching black ring circled his third finger.

AFTER A SIX-hour-plus stressful flight to Virginia, Gage's patience was wearing thin. Sally refused to talk about their situation. It felt like he'd been given the gift of a lifetime and then it had been stolen away. He was elated to find himself married to the woman who had captured his heart from the first day he'd met her, and equally torn apart by how hard she was pushing him away. He drove the rental car down the quiet roads of Oak Falls, Virginia, where they were spending most of the next week putting infrastructure into place for the new youth center before returning to Allure, Colorado, on Friday. He'd thought setting up the new location would be his big break in getting Sally alone and finally asking her out on a real date. He'd never imagined they'd already be married by the time they arrived. Now, if only he could convince her it wasn't the end of life as she knew it.

Gage cut the engine and reached for her hand, brushing his thumb over the faded ink on her finger. She must have scrubbed the hell out of it, because his was still black as night despite his own shower. He met her troubled baby blues, hurting for her. "We need to talk about this, Sal."

She shook her head. "I can't even begin to wrap my head around it. I've not only slept with you and I don't even remember most of it, but we're *married. Married*, Gage. Do you even understand how big a commitment this is? It impacts every aspect of our lives."

"You don't remember *most* of it?" He couldn't stop the grin tugging at his lips. "Then you remember *some* of it?"

She laughed under her breath as she turned away, staring out the window. "Way to skip over the important part. How can you make fun of this? This is a huge mistake. We have to get an annulment. We need a lawyer, and we have so much to do here—"

"Annulment?" *No fucking way.* "I don't want an annulment."

"Gage," she said with an incredulous look. "We've never even dated."

"The hell we haven't. We've spent years unofficially dating. We're closer than most married couples."

She crossed her arms, her gaze darting over the dashboard, out the window, anywhere but to him. He leaned across the console and took her chin between his finger and thumb, turning her toward him, and searched her eyes for the truth. Did she really want an annulment?

"You know it's true, Sally. You can't deny it. We do everything together—go to weddings, visit Rusty, go to the freaking grocery store, for God's sake."

"Those things don't make two people a *couple*. Marriage is complicated and difficult, and you've never even asked me out on a date. We can't be married."

And there it was, the topic they'd been dancing around for too many years to count. Every time he got close to asking her out, she skirted the subject. They did go everywhere together, to the point that everyone else thought of them as a couple, but they'd never bridged that gap. Well, it was about damn time they did.

"I never asked you out because you never seemed ready," he said honestly. He had no idea how much time was enough after someone lost their spouse. He'd played it safe, waiting for a sign. Sally wasn't a drinker, and last night she'd drank a *lot* and hung on to him like he was *hers*, and damn it, from what he could remember, those were pretty big signs.

She threw open her car door, and cold November air rushed in. "Then what makes you think I'm ready for *marriage*? I can't. I just can't..."

She stepped from the car, and he flew out his door and

closed the distance between them. "Sally, listen to me, please. I'm confused about what happened last night, too, but I'm not confused about us. You have to know how badly I've wanted you for all this time."

"I do, but, *Rusty*…" Tears welled in her eyes.

"And what about you? What do *you* want?" *Me. Say you want me.*

She leaned back against the car and tipped her beautiful face up toward the sky. She tucked her straight white-blond hair behind her ear, fidgeting with the ends. An adorable nervous trait.

"I don't know what I want," she said shakily. "My heart and my head are at odds."

Hope swelled inside him. "Then don't make a decision right now. Give us time to digest last night. There has to be a reason you married me, drunk or not."

She pressed her lips together and a single tear slid down her cheek. He cupped her face, wiping it away, his heart aching for both of them.

"Why do you fight us so hard?" The question came without any thought, but now that it was out there, he wanted answers. "How can you step back when all I want to do is move forward?"

Her eyes shifted away again, drifting over the cars parked nearby, but he was still holding her face, and he wasn't about to let go.

"Sal, I never pushed you, did I? I gave you time to grieve for Dave. Wasn't it enough? If you need more time…" It had been almost six years since Dave's accident, and most of the time Sally seemed okay. Though Gage had to admit, there were moments when she'd zone out and he knew in his gut it had to do with losing her husband. Those moments nearly drove him to his knees. He knew she'd been with Dave since she was in high school, and he couldn't imagine the pain she must feel. He didn't want to be a jerk, but he really didn't know how much longer he could go on as friends when he wanted so much more. He hadn't realized until just now how much hope he'd pinned on this trip.

She blinked her eyes dry. "This isn't about Dave. I've moved on from losing him. You of all people know that."

"Are you afraid I'll hurt you the way Dave hurt you when you found out about Chase?" After Dave died, Sally found out that he had been secretly seeing Chase and his mother, Trisha, trying to build a relationship with them before he revealed the truth to his family. Sally had confided in him enough to know that it had cut her to her core, and he had a feeling that hurt still lingered.

"No! Why would I be? You're as honest as the day is long. And it's not like he cheated on me. He was a few years older than me, and he got some woman pregnant before we even met. It wasn't his fault she never told him about the baby. The only thing he did wrong was not telling me right when he found out."

He was at a loss as to why, but it was clear that convincing Sally to let down her guard and explore her feelings for him would be an uphill battle. But Gage was an athlete, and he'd climb as many mountains as it took. With Sally as the prize, he wasn't about to slow down.

"Then what are you afraid of? Tell me so I can fix it. Don't throw us away before we even have a chance to get started."

"I'm not. That's just it. I *love* our friendship," she said softly. "And I've dreamed about it being more. A *lot* more. But I'm terrified. Not just for Rusty, but for me, for *us*."

"Why? Let me in, Sally, because I don't understand. I think last night was fate. We didn't just sleep together. We got *married*. It's what was meant to be. You and I are bigger than rational thoughts of what should or shouldn't be. We always have been. So please, tell me what else is holding you back."

She drew in a deep breath, her gaze trailing over his face, conflicting emotions staring back at him. "I've had a happy marriage, and I lost it. I know how much that hurts. Yes, I've gotten over it, but I don't want a reason to get *over* you. And if we try this, and break up—"

"Then stop pulling away." He stepped closer, holding her as he'd wanted to for so long, as a boyfriend and a lover, not just a friend. *As a husband*, he reminded himself. Something he'd been afraid to dream about.

"There's a world of difference between friendship and spouses, Gage. Sex complicates everything. And marriage? It's a world in and of itself, with misunderstandings, compromises, and finding ways to reignite sparks that dim over time. It's not easy."

"Sally, I haven't been with another woman in years, and nothing about relationships is easy."

"*Years*?" she whispered. "Really?"

He nodded. How could she not know that? He spent nearly every weekend evening hanging out with her. "Yes, and considering neither of us really remembers last night, I'm not sure the sex we had qualifies for the complications you're talking about anyway, unless we do it again. *Sober*." He waggled his brows, earning a small smile, which gave him a thread of hope, and he clung to it like a lifeline.

"Sal, we've got almost a week before we go back to our real

lives. Rusty isn't here. Danica and your friends aren't here. There's just you and me," he said, hoping the worry in her eyes might dissipate with the reminder that no one was there to judge them, or whatever else she might be worried about. "Let's explore what this is, take a leap of faith. Let me take you out on dates and show you how good a boyfriend—a husband—I can be, how good we can be together as a couple. Let's hold hands and make out until you *can't* forget how it feels."

Her smile widened, but she bit her lower lip, blinking up at him with shyness that tugged at his heart. He loved her so much, he wasn't about to let her get away. Stepping even closer, he slid his hand to the nape of her neck and gazed into her eyes.

"We've already slept together, babe. We're married. Putting the sex aside, we can't get any more complicated than we already are. Have dinner with me after we check into our rooms. We'll take a walk, see a movie, or do whatever you want to do on our first real date."

"Gage," she whispered. Her fingers curled around his wrist.

"Say yes, Sally. You know you want to, and you know I'll never let you down."

Her gaze cruised over his face, and when she nodded, her smile reaching all the way up to her eyes, his whole world brightened.

"Okay," she said. "But you can't tell anyone about last night. If Danica finds out she'll think we're completely irresponsible."

"Danica gave up her therapy practice to marry her client and one of the biggest players I've ever known."

Her eyes narrowed. "*Reformed* player. Blake only has eyes for her." Blake Carter was one of the most attentive husbands and fathers Sally had ever met. He and Danica had a little girl named Francesca, *Chessie*, and Danica was now eight months pregnant, which was why she wasn't in Virginia with them.

"Yes, of course," Gage agreed. "The point is, she's not going to judge us. She wants us to be a couple."

"Wanting your friends to get together and knowing your *employees* acted irresponsibly are two separate things. Not to mention she's going to have another baby in a few weeks, and the last thing she needs is to worry about whether our personal life will somehow mess up the opening of the community center. I'd like to keep our personal life out of the office for now. And you know we can't let Rusty get wind of this. He'd never trust me again."

Her gaze softened, and when she looked at him like that—with so much faith there was no denying how close they were—there was nothing he wouldn't do for her.

"Can you please do this for me?" she asked. "Agree to keep the marriage and last night between us until we figure everything out?"

"Now you're making *rules*?" he teased. "I'm glad to see you're taking your role of *wife* seriously."

"Gage!"

"Don't worry, sweetheart. You can make all the rules you want. I'm finally getting to take my best friend on a real date." He grabbed their bags from the trunk, unable to stop grinning as they headed into the hotel.

"Don't get too excited," she said. The spark he loved so much was slowly returning to her voice. "I'm not going to sleep with you tonight."

"Unless I get you drunk."

She rolled her eyes. "I'm never going to live that down, am I?"

"Probably not. Should we cancel your room now and get the honeymoon suite?" The shock and amusement on her face were priceless. Too bad he wasn't kidding.

CHAPTER TWO

SALLY RAN A brush through her hair one last time, so nervous about her date with Gage, she was literally shaking in her boots. He had seen her at her worst, overcome with grief, sick with the flu, and hot and sweaty when they were out hiking. She didn't usually worry too much about what she wore around him, but tonight she'd changed three times before finally deciding on her favorite skinny jeans and a cute white sweater, hoping being comfortable would calm her jitters. The over-the-knee, gray suede boots, however, had been a *very* conscious and embarrassingly calculated decision. Sally was blessed with long legs, and she'd noticed how Gage's glances lingered and his gaze grew hotter when she wore those particular boots. She didn't want to appear too eager, but there was no denying that she hoped he'd find her irresistible, as evident by the lace panties and matching bra she'd chosen to help her *feel* sexy—even if she wasn't planning to jump into bed with him.

She thought about Gage on the other side of the adjoining door to his room, and a swarm of butterflies took flight in her stomach. They always got adjoining rooms when they traveled, although this time he'd pushed hard for the honeymoon suite when they'd checked in. *Come on, Sal. Let's really give this a shot.* His pleading and seductive gaze had *almost* made her give in, but she'd had hours to think on the long plane ride from Vegas to Virginia, and pieces of their night had come back to her. She remembered toasting the new community center with Gage as they'd sat at the bar, and other people at the bar joining in on the celebration. Gage had sat beside her with an arm around her shoulders, which he did often, but it had felt different, being away from home, with all those eyes on them probably assuming they were a couple. It had felt good. *Better than good.* It had felt amazing.

It hadn't been a conscious decision to get drunk, but she'd been a responsible parent since she was eighteen, and it was exciting to finally cut loose with the man she'd been attracted to for so long. All of their friends back home had made comments about the two of them getting together, but the one time Rusty had heard the suggestion, he'd scoffed and walked away, like he didn't even want to think about the possibility of her and Gage as a couple. His reaction had stuck with her, and this marriage was a big risk. How did a person calculate risk when it came to friendships and love? That question was the driving force behind her refusal to share a room with her big, hunky *husband.*

Oh God. I have a husband!

A knock sounded at the door, and her heart leapt. She stared at it as if Gage might have x-ray vision and could see her nervously smoothing her sweater over her hips. She wasn't even sure this date was a good idea, regardless of how much she wanted to go on it. She looked down at her sexy boots. *I'm a walking contradiction.* Risking their friendship scared the hell out of her. Everything hung on their time together.

No pressure or anything.

She drew in a deep, calming breath, second-guessing her outfit. Should she have gotten more dressed up? Worn something sexier? Something younger? Gage was three years younger than her, which wasn't a fact she thought about often, but now that she'd asked herself the question, her nerves reignited.

"Bird? Don't leave me hanging, baby." Gage's deep voice came through the door.

She tried—and failed—to push her worries away, and opened the door. Gage stood before her looking like her every fantasy in a pair of dark jeans and a white dress shirt. The first few buttons were open, exposing a dusting of chest hair. His thick sandy-blond hair looked finger combed in that sexy, tousled way she loved. He hadn't shaved, and his scruff, coupled with his leather jacket, gave him a hard-to-ignore edge. Just like the first time she'd seen him at No Limitz, her heartbeat quickened and her mouth went dry. "Holy smokes" came out before she could stop it.

His lips curved up in a cocky smile as he leaned in, bringing a wave of his manly scent. He kissed her cheek. His whiskers brushed along her skin, unleashing memories of last night's kisses and knocking her a little off-kilter.

"Hi, gorgeous. These are for you." A bouquet of red roses in a beautiful glass vase appeared from behind his back.

It had been ages since she'd received flowers, and her insides warmed with his thoughtfulness. "Thank you. They're beautiful. Come in. I'll just put these on the table."

He followed her in, standing so close behind her as she set the vase down, his heat seared down the length of her body.

"You wore my favorite boots." His minty breath drifted across her cheek. "And you smell incredible."

He might as well have said he wanted to lick her all over, the way her body quivered.

"Gage," she said nervously, turning to face him. He was *right there*. His hands took up residence on her waist. His eyes blazed down at her, *through* her, hindering her ability to think. She needed to get a grip before she did or said something she shouldn't.

She attempted humor, not her strong point. "Is this the way you treat all your first dates?"

"No," he said with a hint of arrogance she wasn't used to—but she liked. *A lot.* "This is the way I treat *you*."

She couldn't stop looking at his mouth, wondering how she could have kissed him and not remembered every detail, no matter how drunk. Forcing her gaze to meet his, she said, "You're making me nervous."

"Nervous is good. The way I see it, I've got several days to make you feel nervous, hot, bothered, happy, and hopefully lots of other new, exciting ways." He tucked her hair behind her ear, smiling like she was all he'd ever wanted. "And I don't plan to waste a second of it."

It was like someone had flicked a switch in him from Gage Ryder, *friend*, to Gage Ryder, *master seducer*. "It's been forever since I've been on a first date." *Like more than twenty years.* "But aren't you being a little pushy?"

"Yes," he said arrogantly.

"Okay, just checking." At least she wasn't off base.

"I don't think I've ever seen you like this. I like you when you're nervous, Sal. You look like you don't know if you want to kiss me or run away."

She pushed past him and grabbed her coat and purse. "Okay, Casanova. Let's get out of here before"—*I make the wrong choice*—"we spontaneously combust."

"Want me to back off?" he asked as they entered the elevator.

No. "A little. Maybe."

He didn't say another word as the elevator descended toward the lobby, though his heated gaze remained trained on her. When the doors opened, a gorgeous redhead was waiting for the elevator. She smiled flirtatiously at Gage, her eyes slowly dragging down his body. He was strikingly handsome, athletic, and confident. The type of man women couldn't help but check out. Sally had noticed it hundreds of times over the years, but now her claws came out. She felt possessive of him in a way she never had before. She lifted her chin, stood up a little straighter, unwilling to be a wallflower.

Gage laced their fingers together and pressed a kiss to the back of her hand. His eyes never left Sally's face. "Are you sure that's what you want, bird?"

She felt the redhead watching them, and it took her a second to realize he was asking if she really wanted him to back off. In her head, she heard herself denying the truth, but when she opened her mouth, no words came. It was all she could do to shake her head.

"Good." He pulled her closer, stepping around the redhead. "Excuse us. Newlyweds coming through."

Ohmygod. What had she done?

GAGE COULDN'T TAKE his eyes off Sally as they ate dinner at a small window-side table in an Italian restaurant. He had eaten dinner with her so many times, he felt like they were already a couple, even though this night, their first real date, brought a rush of new and exciting feelings. Sally had refused his offer for a drink, although he knew she needed one. She'd fidgeted with her hair, her napkin, and barely said anything throughout their meal.

"How can you be this nervous with me, bird? I'm still the same guy I've always been."

The waitress brought their check, and after paying, he moved to the seat beside Sally and held out his hand. Her gaze flicked up to his. A sexy smile lifted her lips as she set her delicate fingers in his palm.

She shook her head, speaking just above a whisper. "No, you're not the same guy. Now you've seen me naked. You've…we've…" She pressed her lips together and glanced out the window, inhaling deeply.

He didn't push, though he wanted to. Instead, he took a moment to really look at her. Sally complained that as a teenager she was pin thin, all legs and arms, but he imagined she was just as beautiful—inside and out—as she was tonight. She wasn't one of those women who flaunted her assets, though she had plenty to flaunt. Her white-blond hair wasn't lifeless, as she often complained. It had gentle waves, like the big slides Gage had ridden down on a sack of burlap as a kid at the county fair. On anyone else her hair might look plain, but it suited Sally perfectly, framing her high cheekbones and full, pouty lips, which he couldn't wait to taste again and again. She was nervously twisting the ends of those gorgeous locks, as she'd done when he'd encroached on her personal space in her hotel room. Did she know how much his effect on her turned him on?

When she faced him again, their eyes connected and held. Heat radiated between them, drawing him closer, and a ragged sigh fell from her lips.

"I hate that after all this time as friends, we ended up in bed together and I don't remember most of it," she said. "I don't even remember our first real kiss."

"I can remedy that."

Heat shone in her eyes, and just as quickly she schooled her expression and leaned back. "Gage, there are some things you don't know about me, and there's still a lot I don't know about you."

He didn't believe there could be a dark secret about the woman who craved cookies like other women craved chocolate, the mother who he was sure had texted her son at least twice since they'd arrived, or the peer he was certain had already checked her email and left no inquiry unanswered. "I have no secrets, Sal, but enlighten me, please."

Her eyes darted over his shoulder to the nearby tables.

"Let's go for a walk," he suggested, and rose to his feet, bringing her up beside him. He gazed into her eyes, his heart thumping harder at the reality that she was his *wife*. The words played in his head loud as thunder—*my wife*.

He helped her with her coat, enjoying every moment of this chance to treat her like she was *his*. He reached up and freed her hair from where it had gotten trapped beneath her collar, soaking in her appreciative smile.

"Shall we?" He took her hand as they left the restaurant, winking when she looked at him questioningly.

"This is weird." She lifted their joined hands. "Suddenly you're acting like we're a couple, and I'm still trying to catch up."

"Hurry your cute little ass up, sweetheart. You don't want to be left behind."

"Okay, *that* is the Gage I know. A little smartass, kinda flirty, but this…" She lifted their hands again. "I don't even know what to do with it."

He tugged her against him and flattened her hand against his chest, beneath his. "How about doing this, my beautiful wife? I remember a few things about last night, one of which was that you knew *exactly* what to do with your pretty little hands."

"Gage!" she whispered with a laugh.

"Come on, bird. You really don't remember our night together? I mean, at first I didn't either, but it's come back to me over the last twelve hours. I know I'll never forget the look in your eyes as you wrapped your legs around my waist, arching up so I could hit that spot, and—"

Her hand landed hard over his mouth as crimson spread up her cheeks. "Don't say another word."

He lightly bit her palm and she gasped. He couldn't help laughing as he lowered her hand to his chest again and held it there. "You are *not* that uptight about sex."

"I'm not uptight, but I don't need a play-by-play of my own sexual encounter, thank you very much."

"Then admit you remember what it was like to be in my arms," he challenged, refusing to allow her to negate their night together. "To kiss me, to feel me loving you like you want me to."

She swallowed hard, looking as innocent as a girl and as sexy as the woman she was. "I remember some. *Most*, I think. But there are alarm bells going off in my head right now, and I don't know what to make of any of it."

"That's what we're here to figure out," he reminded her as they walked along the brick courtyard in the center of town, surrounded by buildings with ornate carvings above colorful awnings.

"We're here to get the community center ready for the

grand opening in March," she reminded him. "We have a full schedule of setting up the offices and interviewing. We just *happened* to get married along the way."

"Boy, do I like the sound of that coming off your lips."

"I'm starting to wonder if this was your plan all along."

"Trust me, bird. My plan would not have been to get you so drunk you didn't remember me making love to you."

Her cheeks pinked up again.

"Although, I have to admit, I'm totally digging the whole marriage thing. Now you can't go out with some other guy."

"We aren't *really* married."

He lifted her hand and brushed his thumb over the ink mark. "What was that?"

"Okay, we are, but it's not like you asked me."

"You sure about that?" He arched a brow, knowing he had, and only now realizing she truly didn't remember it.

Confusion filled her eyes. "You remember?"

"Hell yes. I tried to tell you on the plane, but you kept shutting me down. When we left the bar we were kissing." He guided her past a group of iron tables outside a café, around a landscaped garden, where a tree still clung to a smattering of leaves, and beyond a shiny black streetlight, decorated with tinsel and holly.

"Where are we going?" she asked as he led her around the corner and backed her up against the side of the building. "What are you doing?"

"Showing you how we ended up getting married." He lifted her hands to his shoulders. "We were standing against the side of the building like this." He pressed his body to hers, heat flooding his veins as he brushed his lips over hers. "We were making out, touching each other, without a care about who might see us, because nobody else existed."

He kissed the corner of her mouth, and her breath left her lungs in a faint puff.

"God, bird," he whispered, unable to hold back the truth. "I've always wanted you, but last night you were so carefree and so into me, I wanted to *consume* you. And now…"

His arms circled her waist, holding her tight as he trailed kisses along her neck, to the spot below her ear that had driven her wild last night. She breathed harder, clung to him tighter, rocking her hips and driving him out of his mind. He drew back just far enough to gaze into her lustful eyes. He didn't wonder what she saw. He *knew.* There was no room for anything other than his true emotions.

"You were right there with me, sweetheart. I could feel it in your touch, the way I do right now. I could taste it in your kiss. Last night when I put my cheek against yours, like this"—he touched his cheek to hers—"and I said, 'I want you, Sally. I want to be inside you more than I have ever wanted anything else in my entire life.'"

Her fingers dug into his shoulders. Her breathing shallowed, but she didn't say a word.

"Do you remember that, bird?" He took her face between his hands, gazing deeply into her eyes. "Any of it?"

"Yes," she whispered.

She looked at him like he was her whole world. That was the look that had done him in over the years, each time strengthening their connection, drawing him deeper into love with her. He tried to push past the intoxicating emotions dragging him under, but it was like swimming in tar, and said, "Do you remember what you said next?"

"No, but now I remember kissing you, and being so caught

up in us that I could barely breathe."

Hell yeah, you were caught up in us. Your thigh ran up my outer leg, and I'm pretty sure I have claw marks on the back of my neck. He felt himself smiling. "I remember that, too."

"Pieces of the night are coming back like intermittent flashes I can't hold on to. It's like you say something and it spurs an inkling that appears and then skitters away, and I'm having trouble putting the pieces together. Did I…? Did I try to *climb* you?"

He chuckled. "Yeah. It was the hottest thing I've ever experienced."

"I'm a horrible, skanky drunk, aren't I?" She buried her face in his chest. "I'm way too old to be climbing anyone."

He laughed and pressed a kiss to her head. "If I have it my way, you'll be climbing me when you're so old you'll need a walker."

She smiled up at him. "This is so bad. It's like the walk of shame I never took, but with my best friend, which makes it even more horrifying."

"No, babe. It makes it that much more special, because your best friend finds you hot as fuck."

She bit her lip, her finely manicured brows knitted. "What else did I say or do that I'll never live down? I'd say I need a drink before you tell me, but I don't trust myself with alcohol anymore."

"I'd rather you were clearheaded for this." He knew what he said next would come as a shock, but she deserved to know the truth. "After I said I wanted you, you told me that you'd never sleep with another man outside of wedlock, because you got pregnant with Rusty the summer after high school, before you were married."

The color drained from her face. "I told you that?"

He held her tighter. "Yes."

"Well, I guess it saved me from having to reveal it tonight, but you can never tell Rusty that. He thinks I got pregnant right after Dave and I were married. I have given him so many lectures about safe sex, and they'd be meaningless if he knew the truth."

"He's a college student, babe. He knows what happens when you don't practice safe sex. We've talked about it."

Her eyes nearly bugged out of her head. "You talked about sex with my son?"

"Sure. You didn't think I'd let him go off to college without being fully prepared, did you?"

"I don't know," she said. "I talked to him about it."

"There's a world of difference between Mom telling you to practice safe sex and hearing it from a guy." He paused and then added, "I gave him some advice on what to do when he was so hard he thought he'd die from blue balls and the girl didn't want to go further."

"Seriously? You told him what to do?"

"Yes. Of course."

"What do you mean, *of course*? It's not every day someone talks to my son about sex. Well, don't leave me hanging. How *do* guys handle that situation?"

"Depends on the guy. In college, you can't always rub one out because of roommates or whatever." He paused, waiting for her to hammer him for saying *rub one out*, but her eyes were focused, her face a mask of pure interest. She clearly wanted to know the answer. "I told him to keep an ice pack in the freezer, and after a hot date that didn't end the way his body hoped it would, to put the ice pack on his chest or stomach. It will give his brain something else to focus on, and cool his jets."

Mischief sparked in her eyes. "I'm totally checking your freezer when we get home. You know that, right?"

"Babe, I've been around you for so long, I practically live in the freezer."

She laughed, and he loved it. Her laugh was so *real*, a little loud and breathy, which made it even sexier. And when she'd laughed in bed, it had instantly become one of his favorite naughty pleasures, one he'd like to hear repeatedly for the next hundred years.

"Great. Now I'm not just a woman whose only sexual experience has been limited to one man, but I'm *also* a cock tease."

He ground his teeth together. "Sal?"

"Hm?"

"Don't use that word. It makes me hot."

"Which word?" She paused, and her eyes widened. "You're such a guy."

"Your point?"

She rolled her eyes. He was thrilled that she was loosening up.

"Was that one of the things you didn't think I knew about you? That you got pregnant before you were married and wouldn't sleep with another guy out of wedlock? Because I think that's pretty damn respectable, and explains a lot."

"Mm-hm. Pretty embarrassing is more like it." Her gaze dropped to his chest. "What else did I tell you?"

He slid a finger beneath her chin, lifting her face so she had no choice but to look at him. "Maybe what's more important is what I did next."

She pressed her hands to his chest. "I don't know if I want to hear it."

"Why?"

Her fingers clutched his shirt, hanging on tight. "Because now you know that until last night, I hadn't been with a man since Dave, and I was only *ever* with him. I probably sucked in bed, and God knows what else I revealed to you in my drunken state of sluttiness."

"First, you definitely didn't *suck*, literally or figuratively. I would have remembered having your mouth on me."

"You talk so dirty," she whispered. "Is that because I was so slutty?"

The glimmer of heat in her eyes made him want to talk even dirtier. "You were anything but slutty. You finally gave in to what we both wanted. That's smart, not slutty."

"Oh, *please*! I was so drunk. I probably said all sorts of things."

"Obviously nothing you said turned me away. Don't demean what we did, Sally. So, we were drunk? So what? I'm not drunk now, and I want you more than I did last night."

"Gage…"

"No, don't 'Gage' me. *Hear* me, bird. You said I didn't ask you to marry me, but I did."

Surprise rose in her beautiful eyes, and it killed him that she didn't remember. "When you told me you'd never sleep with another man out of wedlock, I didn't hesitate. I got down on one knee." He knelt before her. "And I took your hand in mine, like this." He held her left hand. "I said, 'Sally Tuft, I have adored you for what feels like forever. Marry me and let me love you for the rest of our lives.'"

She sank down to her knees in front of him. "How do you know you said that? Do you remember saying those beautiful words to me?"

"Most of them, yes. But I don't have to reach far to find what I've wanted to say since Danica and Kaylie's double wedding."

"Since…" Her voice trailed off as a couple came around the corner, whispering as they passed. "That's a really long time," she said incredulously. "What did I say? Last night, I mean."

Now it was his turn to look away. He would never forget her five-word response—*What took you so long?*—but he didn't want to hear those words again until they came from Sally, sober and full of meaning.

"Gage…?"

"I don't remember exactly. One minute I was on my knees, and the next we were climbing into a cab, about to get married." He met her gaze, hating the taste of the first and only lie he'd ever told her. And he vowed to never lie to her again.

CHAPTER THREE

GAGE TOOK SALLY'S hand as they crossed the street to a path that wound through a park. She was getting used to this possessive side of him, but she was still floored by his proposal admission. Even drunk, he was a gentleman. That shouldn't surprise her, given how he'd always treated her, but everything he was doing and saying surprised her tonight.

"Bird?" he said in a way that made her realize she'd zoned out and missed something.

"Sorry." She shook her head to try to clear her thoughts. "Gage, why do you call me bird?"

He released her hand and put an arm around her, tucking her tight against his side, the way he did when it was cold out and they were taking a walk, or when they went to parties or weddings. *Or just about anywhere.* Maybe he was right. Maybe they had been sort of dating for years.

"See how you fit right there?"

"Anyone could fit here. You're giant, and your arms are long." But she knew not everyone fit together like they did. She remembered the first time he'd held her like that. It was after they'd gone to dinner with friends, and as they'd walked to the car, he'd put an arm around her like it was the most natural thing in the world. She hadn't questioned it. In fact, she'd found herself hoping he'd do it more often. And then he did, again and again.

"I hate to tell you this, babe, but you're wrong. I've been with other women, and not one of them fit the way we do." He squeezed her tighter and kissed the top of her head. "You're always curling up beside me when we watch movies and when we go to outdoor concerts. Don't tell me you don't feel it, too. The way my body becomes your nest when we're out?"

Gage ducked beneath a low-hanging branch, and she ducked with him, though it was several inches over her head.

"I do not *always* do it." The fib came out like a joke.

"Whatever helps you sleep at night, little bird. *Anyway*, getting back to why I call you *bird*. You have this way about you. When you're at work, you move from one thing to the next with determination. Even when you just cross the room to get something from the file cabinet, it's like you're on a mission from point A to point B. And when Rusty's around, you're always flapping your wings around him, but never getting close enough to suffocate your young. It's like you want to wrap him up in your arms and never let him go, but now he's a six-foot-one young man and you're not sure how or when it's okay to be Mom."

He ran a hand through his hair, pausing long enough to let his observations sink in. How did he notice everything, right down to the truth about mothering her son?

"I love those things about you. And even though you are one of the strongest women I know, you have this underlying vulnerability that makes me want to hold and protect you like this." He tightened his grip around her. "You're my little bird. And it's more than those things. Sometimes you catch sight of Rusty and I know you see Dave in him, because the longing in your eyes couldn't be anything else."

A spear of guilt sliced through her. There were moments like that, and then there were heavier moments, when she remembered the pain of finding out about Chase.

"I'm sorry. It's not that I haven't moved on, but sometimes it does hurt."

"Don't ever be sorry for missing the man you loved for so long, Sal. That's not why I'm telling you this. You asked why I call you bird, and it's because of all these things. Usually during those times, when you're hurting, you look around for me, or sidle closer, like you need to know I'm there. I don't ever want to take away what you had with Dave. I want you to feel everything you need or want to feel, and I want to be the man you turn to in those times and every other time. But there's more behind the endearment."

Her heart was beating so fast, she settled in a little closer to him. "What else?" As they followed the path around the park, she didn't want their time together to end. She wanted to know what he felt about everything.

"I might be way off base with this, but even though you never talk about moving, I feel like at any time you could flap those pretty wings and fly away to chase a dream or…I don't know what. Sometimes you get this look in your eyes that tells me you want to see and do more. Like I said, I might be totally misreading you, but that's how you feel to me. Like this beautiful, strong bird who likes to spread her wings, but also craves security and comfort."

His piercing blue eyes cut straight to her heart. She was shocked by how well he knew her. Sally's father had been an international investor, and they'd spent her childhood traveling. She had planned to study internationally after high school, traveling on school breaks and seeing as much of the world as she could before settling down. She'd met Dave on the ski slopes the winter of her senior year of high school, and they'd begun dating. The summer after graduation, she'd been on a trip with her parents when she realized she was pregnant. The pregnancy had caused a rift between her and her parents. Dave was a few years older than Sally and well on his way to opening his ski and sporting-goods store with Blake Carter when they'd made their home in Allure. She'd married Dave in a civil ceremony, and her parents had barely spoken to her during her pregnancy. But when Rusty was born and her parents saw their grandson for the first time, they'd come around and their relationship had healed. Although her parents had continued traveling often and they saw each other only once or twice a year, that healing had made it easier for Sally to focus on raising Rusty while going to college part-time. Her life had been full and busy. Unfortunately, between their family, school, and the store, her travel plans had fallen by the wayside, but the desire to travel had never gone away.

"I don't know what to say," she admitted. "You've noticed things no one else ever has." *Not even Dave.*

"You don't have to say anything," he said as they came to a bench at the end of the path across the street from the hotel. They sat down, and he pulled her against his side. "You know how I feel, and now you know why I call you bird. Are there any other mysteries I can help solve?"

"Yes." If they were really laying their cards on the table, she wanted to ask the questions she'd been holding back. Not the obvious questions—*Why are you still single?* and *Why me, out of all the women in the world?*—because she'd been in love before and she knew the heart had a mind of its own. The connection between her and Gage was too strong to deny, and she had no idea how they'd held out this long. She'd thought about him so often, sometimes late at night she wondered what would have happened if she'd met Gage while Dave had been alive. Those were the types of thoughts that could drive her crazy, and she immediately pushed them away. Sometimes not knowing was better than having all the answers.

"You told me you came to Allure to escape a bad relationship, but you never told me what happened."

"You never asked," he said with a thread of tension in his voice, and leaned back, releasing her for what felt like the first time all night.

She'd struck a nerve, and she wanted his arms around her again. If there was one thing she knew about her relationship with Gage, it was that any time they talked about things that really mattered, they became closer. And she wanted that now.

"I'm asking now," she said gently. "I mean, we're married and all, so I should probably know as much about my husband as possible."

"Now you're *owning* up to our marriage?" His tension was replaced with amusement.

"Just using it to my advantage. After all, you know all about my birdlike tendencies. It's only fair that you disclose something private to me, too."

"You do have a point." He rested his forearms on his thighs and stared out toward the street.

"For you to have moved away from Washington State, left your job and started over, something really bad must have gone down."

GAGE HADN'T THOUGHT of Stacy Manerton in years, and she was the last person he wanted to think about now. "It's not that big of a deal. I dated a woman for a long time, and we ended up wanting different things."

"But why move? Did she become a crazy stalker?" She bumped him with her shoulder. "Or did *you* become an obsessive boyfriend who wouldn't let her go?"

He shook his head. "No crazy stalkers. I just needed a fresh start."

"You don't think I'm buying that, do you? Guys never need fresh starts. Come on. You saw me naked. You owe me the truth."

"Listen to my rule-making wife. You saw *me* naked." He sat up, put his mouth right beside her ear, and said, "What do you owe me?"

She turned, bringing their lips a whisper apart. Heat thrummed like a heartbeat between them.

"You're trying to sidetrack me," she said, eyes like burning embers.

"Am I doing a good job of it?"

"Maybe."

He brushed a kiss over her cheek, and her breathing hitched. Man, he liked that reaction. "How about I turn that maybe into a yes?" He fully expected her to put space between them, and when she didn't, he laced their fingers together.

"You really don't want to talk about this, do you?"

He shook his head. "Talking isn't on my mind right now."

"I'm not sleeping with you tonight, if that's what you're thinking."

"Who are you trying to convince?" He touched his lips to her cheek again, reveling in the warmth of her skin. "Me, or you?"

She was quiet for a long moment, holding his gaze as if she were deciding how to respond. The heat in her eyes cooled, only a degree or two, but enough to let him know she wasn't going to let him lead her down that path.

Yet.

"I'm sorry, Gage," she said softly, but he didn't think she was talking about not kissing him. "She must have really hurt you for you to have buried it so deeply you don't want to talk about it."

It took a second for him to switch gears from kissing to his denial, and then to the here and now, and when he did, trying to hide the truth from Sally wasn't an option. "You could say that."

She lifted their joined hands the way he'd done earlier and pressed a kiss to his knuckles. "I've got two good ears if you want to get it off your chest."

He couldn't help but smile. "Isn't that what I said to you the night I found you crying in the parking lot after work a few years ago?" Another night he'd never forget. It was the beginning of their deep friendship. The night he'd first embraced her. The night they'd gone for a two-hour walk and ended up sitting on a park bench, like they were now, and had talked into the wee hours of the morning. She'd had a fight with Rusty, and she'd been sure she would somehow fail her teenage son because she couldn't be both father and mother to him. He remembered telling her, *Rusty doesn't need you to replace his father. He just needs you to be strong enough to love him through his struggles.*

"If you're referring to the night you opened the doors I've never been able to—or wanted to—close between us, then yes." She shifted so she was facing him. "I know you like to think you're indestructible. I've seen you with your family enough to know being a pillar of strength runs like blood through your veins. But no one is impenetrable. You've been there for me so many times. Let me be here for you just this once."

"It's not that big of a deal." He gazed out at the road, watching cars pass by.

She leaned closer. "Try me."

He clenched his jaw at the sick feeling in his gut and decided to get it over with. "Her name was Stacy. She was a strength and conditioning coach and owned her own company, holding programs all over the country. She came to the school where I taught to help out with a summer program, and we started going out. We dated for about two years."

"That's a long time. It must have been serious."

"I thought it was."

Sally ran an assessing gaze over him. "You loved her," she said carefully.

Gage nodded. "I thought I did, but I know now that I was in love with who I thought she was. Or maybe who I wanted her to be. I can be a little pushy."

"It's not so much that you're pushy. You don't give anything *half* an effort. Not the kids you work with at the center, or even the center itself. You set goals and you always achieve them and help others do the same. That's who you are, and your heart only knows one way to be. Look at how you are with me. You're beyond loyal, even if it means waiting years and not really knowing how things will turn out. Because, how can we know? We've been together as friends for a long time, but this?" She lifted their joined hands. "*This* is a whole new world riddled with complexities, the least of which is working together. There's also your relationship with Rusty, and what we both want in our lives moving forward."

"That's where the trouble came in with Stacy," he admitted. "Her lease was up and we had planned to move in together. We'd talked about a future, a family, the whole nine yards. I thought she was it for me, and I never questioned it. The week before she was supposed to move in, she asked me to meet her for lunch, and when I did, she had her car all packed up and ready to leave town."

"Was it too much for her?" Sally asked. "Sometimes it takes *waking up married* to really bring the idea home, you know?"

"I think it had more to do with waking up pregnant."

"Oh, Gage," she said carefully. "You have a child? But I've never seen you with—"

"No, Sal. I don't." His gut clenched, a small reminder of what had once been blinding hurt and anger. "She found out she was pregnant and had an abortion without even discussing it with me."

Sally moved closer, holding their hands against her chest. "That's awful. I'm so sorry."

"It was pretty hard to take at the time." That was putting it mildly. "Maybe if we had talked about the pregnancy and made the decision together, who knows, it might have been easier to take. But I know myself. I would have asked her to have the baby and let me raise it if she didn't want to. She was a free spirit, wanting to try everything, go everywhere, like so many twenty-four-year-olds. I was twenty-nine when we broke up, and I was ready to settle down and have a family. Maybe I've always been the kind of guy who wanted a home base. That's what my brothers and sister have always said. I guess they know me better than I know myself."

Gage had one older brother, Duke, who he was most like

when it came to relationships, and three younger brothers: Blue, a contractor, Cash, a firefighter, and Jake, a search and rescue professional. He also had a younger sister, Trish, who was an actress. She and her rock star husband, Boone, were both nominated for Oscars for a movie they'd costarred in. Their whole family was close, but he'd only told Duke and his father about what had happened with Stacy. It wasn't something he wanted to relive many times over.

"I think you know yourself pretty well," she said. "You once told me that you had never been the type of guy to get off on one-night stands."

"It's the truth, although I had my share of playing around when I was in college. But I don't think that was the type of freedom Stacy wanted. I think it was more about being able to pick up and go places on a whim. She left that afternoon for a five-month contract in Hawaii."

"If she moved away, why did you move? To avoid seeing her when she got back to town?"

He pushed to his feet, pulling her up beside him, and kept hold of her hand as they headed across the street toward the hotel. "I didn't move for another year, when she came back to Washington, pregnant and married."

"Oh, Gage. That's…"

"It's old news, that's what it is," he said firmly. "I can't change who she was or what she did, and I would like to put it behind us. Thanks for listening. I actually feel better having told you. I've kept it bottled up for a long time."

He held the door to the hotel open, and they joined a small crowd boarding the elevator. Gage held Sally from behind in the crowded space, and when they exited the elevator, he held her hand again as they walked down the hall. The discomfort she'd carried when they'd first gone to dinner seemed to have dissipated, but as they neared her room, he felt tension in her hand again.

"I'm glad you shared that with me," she said. "It answers a lot of questions."

When they reached her room, he gathered her in his arms, wanting to take her inside and show her just how right they were for each other. But as much as he wanted to skip ahead, he knew Sally still needed time to adjust to their new relationship. "Then can you answer one question for me?"

"Sure, but when you look at me like that, you make it hard for me to think."

Damn, he liked knowing that. In a split second he threw caution to the wind, casting his request for a kiss good night aside, and said, "Then let's see what this does to you."

He brushed his lips over hers, feeling her shiver against him. "I can't have you forgetting our first *real* kiss," he whispered.

Her tongue swept across her lips, leaving them shiny and tempting and luring him in. He pressed a kiss beside her mouth, wanting to savor the prekiss anticipation vibrating between them.

"I want you to remember the feel of my arms around you," he said, holding her gaze.

He kissed her cheek, and her lips parted, though she was barely breathing. His lips hovered just above hers as he threaded his fingers into her silky hair, drinking in the flush of her skin. Heat radiated between them like a furnace.

"I want you to remember the feel of my hands in your hair, the desire mounting inside you. I want you to see the look in my eyes right now when you go to sleep tonight. And remember what five years of wanting my mouth on you feels like when I finally get my first sober taste."

"*Yes,*" came out as a plea.

He drew her face closer, angling her mouth beneath his, her warm breath coasting over his lips. Her heart thundered against his chest as she reached up and pulled him down to her. *That's it, baby. Take what you want.* Her lips were soft and warm and so fucking perfect he groaned. He tried to go slow, to kiss her gently, to savor the moment, but there was no stopping the lust rushing through his veins. He crushed her to him, earning the sexiest moan he'd ever heard. His fist tightened in her hair, tugging her head back so he could plunder her deeper, possess more of her. His other hand skimmed her back and took hold of her ass. She arched against him, clinging to the back of his neck, as sensual noises streamed from her lungs into their kiss. *Holy hell.*

How would he ever stop kissing her? This was so much more than just a first memorable *kiss.* This was a full-body experience driven by his heart, filling his very soul with the woman he adored. He was disappearing into her warm, eager mouth, consumed by her lush body rocking against him. The scrape of her nails on his neck made his senses reel, and he felt every touch, every breath, more distinctly than the one before.

If he didn't stop now, there was no way he'd ever stop without taking *everything* he wanted. He forced his mouth from hers, instantly missing her taste and the feel of her luscious lips. Her eyes were still closed as a needy whimper escaped. *Fuuck.* How was he supposed to resist *that*?

He went back for one last taste. Taking her slower, kissing her more intensely, memorizing the feel of her mouth against his. They both came away breathless. Needing more, he kissed her cheek, her neck, and blazed a path all the way to her ear.

"What do you think, bird? Meant to be, or a mistake?"

She was trembling all over. He drew back and gazed into her lust-filled eyes. She swallowed hard, licked her lips, and he could see she was having trouble forming words. Damn, he wanted to memorize that look, too.

"Not a mistake" slipped from her lips like a secret.

Her hand fell to his chest, five fingers splayed. A silent message. She needed space. She needed to process their magnificent kisses.

"Okay, bird." He swiped her keycard and followed her inside.

"Gage, I'm not ready—"

Her words were lost by another press of his lips. God, what he'd give to lay her down beneath him and love every inch of her.

"I know, bird. My ice pack awaits." He reached for the adjoining door, blew her a kiss, and answered the question in her eyes. "I always leave my side unlocked. Just in case you *need* me."

CHAPTER FOUR

SALLY SPENT HALF the night lost in dark, sexual dreams with Gage as the object of every filthy one. She woke up wet and needy and lay awake wishing he'd come through the adjoining door between their hotel rooms, unable to stay away from her. But that door stayed closed until the morning, when he asked her to join him for breakfast. They always ate breakfast together when they traveled, but this time sitting across the table from him was mental torture. She couldn't stop thinking about kissing him. And Gage being Gage, he took every opportunity to hold her hand and look at her with those eyes that said, *I want to be inside you.* By the time they got to the new youth center, her insides were humming like live wires. She needed the distraction of setting up the office to keep from attacking him.

The first delivery truck showed up more than an hour late, giving her plenty of time not only to think about what she wanted to do with him, but also to visualize him doing the dirty things he'd done to her in her dream. The rest of the morning was riddled with mixed-up furniture orders and missing products, enough to *almost* keep her sidetracked from her lust-ridden thoughts.

She pressed her cell phone to her ear, filling Danica in on the issues they'd run into. "We should have it all sorted out by the time we leave Friday," Sally reassured her while simultaneously directing furniture deliverymen to the office that would be used for the new administrator. "The network is scheduled to be set up tomorrow, and as long as there are no issues, I hope to start interviews right after that."

"Great. I wanted to talk to you about the grand opening. Kaylie's schedule is crazy, and she has only a few weeks off from her tour. She wants to spend the time at home with the kids instead of traveling to the opening. But she said there's a local band called Surge that is amazing." Danica's younger sister, Kaylie Crew, had become famous when her newest pop-country album hit the charts last year.

"Great. Send me the information and I'll try to connect with them."

"I'll text it after we get off the phone. They're playing tomorrow night at someplace called JJ's Pub. Think you guys can make it?"

Two of the movers headed back out to the truck, while another maneuvered a desk on a handcart through the glass doors.

"Hold on, Danica." Sally directed the movers to another office, then focused on Danica again. "I have to check with Gage about his schedule. He's out right now meeting with a local sports club, but I'm sure it's fine. If he has a meeting, I'll go."

"Do you still think this week will be enough time?" Danica asked.

Gage's voice sailed through her mind. *There's just you and me. Let's explore what this is together, take a leap of faith...Let's hold hands and make out until you can't forget how it feels.*

"I hope so," she said honestly.

"Do you think you need more time?"

"No. We should be fine. Besides"—she stopped short of blowing Danica's surprise by saying, *Do you really think I'd miss your baby shower?* Blake had gone to great lengths to set up Danica's surprise baby shower, which was taking place two weeks after they returned to Colorado. "I want to get a few things done before Rusty gets home for the holidays, and Gage is hosting Christmas this year for his family. I promised I'd help him get ready."

She mentally ran through the other things they needed to get done. Gage's younger brother, Blue, was marrying his fiancée, Lizzie Barber, right after the New Year. She and Gage needed to find a gift for the wedding. Sally had known Gage's family nearly as long as she'd known him. She'd gone with Gage to the weddings of his brother Duke and his sister, Trish, this past summer. The ceremonies were beautiful, and she couldn't deny that she'd allowed her mind to wander down the *what if* path. *What would it be like to be married to her best friend? To be part of his big, loving family?* And while the answers had been blurry at best, one had continually shone through—those dreams would not be worth the risk of Rusty losing Gage altogether if her and Gage's relationship went south.

"I still can't believe Rusty is not coming home until Christmas *week*. Remember the first year he went away to college? He couldn't wait to come home for winter break."

"That was before he had his own apartment, a job, and a close group of friends. I know I'm supposed to tell you that you should be glad he's independent. It means you raised him well." Danica sighed. "But all I can think about is how glad I am that I have years before Chessie goes away to college. I can't imagine how it will feel when she and our new baby have their own grown-up lives and we'll only see them on the holidays. Thank God you have Gage," Danica said. "You'd be so lonely without him."

Sally hadn't thought about the way Gage had filled the time Rusty had once occupied, but Danica was right. Where Sally had once been busy driving Rusty all over town, hounding him to do homework, or connecting for dinner, now her schedule was her own. And more often than not, she worked late, grabbed something on her way home. *Or joined Gage for a quick bite at a local café or at one of our houses.* She *would* be lonely without him, not just because of the time they spent together, but also because of the way he made her feel happy and loved. Even when she was alone, she never felt truly alone.

She watched the movers carrying in more furniture. "Yeah. He's a good friend."

"You know," Danica said with a mischievous arc to her voice, "you're all the way out in Virginia, alone with Gage. You two could finally take your relationship to the next level."

"Danica, you're my friend, and I appreciate you wanting to see me and Gage together, but you're also our boss, and I'm sure you don't really want us to jeopardize our working relationship."

"What? *Hello?* Where have you been for the past few years? I've practically pushed you two to finally take a chance on each other."

Sally walked to the far end of the room, away from the movers. "You don't mean that." *Do you? Please tell me you do.* "What if we got together and then broke up? It would be awful working together and watching him get together with someone else."

"Seriously? That could happen *tomorrow*. I know you love

your job, but you two have been playing cat and mouse for years. It's time to eat the cheese."

"That sounds disgusting." Sally laughed.

"Eat the meat?"

"Ohmygod. What happened to the conservative woman I met years ago?"

"Blake Carter happened," Danica said sassily. "My man's got a dirty mouth."

Sally absently touched her lips, remembering the feel of Gage's delicious mouth on hers, and his voice followed. *I know I'll never forget the look in your eyes as you wrapped your silky thighs around my waist, arching up so I could hit the spot, and—*

"My man has a dirty mouth, too."

"What?" Danica said.

Oh shit. She hadn't meant to say it out loud. "Um. I said that man's got dirt on his mouth. The mover. I'd better go see what's going on. Sorry, Danica. Can we catch up after I get things under control around here?" *Holy cow.* She was losing her mind.

Several hours later, Sally sat on a couch in the reception area poring over résumés of the final candidates for the administrator position. Her stomach growled so loud it startled her. Gage had called earlier and asked her to have dinner with him. She knew he had several meetings, but it was six thirty, and she was beginning to wonder if he'd forgotten he'd asked. She looked at the fading ink on her finger, and a wave of longing washed through her.

The sound of the door to the gym opening down the hall sent Sally to her feet, her heart racing as she tried to remember if she'd locked the outside door. She heard Gage's determined footsteps seconds before he appeared from the hallway. Their eyes connected, and an irresistible smile spread across his handsome face, sending her already speeding heart into overdrive.

He tossed his coat on the desk, faded denim hugging his powerful thighs as he ate up the distance between them. He stood before her in a dark button-down, the hint of a five o'clock shadow peppering his cheeks. Her stomach fluttered like a teenager with a crush, only her thoughts were nothing like a young girl's. She hadn't been able to stop thinking about his mouth, or his dirty talk, since she'd spoken with Danica. And the more she thought about him in that way, the more she wanted him.

When he took her hand, one strong arm circling her waist like she was *his*, she swore the temperature amped up fifty degrees. He pressed his warm lips to her cheek, and she closed her eyes, soaking in every second of his touch, breathing in his rugged, sexy scent.

"Hey, beautiful."

"Hi." She sounded breathless. How could she be this nervous with just a hello? They were only having dinner together, and they'd eaten together a million times. *But not after I spent all day contemplating my boss's approval of taking our relationship further.*

"How did your meetings go?" she asked to distract herself from the dire urge to kiss him until neither one remembered their own name.

"Fine. But I don't want to talk about work."

He was looking at her like he didn't want to *talk* at all. His smoldering gaze raked down her chest slow as sap dripping from a tree. Long, adrenaline-drenched seconds passed before his eyes met hers, lingering with lethal calmness, prolonging the intensity of the moment so long she felt unsteady, even in his arms.

GAGE HAD MADE a mistake last night. He'd allowed his past to steal some of their time. He wasn't about to let anything come between them again, not when everything he wanted was right there in his arms. Sally was special, and what he felt for her was miles above what he'd ever felt for any other woman. He didn't want her to feel like someone came before her in his heart, but he hadn't wanted to lie, even if his love for Stacy didn't compare to his love for her. Did that have any bearing on why Sally was suddenly fidgeting with the ends of her hair?

"I'm making you nervous," he said carefully.

"No, you're not. Why would you say that?" *Fidget. Fidget.*

"Bird, it's just me." He took her hands and placed them on his chest. "When you get nervous, put your hands here. Let me play with your hair." He tangled his fingers into her long locks, angling her beautiful face up, and brushed his lips over hers. "I want to give you something to be nervous about."

"Gage," she whispered as he lowered his lips to hers.

The first touch was electric, sizzling through him as he took the kiss deeper. Her fingers fisted in his shirt, and he cupped the base of her skull, sliding his other hand to her lower back and holding her sweet softness against him. She followed his lead, her tongue gliding over his, her body moving with the rhythm of his hips. He'd promised himself on the way over that he wouldn't take things too fast. He'd respect her need for space and time and let her lead their intimacy. But she made the sexiest little noises, and when her thigh rode up the outside of his leg, he couldn't resist spreading his hand over her ass. This wasn't a kiss of a woman who didn't want more. This was a lustful, greedy *taking*. A kiss that topped all others, it was real and hot and so damn hungry.

Hungry.

Hell, he'd promised her dinner.

Groaning, he reluctantly forced himself to pull back. Her lips were swollen and pink, and *God*, he loved them. The lusty look in her eyes brought his mouth back to hers, softer this time, lingering in the heady space between *taking* and *giving*.

"Wow," she said breathily. "Just... *Wow*. Is that how we say hello now?"

"Do you want it to be?"

She reached for her hair and he grabbed her wrist, stopping her midair, and laced their fingers together, waiting for her answer. He was a patient man, but she'd unleashed the darkest parts of him. The parts he'd kept chained up for far too long.

"Maybe," she said. "We'll see how good the next one is."

He kissed her harder, more demanding, until she clawed at his shoulders as she'd done the other night. He was right there with her, groping her ass and pressing her body impossibly closer. He didn't want to stop for dinner, didn't want to eat anything but *her*. But this was Sally, and blowing it wasn't on his agenda. He reluctantly eased his efforts to an intoxicating rhythm.

When they finally drew apart, they were both unsteady.

"That was..." She touched her lips as if they burned for more. "Pretty good. We'll have to keep practicing."

He chuckled. "My pleasure, my demanding little bird. I've got something to show you." With a hand around her waist, he led her toward the gym.

She cocked her head. "What do I hear?"

He opened the door, and the sounds of an Etta James song greeted them. He guided Sally into the candle-lit gym. An awed expression settled over her features as her gaze swept over the two hundred white balloons covering the gymnasium floor and the wedding canopy he'd erected in the middle of the room. White and peach silk drapes hung from the frame. Bouquets of roses and tendrils of ivy decorated the corners. Beneath the canopy, he'd set a table with dinner for two on silver platters from the finest restaurant in Oak Falls. A small wedding cake sat in the center of the table. He'd had to practically beg to get the cake and balloons on such short notice, but the smile lifting Sally's lips was worth it.

"Gage," came out in a whisper. "How…?"

"Don't you know me yet?" He led her farther into the room, sending balloons scattering around them. "There's nothing I can't do. Especially for you."

"But how did you do this with all your meetings? How did I not hear you setting it up?"

"I only had two meetings, but I figured this was worth a little white lie, and I was in super-stealth mode."

"It's unbelievably gorgeous. I don't know what to say."

"Don't say a word, babe. I don't know how much of our wedding either of us will ever remember, and I can't change that. But I can give you a night you'll never forget."

He swept her into his arms as "At Last" by Etta James began playing. They'd danced together so many times, they fell effortlessly into sync. Balloons floated into the air like a river of white. Sally melted against him, fitting perfectly in his arms and looking at him like he was her whole world again. He'd never get enough of that look, and when she was with him like this—

in mind and heart—he knew they'd be together forever.

"This song…" Her voice was full of wonder. "It's beautiful and *telling*."

Etta James sang about love coming along and lonely days being over. He really did feel like his life was a song right then. "I've made no effort to hide what I want with you. I'm done pretending I'm okay with only being friends."

"Oh" came out full of wonder. "I didn't know you were so romantic."

"Only for you, bird."

Their dance became a slow rock, a blending of their bodies, an acceptance of the love between them.

"When you said there was a lot about me you didn't know, I thought you were wrong," Gage admitted. "But this afternoon, as I was getting ready to surprise you, I realized there's a lot of me you haven't gotten to know, because I've been holding back. I'm done holding back, Sally. You're getting all of me, and you'll need to slam the brakes if I come on too strong, because I swear I feel like I've been let out of jail, and holding back is the last thing I want to do."

"Gage, you know I'm worried about how our relationship will impact Rusty and what that means for us in the long run. But I don't want you to hold back. You were right. We're here without anyone getting in our way. I want to take this leap of faith with you and see where we end up."

"Aw, baby…" His voice trailed off as he choked up, but no more words were necessary as he danced with his *wife*.

They danced until Sally's stomach growled too loud to ignore. They talked and drank champagne, sharing filet mignon and salmon.

"I'm too far away." Gage came to Sally's side. "And I've

never seen you smile so much. I need pictures with my bride." He crouched beside her chair and leaned in close for a selfie.

"I take back what I said about you not being pushy."

He took another picture as he kissed her cheek.

"How many pictures are you going to take?"

"As many as you'll let me." He took another. "Too much?"

"No. I like your pushy love. I don't know if I'm really ready for it, because there are so many complications if it goes wrong. Not just for Rusty. I really like my job, and our friendship, and I don't want to screw any of that up. But I have loved you for so long, I can't imagine not loving you. And even if it's only for now, while we're here and it doesn't impact anyone else, I want to pretend it's real."

Her cautiousness might make another man upset, but Gage was so full of love for Sally, her love for her son and friends just made him fall that much harder for her. "After next week, you won't be able to pretend you *don't* love me."

"Maybe I should have kept my thoughts to myself. Your ego might be getting too big for this gymnasium. Get the camera ready, hot stuff." She leaned in for a kiss. "You're not the only one who gets to be pushy."

They kissed and laughed, and kissed some more. It was like he'd untethered something inside her that allowed her to be freer with him. Even with her stipulations it was forward momentum, and he intended to keep it moving in that direction. When he reached for the cake she grabbed his phone.

"We need pictures of our wedding cake." She took pictures of the little plastic couple on the top of the cake and of the sides of the cake where he'd had the baker write their names beside a heart.

She handed him the knife, and he covered her hand with

his, taking the phone from her.

He focused the lens on their joined hands. "Now, that's a picture."

"You know, if word gets out about this, your brothers are going to give you the hardest time about being so sappy."

"If word gets out about this, it means you decided you were all in, and I won't care what anyone says."

"We have a lot of things to figure out before we jump ahead. This is a start. If we're as good together as a couple as we are as friends, then it'll be easy, right?"

She reached for her hair and stopped, placing her hand on his chest instead. That simple motion made his insides turn to mush. He'd always known she trusted him, but this—taking this leap of faith with her heart, when her worries about her son lay in the balance—was *huge*.

He eyed the cake, and she raised her brows, a smile playing at the edges of her mouth.

"Shall we?" he asked, and cut them each a piece.

"Don't even think about smashing that in my face," she warned with a fierce look in her pretty eyes.

He handed her a piece of cake. "Would I do that?"

"Heck, yes, you would do that. Look at all of this. We're standing in a sea of balloons, listening to romantic music by candlelight beneath a wedding canopy in a building we've been in for less than a day. You even got me to drink champagne, which is really amazing considering I vowed not to have another drink around you for at least a lifetime. I don't think there's anything you *won't* do."

He laughed, loving her more with each passing second. "Here's to us, sweetheart."

He lifted the cake to her mouth as she reached up and

smashed her piece to his lips and chin. She squealed when he did the same, and tried to dash away. He trapped her against him with one arm, nipping at the pieces of cake and icing hanging off her lips. She went up on her toes and licked the cake from his chin, her laughter quieting to something much more seductive.

"Kiss me, secret husband," she whispered. "Kiss me like you never want me to forget this magical moment."

He kissed off the remaining cake and traced her lower lip with his tongue, loving the needy sigh she emitted. When he did the same to her upper lip, she clung to the back of his neck, pulling him into a scorching-hot and heavy kiss. She tasted like sweet sugar and sinful nights, and he couldn't hold back. His hands moved over her body, wanting to touch all of her at once. She was right there with him, succumbing to the inferno blazing between them, touching him like she owned him, and he fucking loved it. She pushed against him, arching her back, thrusting her magnificent breasts so hard he couldn't resist taking what she was offering. He tugged her shirt from her jeans and pushed his hand beneath, filling his palm with her lace-covered breast. His cock throbbed as his thumb grazed over her taut nipple, straining against the material.

He tore back from the kiss long enough to say, "You're killing me."

Their mouths collided as he backed her up against the wall, sending balloons flying around their feet. A seductive beat played around them as he devoured her, grinding against her hips with wicked intent. She moaned and mewled, spurring him on. He fisted his hand in her hair. Gorgeous blond ropes tumbled over his fingers, and no part of him wanted to hold back, but he had to be careful—too much more of this and he'd strip away those sexy jeans and bury himself to the hilt. She was his best friend, and he'd waited years to have her. He wasn't about to make love to her for the first time they'd both remember in a gymnasium, but he needed more, and he needed it *now*.

He kissed her neck as he lifted her shirt up over her breasts, and she grabbed his ass. *Oh yeah, baby. Possess me.* Their eyes caught for a hot second, and then hers fluttered closed and she bowed off the wall. Her skin was flushed, her lips parted, and her breasts strained against pink lace. Christ, she was the sexiest woman he'd ever seen. He placed openmouthed kisses along the swell of her beautiful breasts and tugged the lace down on both sides, freeing them for him to taste. He dragged his tongue around each taut peak. Her hands slid off his ass, falling limply by her sides, like it was all she could do to remain standing. He cradled her breast and lowered his mouth over the peak, sucking hard. A cry escaped her lips, and he eased up.

"Don't stop," she panted out.

He'd dreamed about touching her, tasting her, but nothing came close to the sinful noises she made as he lavished her other breast with the same attention. He wedged his knee between her legs, and she ground against him. *Fuck.* He was painfully hard, and soon there would be no stopping him. Like a movie on fast-forward, in his mind he was stripping off her jeans, kneeling between her legs, and feasting on her sweetness. He wanted to hear his name sail desperately from her lungs in the throes of passion, the way it had when they'd made love. He remembered that sound. He might not remember every second of that night, but *hell yes*, he remembered his name coming off her lips, and there was no way he'd ever forget it.

The thrill of the memory snapped his brain into gear. They

were both panting, ready to fuck, only he didn't want to *fuck* her in a gym. He wanted to *love* her, *take* her, and yes, eventually *fuck* her many, many times in every location when the feeling hit, including a goddamn gym. But not the first time they'd both clearly remember for the rest of their lives.

He kissed her breasts, every fleck of skin, telling himself to back off and fighting himself in equal measure. But he knew what he had to do, and he righted her bra and lowered her shirt, trying not to feel like a dick because of the confusion—*disappointment?*—in her eyes. It was awkward, stopping when they were both so revved up, but he loved her too much to chance doing the wrong thing.

"Not here, baby. Not like this."

"Oh, um, no. Of course not." She stepped away, her hair curtaining her face, but not before he caught sight of the blush on her cheeks. "I'm sorry. It's been a long time since I've done anything like this."

He reached for her, but she moved around him. *Goddamn it.*

"We need to clean up. No janitors on board yet," she said with feigned casualness.

He pulled her into his arms, and he felt her embarrassment like a barrier between them. It killed him knowing he'd caused it. "Sal."

She stared at his chest.

"Baby, look at me." When she met his gaze, the pain in her eyes cut him to his core. "Sally, I want you right here and right now, but what I want more than that is to wake up with you in my arms every single day. I can't take a chance that you'll regret anything that we do."

She huffed out a breath and drew her shoulders back, her

confidence filling the space between them. "Gage, I don't know how to navigate the dating world, so maybe I'm considered a slut for saying this, but I'm thirty-eight years old. If I give you the okay to touch me, then trust me, I've weeded through the regrets and made a decision." A smile lifted her lips and she added, "That is, as long as I'm not three sheets to the wind on hard liquor in Vegas."

"Well, hell, bird. I was so worried about you waking up tomorrow and regretting doing it in a gym, I didn't think about *that.*" His arms came around her again, and he went in for another kiss, ready to play, but she twisted away.

"The moment passed." She crossed and uncrossed her arms, as if they were foreign objects and she had no idea what to do with them. "None of this is easy for me. Other than the night we were drunk, no man has so much as *seen* me naked since Dave. It was a really big deal for me to build up the courage to let you do as much as we just did, so forgive me for being flustered and ridiculous."

"I know it was, babe. And it was a huge deal for me, too. That's why I stopped. I don't want to mess this up. I'm sorry that I read you wrong, but you are not ridiculous. I'm just an idiot."

She sighed heavily. "Can we just clean up and go back to the hotel so I can take a hot bath and enjoy my mortification alone?"

He waggled his brows in an effort to lighten the mood and take the emphasis off of what an ass he was. "How about taking a bath *together*?"

She rolled her eyes, and a soft laugh slipped out. "See? Getting used to each other in this way is going to be a lot harder than you thought."

The hell with pussyfooting around. He hauled her against him so she could feel what she did to him. Heat rose in her eyes. "I'm glad you noticed. *Hard* is *very* good, and I look forward to getting *used to* you as often as you'll let me."

Chapter Five

TUESDAY AFTERNOON SALLY wondered if every day from now on was going to be a test of her ability to function at work while experiencing sexual tension thick enough to cut with a knife. Getting through setting up the network and coordinating interviews was painful, since all she wanted to do was be back in Gage's arms. Gage had been busy all day as well, meeting with vendors and potential clients. Every time they passed in the hall, she wanted to jump him, and his furtive touches and stolen glances told her he wanted to do the same. But the darn computer technicians were right there, like mice infiltrating every square inch of the place.

She gathered her things at the end of the day, thinking about what to wear to JJ's Pub to check out the band for the grand opening. Gage was excited to see the band, but he seemed even more thrilled at the prospect of another date night with Sally, which he had pointed out every chance he got. *Our third date as a married couple.* Even thinking about the things he said and the way he said them made her pulse race, which was exactly why she was having a hard time deciding what to wear. This openly affectionate, seductive side of him was addicting, and brought out a part of her she wasn't sure she'd ever tapped into.

Tapped into? Heck, I never even knew it existed.

She left her office and went to find her new secret husband. The center was bigger than the one in Allure to accommodate the larger small town. She peeked into the gymnasium and her heart swelled. Neither she nor Gage had wanted to clear away the memories of last night. No one had ever done anything so romantic for her. She had been so young when she married Dave, and real life had come at them quickly—caring for a baby, chasing a toddler, taking night classes while Dave got his business up and running. She couldn't remember ever thinking about romance, much less feeling like she'd missed it. But with Gage everything felt romantic. Even silly things, like cleaning up from dinner and their messy cake smashing together. They'd left the balloons and canopy in place, and they talked for hours about silly things, like favorite colors and most hated foods—his was blue and eggplant. By the time they returned to the hotel, they were both exhausted, and all she wanted to do was take a hot bath and curl up in Gage's arms and sleep. But she'd begged off his offer to do just that, knowing sleeping would be the last thing on her mind if she was in his bed. Although her solo bath had only woken her up and stirred her desire for the man on the other side of the adjoining door. The orgasm she'd given herself hadn't come close to what she'd needed.

She followed the sound of Gage's voice down the hall, which sent her stomach into a wild flurry. How could a voice she'd heard every day for years suddenly turn her inside out?

Gage sat on the edge of the desk gazing out the window and talking on his cell phone. His long-sleeved T-shirt was stretched tight over his broad back, long, jeans-clad legs stretched out before him. She wanted to walk right up and stand between those legs, run her hands up his thighs, and distract him from the phone call, doling out some of the sexual torture he'd given her last night.

He turned, an easy smile lifting his lips, and waved her in. Her mind was still playing naughty games, and she wasn't sure her legs would carry her across the floor. She leaned against the doorframe, crossing her legs at the ankles, and mouthed, *Take your time*, as she enjoyed the view.

His gaze slid down her body, lingering on the open neckline of her blouse. He licked his lips, and she felt her nipples rise to greet him. Memories of what that hot mouth of his felt like stroked the inferno that had been simmering all day long.

"Okay, buddy. Sure," Gage said into the phone as he pushed to his feet, approaching her like a panther on the prowl.

Her pulse spiked with each step. Lord, there must have been testosterone in whatever he'd had for lunch, because he exuded sexuality even more than ever before.

"Your mom is right here. Want to say hi?"

Her brain snapped into Mommy mode, and she pushed from the wall. "Is that Rusty?"

Gage nodded. "He said he spoke to you a few hours ago. Do you want to talk to him?"

"Not unless he wants to talk to me," she said, wondering what they were talking about. "But tell him I love him."

Gage said, "He heard you," to Sally, then into the phone he said, "Okay, buddy. Be safe."

Be safe. Did he know that watching out for her son, even making time for him the way Gage did so often, was like mommy porn? Oh yes, she was wearing those over-the-knee boots again just for him tonight. And maybe her sweater minidress, too. The one she'd worn a few weeks ago, when he hadn't been able to stop staring.

Gage tucked his phone into his pocket and put his arms

around her. "How's my gorgeous wife?"

Hearing him say that made her heart race again. She reached for her hair, and he intercepted her hand, putting it on his chest. He was hard and warm, and her mind went straight to the gutter. *Hard is very good.* Then his long, strong fingers pushed into her hair and his blue eyes narrowed, drawing her right in. *Pure. Seduction.*

"I'm wondering what you and Rusty were talking about," she managed.

A coy smile played at the edges of his mouth. "Oh? You mean my *stepson*?"

Holy cow. She hadn't put a name to what he was to Rusty now—legally speaking. A storm of emotions barraged her. "Please tell me you did *not* tell him about Vegas."

He tugged her hair, bringing her so close, she saw starbursts of white in his irises. "Tell my stepson about his mother waking up naked in my bed?" he said in a voice as rich as melted chocolate. "I want to do a lot of things to you, but disrespecting you is not one of them."

Her mind screamed, *Kiss me!* but the words got lost in her desire.

He pressed his lips to the corner of her mouth. "No, bird. I did not tell him you and I are married." He kissed her neck, and she leaned to the side, giving him better access. "You asked me not to, and I'm a pretty good listener."

He gave her hair another gentle tug, opening her up to him even more, and proceeded to drive her out of her mind one kiss at a time. She closed her eyes and felt him go hard against her as he tasted every inch of flesh between her chin and breastbone.

"Gage," she said breathlessly. "Rusty? Is he okay?"

He cradled her face in his hands and gazed into her eyes.

"Yes, babe. His buddy's selling a Jeep and he wanted advice on cars. He said he told you he was thinking of buying one. Did he?"

"Yes. Thank you for helping him."

"Hey," he said between kisses. "I'd never hide anything about your son from you. There's no secret stuff going on. You know that, don't you? I would have told you about our conversation about sex if you'd asked, which now that I'm thinking about it, is probably wrong on some level. I should have clued you in back then."

She smiled and shook her head. "No. Believe it or not, there are certain things a mom doesn't need to know. Now, if you'd have told him to sleep with as many women as he could, I would have been upset. But you wouldn't do that. It's not the Ryder way."

He grinned. "You have met Jake, right?"

Jake was his youngest brother, and before he'd fallen in love with his fiancée, Addison Dahl, he'd been one of the biggest players Sally had ever met. Right up there with Blake Carter. "He's grown up, and now he's as loyal as a retriever," she reminded him. "We'd better get a move on if we're going to the bar. I'm starved and want to grab something on the way back to the hotel."

He took her hand as they headed for the exit, shutting off lights on their way. "Have I ever told you that I love how you eat when you're hungry?"

"As opposed to?"

"Being one of those women who exist on air." He grabbed her ass as they walked out to the parking lot. "Don't ever lose this perfect ass, baby."

"That's like a license to eat, you know. I could get huge."

He unlocked the car door and held it open for her, his mouth curling into a devilish grin. "More of you to love."

"I could develop fat rolls." She slid into the passenger seat, and he leaned in and squeezed her upper thigh.

"More to hang on to when we're making love."

"You say all the right things, but I've never seen you with a heavyset woman."

"You've never seen me with *any* woman," he said seriously, as if he'd taken offense by her comment. "Because there's only one woman I want. Fat, thin, round with our babies, old and wrinkly. Only you, little bird."

He pressed his lips to hers and she wondered if Danica would be upset if they skipped going to see the band and made out all night instead.

GAGE SAT IN his hotel room Skyping with his brothers Duke and Cash. Their wives, Gabriella and Siena, had gone out shopping. Cash was on dad duty with his almost eight-month-old twins, Coco and Seth. The first time Gage had held his niece and nephew, he'd expected to feel a pang of sadness over what he'd lost, but it had never come. All he'd felt was anticipation of one day having his own babies to love and raise.

"We're thinking of giving Blue and Lizzie a three-week cruise as their wedding present. Have you gotten them a gift?" Cash bounced Coco on his knee. Her sandy-blond curls springing around her chubby cheeks and her sweet baby giggles made Gage laugh. Coco took after Cash, while Seth's hair was darker brown like Siena's.

"Not yet. Sally and I are in Virginia setting up the new

center. We'll get to it." Gage couldn't take his eyes off his adorable niece. There'd been a time when he'd thought he'd be the first one in his family to the altar. Strangely, that hadn't been when he was with Stacy, but a year after he'd known Sally. He had no one to blame but himself. He'd wasted a lot of time waiting for a sign, some indication that she was ready. *Sometimes it takes waking up married to really bring the idea home.*

Not that he'd planned their impromptu wedding, but damn, if he'd known how that night would turn out, he'd have taken her to Vegas years ago.

Duke's face appeared beside Cash. His oldest brother looked a lot like their father, dark and serious. "You act like you're already married."

It was hell holding his tongue when he wanted to shout his confirmation from the rooftops. "What can I say, bro? Wishful thinking, I guess." Gage checked his watch. It was nearly eight o'clock. Sally had gone back to her room after dinner to shower and change. She'd been in there forever, and every minute away from her felt like an hour. "So, what's up? Why'd you want to Skype?"

"Because I wanted to show you this." Duke held up a sonogram picture, pride gleaming in his eyes, alongside something more serious.

An unspoken, misdirected apology, maybe?

Gage smiled, nodding in a way he knew Duke would interpret just as he should—that Gage was more than fine with the news, and thrilled for him. "Gabby's pregnant? Man, that's awesome! Congratulations. When's the baby due?"

"Early May," Duke answered. "We wanted to wait until we passed the first trimester. Doc says everything looks good."

"Dude, I'm so happy for you."

"Yeah, this guy has no idea what he's in for." Cash handed Coco to Duke and turned to pick up Seth from the playpen behind him. "My kids have decided they no longer need to go to bed until they've worn me and Siena out."

"I'm sure it's worth it, though," Gage said. "Listen, I've got to get Sally to hurry up. We're going to check out a band for the grand opening. Kiss my niece and nephew for me, and, Duke, give Gabby a big hug for me."

"Will do," Duke said.

After he ended the call, he grabbed his wallet and knocked on the adjoining door. "Sal? You almost ready?"

The door swung open and she stood before him in a slinky little sweaterdress that showed off her gorgeous legs.

"Sorry. I was on the phone with Gabby and Siena." Her head was tilted to the side as she fiddled with her earring, leaving her neck exposed.

He didn't waste a second before going in for a taste. "You heard the news?" He wasn't surprised. She was as close to his sisters-in-law as his own sister was.

"Yes. Isn't it exciting?" She held on to his forearm as he covered her neck with kisses. "Gabby said Duke was going to tell you tonight, too."

"Mm. He did. They're very lucky. Almost as lucky as me. I have the hottest wife on the planet." His hands roamed over her bottom. "You look good enough to eat, baby. Maybe we should blow off the band. We are newlyweds after all."

She stilled, and trapped her lip between her teeth, like she loved the sound of that. A long moment later, she said, "We can't," and shook out her hair. It fell lustrous and shiny over her shoulders. "I went online to check out the band and found out this is their last gig until after the holidays." She grabbed a brush from the dresser and hurried into the bathroom.

He watched her brush her hair, and when her eyes drifted over the counter, brows furrowed, he looked around the bedroom and spotted her favorite hair product. He snagged the bottle and handed it to her. He'd seen her get ready so many times he knew her routine by heart. She'd flip her head upside down, spray three times, then flip it back over, magically making her hair appear fuller.

"That's a shame," he said as she flipped, spritzed, and directed her long locks away from her face. "Because I can think of at least a dozen things I'd like to do with my wife right now."

She set the spray can on the counter, watching him in the mirror as he stepped behind her and placed his hands on her hips. "You smell like summer rain and newlywed."

"What's with you and all this newlywed talk?" She turned in his arms, smiling up at him. "You probably shouldn't call me your wife around the band tonight in case they're really good and they agree to play at the grand opening, and you know…something goes wrong."

"You really need to stop worrying about that. The opening is months away. You'll be telling *everyone* way before that," he said confidently.

"I'm sure you're right," she said with a glimmer of happiness in her eyes. "But still."

He clung to that glimmer, and her admission, and took her left hand in his, noticing the ink was almost gone from her finger. His gut clenched, and he took a stab at getting her to change her mind. "Are we suggesting we pretend we're single tonight? Because I have to warn you, I'm a major chick magnet."

She laughed. "That you are." She went into the bedroom

and bent to pick up one of her fuck-me boots. "Not single, just not married."

She sat on the edge of the bed and pulled on the boot. Every time she wore those boots, he imagined making love to her when she was naked, except for those sexy suede boots. *One day…*

She pointed to her other boot, giving him a don't-count-your-chickens look. "Can you please hand me my boot?"

He picked it up and said, "The *husband* hands the *wife* her boot."

She laughed and he knelt before her. "The *husband* helps his beautiful *wife* put on her boot." He ran his hands slowly up her leg and back down. "As long as I'm down here…" He bent forward and kissed her inner thigh, running his hands up her leg again.

She put her hands over his, her eyes warning and pleading at once.

He scooched forward on his knees, perched between her legs, and wound his arms around her waist. "I'm not going to miss any signals this time."

"You're making me nervous again," she whispered.

"And…?"

"And we can't miss the band. I promised Danica."

"And…? I'm not missing any signals tonight, remember? I'm picking up on one that I can't read. Help me interpret it."

"I'm not used to you like this," she said, and lowered her voice to just above a whisper. "I can't just let you do *that*."

"Ah, my girl needs kisses and foreplay. Duly noted."

She pressed her hands to his cheeks with an unstoppable smile and said, "Stop embarrassing me!"

He gave her a chaste kiss and sat back on his heels to help

her with her boot. "Fine, but you're cute when you're embarrassed, and you're wearing fuck-me boots, which is like visual torture. I'll be turned on all night."

"Good," she said.

"Bird, you naughty girl." He leaned in, and she drew back, shaking her head. "Damn, baby. I'm just going to warn you now. By the time we get together, I'm going to be incapable of holding back."

Her fingers dug into the edge of the bed, and heat flared in her sweet baby blues.

"You're still my wife, whether or not I'm allowed to call you that. So let's not play the single game at the bar tonight."

She leaned in so close, he thought she was going to kiss him, but her gaze moved over his face, and a sassy smile formed on her lips. "Someone's afraid of getting jealous because his wife is a *dude magnet.*"

He scoffed and pushed to his feet. Guys were always checking Sally out, but there was no doubt in his mind—or apparently in hers—that he'd become more possessive of her since Vegas. The only difference was that now he could show it, whereas before he'd kept those feelings chained up.

She smoothed the front of the slinky little number she was wearing and fluttered her long lashes as she handed him her hotel keycard. "This is going to be *so* fun."

CHAPTER SIX

WHILE THE QUAINT small town of Oak Falls reminded Sally of home, JJ's Pub was like a whole different world. It smelled of leather, a hard day's work, and lost inhibitions. Music blared from the band in the back of the bar, where colored lights misted down on a stage she couldn't see. Gage held her hand, leading her through a crowd of twentysome-things who were bobbing to a country song. Gage's broad shoulders and the determined set of his jaw gave off an authoritative air, and the crowd parted for them. Sally clung tightly to him as women cast lustful gazes his way and men sized him up. They passed an archway, and she caught a glimpse of a burly, bearded guy riding a mechanical bull in the next room as a throng of women cheered him on. For the first time in a long time, Sally felt her age, and completely out of her element. She'd had Rusty so young, she'd missed out on the single years of bars and parties and skipped straight ahead to soccer mom and then widowed parent.

Gage's arm came around her waist, guiding her in front of him, his body forming a protective shield around her, as if he knew exactly what she was feeling.

He put his mouth beside her ear and said, "Stay close to me, bird. I'd hate to have to kill some guy for touching you."

She couldn't help but laugh at that. Did he not feel the

stares of all the young, beautiful women checking him out?

The line at the bar was five people deep. Gage slid one large hand to her stomach and the other across her chest, like a seat belt. She could feel his heart beating against her back. It was such an intimate embrace, it reminded her of their night out in Vegas, when he'd also been overly possessive. Her nerves went a little crazy, as they had earlier, when he'd been on his knees putting on her boots and he'd made the innuendo about what he could do while he was *down there.* She remembered with shocking clarity exactly how good he'd been at the particular thing he had offered. She didn't have to reach far to recall the scratch of his scruff on her thighs or his talented mouth driving her out of her mind. A streak of heat coursed through her. *Great.* Now she was getting all hot and bothered again.

"The line's not moving," Gage said, his warm breath caressing her cheek, making her even more aware of every inch of him.

His fingers covered the span of her stomach, pressing into her belly, his arm sank into the pillows of her breasts, and his chest muscles contracted as he held her captive against his hard body.

Suddenly Gage was on the move, weaving deeper into the crowd, closer to the stage, keeping Sally trapped against his chest. The driving pulse of the music thrummed, rough and alive, drilling beneath her skin, until she breathed to the same staccato beat. Gage turned her in his arms, never once fully releasing her as he brought her tight against him in another proprietary embrace. His piercing blue eyes were entrancing, more libidinous than ever, as if the oppressive heat of the crowd, the provocative bumping and grinding around them, was a drug in and of itself, luring him in and leaving his inhibitions behind.

When he lowered his face beside hers, the scratch of his whiskers brought memories of his rough kisses. She wound her arms around his neck, giving herself over to the hypnotic riff of the guitar, and closed her eyes.

"In case you've forgotten"—Gage's deep voice slid into her ear—"I'm crazy about you, bird."

She was sure she'd melt into a puddle right there on the dance floor. His hands moved over her back, into her hair, tugging and tangling, and eventually skimmed down her hips and caressed her bottom. She didn't want to think about the youth center, or the band they were checking out, or the way she'd felt old and out of place when they'd first arrived. She wanted to disappear into the long, sensual strokes of Gage's hands and give herself over to the intoxicating draw of his masterful seduction.

His lips grazed her cheek. "My wife is the most beautiful woman in here."

Oh, this man! He'd always had a way of making her feel special, but when he turned on the charm she was powerless to resist him. They swayed to the erotic beat of desire, with an undercurrent of freedom that could only come from being far away from their real world. When he pressed his warm, soft lips to her neck, lust pooled deep inside her. And when he brought those lips to hers, she didn't hesitate opening up for him. She wanted this. The dancing. The titillation of what would come next. The full-body anticipation rattling her from the inside out, making her body throb and ache and swallowing her whole.

When the song came to an end, Gage and Sally didn't stop moving to their own private beat. He gazed into her eyes, holding her even tighter as people moved around them and the band began playing another song. He spoke into her ear, rough and soft at once. "I don't know how to draw the line again, Sally. I've wanted you for so long, in my head you're already mine. Everything changed when that door opened, and I don't want to close it. I know I can't call you my wife while we're here, but I need to kiss you, bird. Right here, right now—"

Sally turned and their mouths collided. Her hands pushed into his hair as he took control, angling their bodies exactly where he wanted them and fitting them together like a puzzle, so close heat whipped through her like a hurricane and stole her breath, then gave it back in fits and spurts. Desire radiated from her core, pulling her further in to him. Somewhere in the recesses of her mind a whisper of a warning sounded. They shouldn't be making this type of public display in the town where they were setting up the center, but she didn't want to stop. She felt every inch of his hard heat against her belly, and that warning melted away.

A tormented sound escaped his lips as he tore his mouth away. His hands fisted in her hair, his gaze hot and conflicted. "The band," he said before taking her in another scorching kiss, like he couldn't stand even the few seconds they were apart.

He pulled away again, which was good, because Sally didn't have the strength to do it herself. All around them couples danced and groped, and she realized no one was watching them. They actually fit in with this steamy, needy crowd in which she'd felt so out of place.

They both shot a look toward the stage, each silently waging their own internal battle. Even through her lusty haze Sally recognized Sable Montgomery from the pictures she'd seen online. Long dark hair tumbled out from beneath a black cowgirl hat, hanging wild and thick like a horse's mane. She played the guitar like it was an appendage she'd been born with, and belted out the song in a voice as sweet and rough as whiskey. Sally knew this was the band's last gig while she and Gage were in town, and they needed to connect with them. But when Gage's hand moved to the nape of her neck, drawing her mouth back to his, her desire took over, pushing that responsible, practical woman out of the way. Hell, she'd knock that bitch down if that's what it took, because Gage's mouth was hot and hungry and his lips sweet and demanding. She wanted to stay there all night long, lost in him, loved by him, feeling free for the first time since she was a teenager.

She didn't know what had changed, but this was too right to ignore. She wasn't going to feel guilty for loving Gage. But she would feel guilty for not following through on her responsibility to Danica.

She reluctantly broke their connection. "We promised Danica."

His gaze flicked to the stage, then back to Sally, and she knew he was struggling with the same commitment. The muscles in his jaw bunched. He cursed under his breath and lowered his mouth beside her ear again. She was coming to crave those private whispers.

"We've worked all day. The only *work* I want to do is loving *you*, bird."

Yes, please. She glanced at the stage again, her mind racing through possible excuses she could give Danica. There were plenty that Danica would probably buy, but that wasn't how Sally lived her life, telling lies. She shifted her gaze to Gage again, and he untangled her finger from where she'd been absently twisting her hair around it.

With a look full of repressed sexual desire and reluctant

defeat, he gathered her in his arms and said, "Think they have an ice pack behind the bar?"

GAGE STOOD BY the bar thinking of hairy, sweaty men in an effort to calm his raging erection. The area was so crowded, Sally stood sideways, her softness pressed against him. Every time she moved, he had to refocus on those imaginary erection reducers. It was a losing battle.

"Don't you want a drink?" she asked, her nervous gaze moving to the bar.

A guy brushed against her shoulder and Gage pulled her against him, glaring at the offender. Sally's hands covered his chest, her eyes glossed over, soft and seductive, holding his rapt attention.

"No drinks," he ground out. "When I have you in my bed, I want to be stone-cold sober."

Her eyes widened as she climbed out of her comfort zone and into the darker place he was pushing her. He knew what she wanted, what she needed, and he wasn't about to let up. If it weren't for their responsibility to Danica, he'd have hauled her pretty little ass off the dance floor and she'd be back at the hotel enjoying orgasm number two or three by now.

Aw fuck.

He conjured more images of ugly men, and when that didn't work, he hit himself with the image that always calmed his jets. His parents.

Another song ended, and the band announced a break. A group of women came off the dance floor, laughing and fanning their faces. A gorgeous blonde wedged herself between Sally and the guy behind her, flashing a flirtatious smile at Gage. She had eyes that spelled trouble and a smile that said she meant it.

This girl had balls, considering Sally was plastered against him, and he was sure he had about ten years on her. Sally was busy watching the band come off the stage. Gage cradled Sally's much more beautiful face and kissed her. He felt Sally startle, and he kissed her more sensually, disappearing into her as she went boneless against him. They remained entwined for a long time, deepening the kiss and getting lost in each other all over again. Gage came away slowly, pressing several softer kisses to Sally's luscious mouth before finally meeting the blonde's gaze. There was no way she didn't get the message.

Holy shit. She looked like she was turned on. That was not the reaction he was hoping for.

The blonde flashed that smile again and hollered, "JJ!" to the bartender.

JJ sauntered over, eyeing her like he knew her well. "What can I get for you, darlin'?"

She pointed to Sally and said, "I want whatever she had."

Sally followed Gage's gaze over her shoulder toward the girl, and the confidence drained from her face. Didn't she know how beautiful she was? How spectacular of a woman, mother, and friend she was? Not to mention those smoking-hot kisses. That young girl had nothing on Sally. Hell, no one in the *state* did.

"Hey." Gage waited for Sally to meet his gaze. "I kissed *you*, bird. Every woman in here could be naked and you'd still be the only one I see." He pulled her in closer. "And the only one I'll ever want."

"Damn," the blonde said. "Forget the drink, JJ. I need to crawl into this woman's skin and see what her secret is." She flashed a friendlier, less flirtatious smile and moved closer to

Sally, like she was sharing a secret. "I have gone out with a lot of guys, and never once have I heard anything even close to that. What's your secret?"

Gage was glad she wasn't a bitch, because if she'd said something spiteful, he'd have told her off.

Sally's eyes darted up to him, and she drew her shoulders back, standing taller, *prideful.* "There's no secret. The best relationships always begin with friendship."

"Honey," the blonde said as the female guitarist broke through the crowd and put an arm around her, "I've been sleeping with my best friend for years and he's never said anything like that to me."

"That's because you also treat flirting like it's a career, baby sister," the guitarist said, flashing the same friendly smile as the blonde at Sally. "Is Brindle hitting on your man?" Her eyes raked down Gage. "Damn, you are hot, but clearly taken." She turned Brindle by the shoulders and pointed to a handsome dark-haired guy standing at the other end of the bar. "Go get Trace and leave these two alone."

The well-honed older-sister tone of her voice reminded Gage of Duke when they were younger and he'd admonish him in much the same I-know-what's-best way.

"Trace Jericho and I are done." Brindle crossed her arms with an irritated expression.

"This week," the guitarist said sarcastically. She lifted her chin at the bartender. "Justus, make sure she doesn't have any more to drink, got it? Her radar is a little off tonight."

"You got it, Sable," the bartender said.

Gage connected the dots and realized the bartender, JJ—*Justus*—was also the owner of the pub.

Brindle stalked away and Sable turned her attention back to

Sally and Gage. "Sorry, guys. My sister is a bit of a wild one, but beneath all that flirtation, she's a good egg."

"That's okay." Gage held out his hand. "I'm Gage Ryder, and this is"—*my wife*—"Sally Tuft. We came tonight to check out your band. We're opening a new youth center across town called No Limitz, and we wanted to talk to you about playing at the grand opening in March."

"Ah, you're with the company Brindle has been talking about. She's excited about the opportunity to hold more kids' programs." She glanced at her sister, who was now busy chatting with a group of girls. "She teaches English and runs the drama club at the elementary school. Believe it or not, she's an amazing teacher."

"I'm sure she is." Sally turned a heated gaze on Gage. "Alcohol loosens everyone up."

Damn, baby. That look...

He realized he wasn't the only one enjoying that look and glared at the two guys checking Sally out from a few feet away. He put his arm possessively around her waist.

"Oh, Brindle's always a spitfire, but she's all talk. Don't worry. Now that she knows Gage is taken, she won't try to pick him up." Sable took her cowgirl hat off and ran a hand through her long brown hair. "I've got to get back to the band, but I'd love to talk about the opening." She put her hand on the shoulders of two men who were seated at the bar, pushing them farther apart. "Excuse me, boys." She hiked herself onto her belly on the bar, reaching for something beneath the edge.

"Sable!" Justus hollered from the other end of the bar. He shook his head and headed toward them.

Sable's legs kicked up and Gage pulled Sally aside to keep her from getting struck.

"One of these days you're going to get yourself in trouble doing that," the larger of the two men said as he slapped Sable's ass.

Sable landed on her boots with a *clunk*, exhaled loudly, and got right in the guy's face. "Frazier Young, you touch my ass again and I'll kick yours so far out of town you won't be able to find your way back."

Frazier held up his hands in surrender. "Can't blame a guy for trying."

"Can't blame a girl for kickin' a guy's ass, either." Sable handed Sally a flyer. "That's got our band's information and my cell number as well as the number at my auto shop."

"Sable, how about you keep your feet on the ground, darlin'?" Justus put a stack of flyers on the bar and glared at Frazier. Justus was a big dude, with deep-set eyes and an athletic build, but even his size and serious stare didn't seem to faze Frazier. "Don't start shit with her. She'll knock you flat on your back."

Frazier smirked. "Just as long as she climbs on top afterward, I'm cool with that."

Sable waved him off. "Justus Jericho, this is Gage Ryder and Sally Tuft. Gage and Sally are setting up the new youth center. Justus owns this pub, and he and his brothers can break a horse about as fast as I can rebuild an engine. I've got to get back onstage, but it was nice meeting you both. Give me a call tomorrow afternoon and we can talk."

"See ya, Sable." After she walked away, Justus said, "She's a hell of a mechanic if you ever need one, and her band is the best around. Word around town is that you're looking for someone to run your sports programs at the youth center."

"Yes," Gage said. "We're holding interviews this week. Do you know anyone?"

"This town's about as big as my fist. I know everyone." Justus set a beer on the bar for a customer. "There's only one guy around here you need to interview." He pointed across the room at a burly, dark-haired man who looked like he belonged on a football field. He was in deep conversation with a petite blonde. "Sinclair Vernon. *Sin.*"

"That's Sin Vernon? The same Sin Vernon who runs the athletic program for Virginia State?" Gage had heard great things about the guy.

"*Ran* the program," Justus clarified. "He just resigned. I can call him over and introduce y'all."

"That's okay. He looks busy." Gage knew if they started talking sports they'd be there for hours, and the only thing he wanted to do for hours was Sally. He withdrew a business card from his wallet and handed it to Justus. "Would you mind passing my number along to him? I'd love to speak with him." He put an arm around Sally, pulling her close again. Duty done, he couldn't wait to get her alone. When their eyes met, he was sure they'd set off the smoke alarms.

"Thanks, man," he said to Justus. "It was nice meeting you, but we've got to run. Sally and I have some pressing business to take care of."

CHAPTER SEVEN

SALLY HURRIED TO keep up with Gage. The cold night air stung her cheeks as they crossed the parking lot. "Pressing business?"

He hauled her against him and captured her mouth, kissing her so deeply, her legs turned to butter. She wound her arms around his neck, his urgency feeding hers. When he grabbed her bottom, holding her so close to his big, hard body even air couldn't fit between them, a moan slipped from her lungs. She felt him smile against her lips as they stumbled toward the car. He trapped her against the passenger door, grinding into her, and made a purely male sound that sent rivers of heat pooling between her legs. Without breaking their kiss, he lifted her up and set her on the hood, reached around her, his hand flat on the small of her back, and hauled her forward. His wide hips were nestled between her legs, and his mouth blazed a trail down her neck. *Oh, yes. More, more, more.* He grabbed her leg and lifted it to his hip, pressing his hard length against her center, and *oh Lord*, he was *hard*, and she was ready.

Her eyes fluttered closed as he sealed his mouth over her neck and sucked.

"*Gage*," came out in a rush, but he didn't relent the titillating torture.

"Not stopping," he growled.

His mouth came down over hers again, taking and exploring like he wanted to climb inside and live there. The muscles in his neck corded beneath her fingers. The feel of his hot skin made her want to taste more of him in ways other than kisses. The faint beat of the band sounded in the distance, competing with her thundering heart. Gage drew back and framed her face between his large hands. He touched his forehead to hers, breathing heavily.

"Salbird," came out full of lust and love. The way it had in her fantasies, only better, because this was real.

Desire ran rampant through her, muddling her thoughts and making her tremble with need. "Take me to the hotel" came out somewhere between a demand and a plea.

She didn't have to ask twice. The second they were in the car they both reached across the console, unable to keep their hands off each other. *This is it*, her lust-addled brain chanted. She was finally going to make love to the man she'd wanted for so long, her body throbbed and ached for him. She was as nervous as she was excited. Gage kissed her hard and possessively as he guided her seat belt across her body, latching it into place.

"Can't have my wife getting hurt."

She watched his lips, taunted by their fullness and the pleasures she knew they would bring.

"Hurry," she urged. If he didn't drive, she was either going to chicken out or pull him into another kiss. She definitely didn't want to chicken out, and if she kissed him again, she wasn't sure she'd be able to stop. The only way to top having sex and getting married while flat-out drunk was to get caught having sex in a parking lot. She was just unlucky enough for that to happen.

Gage drove the whole way with one hand on her thigh, the tips of his fingers beneath the edge of her sweaterdress, a fraction of an inch from the juncture of her thighs. It was impossible not to think about his hot hand as it practically branded her through her stockings. *Maybe I should have worn thigh-highs.* One shift in her seat and she'd feel his fingers against her panties, even if through her stockings. She debated the shift and felt her cheeks burn as he pulled into the hotel parking lot and cut the engine.

Gage leaned across the console and slowly unwound her hair from around her finger with a sinful look in his eyes. Her pulse sprinted. She couldn't wait to see that look from beneath his naked body as his thick cock drove into her. He pressed a kiss to her hand and tucked her hair behind her ear. A softer look came over him as he dragged the back of his knuckles along her cheek.

"Still with me, bird? No pressure if you're having second thoughts."

"No second thoughts." She was surprised she could form words she was so nervous. She could overthink what was coming next forever, but hadn't she already spent years doing just that? There was no chance of anyone they knew suddenly knocking on their door, or of her son coming home and catching them in bed together. It didn't get much safer than this. Nothing short of a comet plummeting to earth would stop her now.

He kissed her then, soft and sweet and so deliciously, her entire body tingled from her head to her toes.

A few minutes later they were making out in the elevator, hands and mouths moving too fast to slow down. The doors opened and they stumbled out in a tangle of limbs and fiery kisses. And then they were in Gage's hotel room, the door clicking shut behind them as he drew back only long enough to strip off their coats. The room smelled like Gage, rugged and tempting. It was dark, save for the moonlight casting a dim bluish hue through the open curtains, and Sally was shaking like a leaf in the wind.

Gage's hands ran down her arms. "You okay, sweetheart?"

"Nervous," she said honestly, swallowing hard.

"Me too."

Laughter bubbled out before she could stop it. "Uh-huh."

He stepped closer, their bodies touching from thigh to chest. "I've got the woman of my dreams in a hotel room, and she's not drunk or even tipsy." He took her hand in his, leading her farther into the room. "Five long years of wanting you all comes down to what happens next. Am I going to screw up? Move too fast?" He began unbuttoning his shirt, stopping after two buttons. "Too slow?"

He led her to the bed and she sat on the edge as he knelt before her, her pulse quickening with every breath. This was where they'd started out the night, and as he lifted her foot and ran his hand up the back of her calf, memories of what he'd wanted to do earlier when he was in that position came rushing back. Heat flooded her body. She didn't think it was possible to feel so much, to be turned on to the point of already being wet and shaky and nearly unable to speak. But as his hand moved up her leg, she knew he'd only begun his masterful seduction.

"Am I going to bring you enough pleasure?" he said, continuing to list his reasons for being nervous.

He unzipped her boot and pulled it off. There was something unexpected and sensual about his honesty and about the feel of his hands moving so carefully as he lifted her other foot and unzipped the boot ever so slowly.

"Am I going to *last* the first time I bury myself deep inside you?" He arched a brow, a wicked smile lifting his lips.

Oh God. Hearing him say that took her even higher. Could he take her right up to the edge with words alone?

He pulled off her boot and sat beside her on the bed, toeing off his shoes, then tugging off his socks. She was so nervous she could barely breathe.

He brushed her hair from her shoulder, his touch gentle yet determinedly seductive. "Am I going to figure out how to get those stockings off you without tearing them?"

Oh! She hadn't thought about that. She should have thought about this moment, not just the dress. She really needed to up her game. *Tear them, please! With your teeth.* She wanted to say the words, but his chest came down over hers, lowering her to her back, and her voice was lost beneath her frantic heartbeat.

He laced their fingers together and brushed his lips over hers. She loved when he did that feathery tease of a kiss.

"I've got plenty to be nervous about, baby, but that's not going to stop me from enjoying every second of this night."

He released one of her hands, sliding his palm along her ribs and down her hip, then back up again, grazing the side of her breast. She shuddered with anticipation. He didn't say a word for the longest time, just gazed into her eyes as he explored the curve of her waist, the swell of her breast, the top of her thigh.

Oh God…

His eyes trailed down her body, their hampered breathing and the sound of his hand sliding along her dress the only noises in the room. He touched her cheek, gazing at her like she was a treasure. Her heart beat faster with every passing second.

"I can't decide where to start." He brushed his thumb over her lips. "Your mouth?" He dragged his tongue along the seam of her lips, and she leaned up, trying to catch a kiss, but he lifted just out of reach. "Your neck?" He gently sucked the column of her neck.

She squirmed beneath him.

"Or do I strip you bare and start lower?" He gathered her dress above her thighs. His eyes locked on Sally's, which was about the sexiest thing she'd ever seen. He lifted it higher and ran his fingers along the waist of her stockings. "These have got to go."

She reached down to remove them and he caught her hand.

"Not a chance, beautiful."

He lowered his mouth to hers. His tongue was smooth and demanding over hers as his hand stroked an intoxicating rhythm between her navel and thighs. She tried to concentrate on their kisses, but her mind kept drifting south, where his fingers trailed close to her sex and then up again, taunting her over and over until she held her breath with every downward pet. His leg moved over her thigh, his arousal pulsing against her, hot and hard, obliterating the last shred of her sanity. She went a little wild, grabbing at his body, bowing off the bed. When she tugged at her stockings, he tried to roll them down her hips, moving slowly and carefully, but he accidentally latched on to her thong, too, and they got twisted and stuck. His brows knitted. He tried to roll them back up, and his fingers tore through the nylon.

Her first sober sexual encounter in years and she couldn't even get there! She tried to help him, lifting her butt from the mattress and wiggling, but it only made things worse. Their eyes connected, and just as mortification began to steal her breath, laughter burst out.

"I can't even have sex *sober*," she said through hysterical laughter.

"Oh, you're going to have sex all right. The best sex of your life if I can get these suckers off." He thrust his fingers through the hole, shredding them one yank at a time, but the waist remained intact. "What the…?"

His gaze flicked to hers, and she fell back laughing so hard tears streamed down her cheeks. His eyes narrowed with determination, making her laugh even harder. He tore at the waist like his life depended on it, while Sally held on to the mattress in fits of laughter, making him laugh, too. When he *finally* managed to get them, *and* her thong, off, he dragged a long strip of the silky material over her sex and thighs. The lascivious look in his eyes stopped her cold as he climbed up her body and perched above her, his heated gaze so open and honest, so *real*, she felt her world coming together like never before.

"Sorry, baby."

A laugh slipped out before she could stop it. "It's okay."

"I can think of something we can do with this." He brushed the shredded material over her wrist and her pulse spiked. "But I'm afraid I'd never get you untied."

That spurred another round of laughter.

She pushed playfully at his chest, rolling him onto his back, and began unbuttoning his shirt. "Good thing I didn't wear Spanx."

"Next time I'm bringing scissors."

God, she loved this beautiful man. *Loved* him! This wasn't infatuation or loneliness. This was heart-and-soul, to-the-ends-of-the-earth, bone-deep love. She finished unbuttoning his shirt and pressed a kiss to the center of his chest.

He shrugged off his shirt and tossed it to the floor.

She couldn't resist teasing him. "You still want there to be a next time? Even after the *stocking* fiasco?"

"Every day for the rest of my life."

GAGE HELD SALLY'S gaze as he undressed. Her dress was bunched around her thighs, her legs tucked beneath her. Her big blue eyes were innocent and hungry at once, trailing down his body, lingering on his erection, and making him even harder. Her chest rose with an uneven inhalation as she went up on her knees and pulled that slinky little dress over her head, revealing a black lace bra stretched tight over her full breasts. Without a moment's hesitation, she dropped the silky lingerie to the bed. Holy hell, she was *stunning*. He drank in every inch, from her rosy nipples to the curve of her waist and the fine white stretch marks barely visible along her lower belly. *Marks of motherhood.* Those scars made him love her even more.

His gaze moved lower, to the tuft of blond at the apex of her thighs. She trapped her lower lip between her teeth, absently winding her long hair around her finger as she covered her belly with her other hand.

His body ached to finally make love to her, but it was his thundering heart that had him moving her hand so he could kiss every mark.

"You're beyond gorgeous, bird."

She was trembling harder again, and he lay her gently on the bed and kissed her until her trembling eased.

"I love you, sweetheart, and if you need a moment, or a day, give me the word."

The sweetest smile appeared, and she shook her head. "All I need is you, Gage. Love me like you promised."

Like you promised. She knew she could count on him—even for this. That meant so much to him, he got a little choked up. "Always, baby."

He loved his way down her body, memorizing the feel of her, soft and wanting, beneath him. Her hands played in his hair as he learned what made her hold her breath—loving her breasts with his mouth—and what made her arch off the bed—when he licked and kissed her hips. Goose bumps chased his lips around her belly button to the tops of her thighs. When he shifted between her legs, she opened them wider to accommodate his broad body and closed her eyes. He reached up and laced the fingers of his right hand with hers, loving her so deeply he wanted to be connected on every level.

As he lowered his mouth to her inner thigh, she tightened her fingers around his. He stole a glance at her flushed cheeks, her teeth trapping her lower lip. Her left arm rested beside her head, a lock of hair caught between her fingers. His heart squeezed. She was so trusting. He knew he'd spend the rest of his life making sure she never doubted that trust.

He pressed a kiss to the tuft of blond between her legs and slicked his tongue along her glistening sex, taking his first sober taste of her. *Sweet perfection.* He loved her slowly, licking and kissing, teasing and taunting with his hand and mouth, until she was writhing and moaning. Her sexy little murmurs made his pulse skyrocket as she angled her hips, arching and rocking, guiding him in ways he knew she was too shy to verbalize. He slid two fingers inside her, taking her higher, until every breath was stilted and her thighs tightened around his head. Another slick of his tongue, a furtive stroke of his fingers along that magical spot, and his name flew from her lips like the wind.

"*Gage! Ohhhh—*"

The seductive sound shot through him like a bullet. He stayed with her, riding the waves of their passion and taking her right up to the peak again. Her nails dug into his knuckles. He was sure she'd leave scars, and he didn't care. He wanted them—*everywhere.*

"Gage," she panted out. "I need *you.*"

He grabbed a condom from the bedside drawer and rolled it on. Sally's eyes fluttered open, and his heart tumbled in his chest as she reached for him. He'd waited so long for this moment, he had a veritable list of things he thought he'd say when they got here. But as he gazed into her loving eyes, he couldn't form a single word. And as he pushed into her tight heat, he filled her so completely, so perfectly, he could barely breathe. Their bodies moved in sync, better than he'd dreamed. Better than anything he could imagine. Her legs wound around his waist as their mouths came together in a scorching kiss. He pushed one hand beneath her ass, and the other cradled her body as he loved her so thoroughly, he had to grit his teeth to keep from coming too fast. Bound by a tempo of urgency, a flood tide of emotions swamping him, he struggled to slow his pace, catching a hitch in her breathing every time he thrust. The feel of her body tightening around him took him right up to the edge.

"Open your eyes, baby."

Her eyes opened, and the love in them would have knocked him to his knees had he been upright.

"You're everything, Sally. My heart, my soul, my reason for being."

Her eyes went damp, and he kissed her softly.

"I love you, too, Gage."

The raw sensuousness of her voice slid over his lips, beneath his skin, all the way to his bones, carrying him to even greater heights. He thrust harder, loved her deeper, wanting to become a permanent part of her. The sounds of their lovemaking filled the room, their bodies slick with heat, hands groping for purchase. Her breaths came in long, surrendering moans, carrying him right along with them. Gage's thoughts spun away as they yielded to the searing need that had been building for years, and blissfully succumbed to the explosive passion of their love.

They lay tangled together for a long while afterward as their breathing calmed. Gage couldn't stop kissing her. He didn't want to break away long enough to even take care of the condom. He was so full of Sally, he wanted to keep her in the nest of his love forever. She snuggled against him, murmuring against his neck and holding him so tight he knew she felt the magnitude of their connection just as deeply.

Sometime later, after ridding himself of the condom, Gage gathered her in his arms again, her body cradled against him, their hearts beating as one.

"Saying I love you seems too small for what I feel," he admitted. "I'm *yours*, bird, in every sense of the word."

CHAPTER EIGHT

SALLY WOKE WITH a smile on her face after the best sleep she'd had in ages and the best sex...*ever.* Being cradled within the confines of Gage's body was nothing like she'd imagined. He was a big man, and she'd thought he'd cuddle her for a little while and then he'd fall into whatever was his natural sleeping position. But as the sun crept in, Gage was still wrapped around her. The hair on his legs tickled the backs of her thighs. His chest was hot, his arms heavy and comforting. *Safe. Loving.* He hadn't moved all night, save for the warm kisses he'd pressed to her shoulder, which she thought he'd done in his sleep. She would pinch herself to make sure she wasn't dreaming, but she didn't dare move. He felt too good to risk waking him. Besides, what if their lovemaking wasn't as good for him as it was for her? She'd gone so long without, her ability to decipher good from bad might be off. Although for her, sex with Gage wasn't just *good.* It was *unfreakingbelievable.* And she was sure it was because she'd loved him for so long before they'd crossed that line.

His arms tightened around her, and she felt him go hard against her bottom. Heat and ice wound together inside her as she recalled every perfect moment of the night before. She'd imagined making love with him so many times, but when their bodies came together, it was nothing like she'd thought it would be. He smelled more masculine, and his touch was rougher, more controlling, in the very best way. And his laughter? She'd never laughed during sex before, at least not that she could remember.

There was nothing predictable about Gage, and when they were making love, she felt things she never had before. A trickle of guilt accompanied that admission, but she and Dave had been so young, she'd had no idea how to have an orgasm, much less how to move her body to help get her there. Truth be known, she'd never really thought about or discovered the nuances of the big O until after Dave had died. A few months after Dave's accident, she'd been lonely, desperate for human touch, and only then had she explored her own body. She'd taken it further, researching to find out how to best pleasure herself. She'd been amazed by what she was capable of feeling, and she'd felt guilty for not knowing how to enhance her pleasures when she'd been with Dave. He'd never complained about their sex life, but she couldn't help wondering if he'd missed out on something, too.

"How's my wife?" Gage asked in a sleepy voice.

"Good," she said nervously, suddenly peppered with worries. *Are we still okay? Was it good for you? Oh God! Did I taste okay?*

"Breathe, bird. You heart is beating too fast."

"Shh. You'll make me more nervous."

"Turn around, sweetheart."

She turned in his arms and he gathered her against him, seemingly either unaware of, or at least not bothered by, his erection.

"Talk to me, Sal."

No way could she voice her worries. "How about if I just go

get ready for work? We both have a long day of interviews ahead of us."

"Is that what you want, Sal? To fly away and pretend this never happened?" He kissed her softly. "Because if you're overthinking last night, please don't."

She touched her forehead to his chest, wishing she could crawl beneath his skin and hide until all her worries were put to rest.

"Sally, talk to me. Are you having second thoughts?"

She shook her head, and she nervously glanced up at him. "Are you?"

"No, babe, so don't panic. Making love to you was the most incredible feeling in the world."

"So…I didn't suck?"

"Unfortunately, not last night," he said with a wolfish grin. "But if you want to…" He flipped the sheet off them, exposing their naked bodies, and just like that, her questions were silenced by desire.

"Gage!" She tugged at the sheet and he covered them up again, chuckling.

He moved over her, pinning her to the mattress beneath him, an easy, reassuring smile on his handsome face. "Did it suck for you?"

"What? No!"

"Was I too pushy?"

"No."

"Was it the stockings?"

She laughed. "No. That was funny, though."

He nipped at her lower lip. "Then what is it, bird? What's got you all tied up?" He arched a brow. "There's an idea."

She loved that he knew how to ease her worries. "Actually,

I've never been tied up."

"Good. Something to look forward to."

Her insides flamed. "So, it wasn't bad? Really? You weren't lying there thinking I'm…I don't know. Not fun enough in bed? Not exciting enough? I've had a baby, things might not be, *you know…*" She whispered that last part.

He pressed a kiss to the center of her chin. "Baby, you're fun and exciting. And as far as your body goes, you're perfect. Didn't it feel good to you?"

"Yes. But what do I know? I've only been with one man in my entire life."

"Two," he reminded her. "Any other questions?"

She was quiet for a beat, drawing her courage. "Just one…"

"Anything."

She gave in to the smile tugging at her lips and said, "Can we do it again?"

"God, I love you."

His mouth came down over hers, and she felt the broad head of his arousal at her entrance.

"Protection," she said urgently.

He groaned and reached into the open drawer. Perched on his knees, he tore the condom open with his teeth.

"You know," he said with a hopeful grin. "We're married. We could just throw caution to the wind and start our family."

She loved Gage so much, she was tempted to agree, but she knew better. "I can't even think about having more children until we tell Rusty we're married." Rusty had been so angry at his father after he died, and while some of that was normal anger at losing him so unexpectedly, the aftermath of meeting Trisha and Chase had been overwhelming for both of them. She couldn't expect her son to deal with news of their marriage and a child all at once.

Gage sheathed his hard length and came down over her as he kissed her tenderly. "I was only teasing, baby. I don't want to make Rusty uncomfortable."

"Thank you. I'm still a little in shock about being married, even if you're taking it all in stride."

"In stride? Hell, baby. I want to shout it from the rooftops."

She mentally snapped a picture of the loving look in his eyes and tucked it beside her very full heart. "I'm sorry. I know this can't be easy for you."

"Relationships are supposed to be easy?" He kissed her again. "I love you, Sally. We'll do whatever it takes to make sure we're *all* okay, most of all, Rusty."

"Good. Now please proceed in convincing me that this marriage is the best *oops* moment in the world."

"Ah, birdie. What am I going to do with you?"

"Hopefully all those things you did last night. Especially that thing you did with your tongue."

THE REST OF the day passed in a blur. Sally and Gage worked diligently through their schedules, stealing kisses every chance they got. Gage had caught Sally peeking into the gym several times, and it warmed him all over knowing how much his efforts had meant to her. He hated the idea of clearing it all away Friday afternoon, but every day that passed brought them closer to the date they'd see Rusty, and one step closer to building their future together. Sally had spoken with Sable Montgomery, and Danica was putting together a contract for Surge to play at the grand opening. Gage coordinated meetings with several youth groups for after the holidays, and after a string of disappointing interviews, he received a call from Sinclair "Sin" Vernon. They scheduled a meeting for Friday morning, right before Sally and Gage were scheduled to leave town. Gage knew Sin fit the bill perfectly, and hoped the position was what he was looking for.

By the end of the day, they were both ready for some time away from the office, and in each other's arms. But first they hit the local shops to find presents for Danica and Blake's baby shower and Blue and Lizzie's wedding.

"I can't believe we waited so long to buy their gifts," Sally said as they headed into the mall. "It's so unlike us."

"You do realize, lovely wife of mine, that you sound like we've been married forever." He draped an arm over her shoulder. "From the day we met, it's always been *us*."

"Whatever, *pushy secret husband* of mine. It *is* unlike us. We always make sure we have gifts well ahead of time, and Danica's baby shower is right around the corner."

"I think a spur-of-the-moment wedding and finally getting together is cause for forgotten priorities."

She went up on her toes and kissed him. "Definitely. We should really find something for Chessie, too, so she doesn't feel left out."

"That big heart of yours is just one reason I adore you."

They went into a gift shop and then a department store looking for gift ideas, but Gage had no idea what to get his brother. "Cash and Siena are getting them a three-week cruise."

"Wow, that's an expensive gift."

"It's something Blue and Lizzie would never treat themselves with, so it's the perfect gift. What do you think we should get them?"

"Gosh," she said as they left the department store empty-handed. "I have no idea. They didn't register anywhere because they didn't want gifts, but Blue should know better. Giving gifts is the best part of your friends getting married. What about something clever instead of big, like matching aprons that say 'Kiss the Cook' since Lizzie used to do the Naked Baker webcast? Or cooking classes for the two of them?"

"Hm, maybe. Those are good ideas. What are you going to want as a wedding gift when we have our real wedding?"

"We're already married," she reminded him.

"If you think I'm going to make you miss out on walking down a real aisle in front of our friends and family, in a beautiful wedding dress, you're wrong." He tipped up her face and kissed her until she went soft in his arms. "Besides, I want to feel my heart pound as I watch you walk down the aisle. I want to know that you're sober and nothing could stop you from marrying me. So, tell me, my sweet bird. What would you want if it were your wedding?"

"You gave me that beautiful night in the gym. You don't have to do more."

"Baby, don't you see? I want *everything* with you. When we're old and gray, I want you to look back and feel like you never missed a thing."

Her gaze warmed. "But I don't love you because of how much you do for me. I love you because of the man that you are."

"I know, but I'm going to do things for you, with you, *to* you…" He kissed her again. "Why don't you think about what you'll want for a wedding gift, and we can get Blue and Lizzie something Blue would appreciate, like lingerie for his new wife." He waggled his brows.

"I guess I know what you'll want for a wedding gift." Her eyes widened. "Oh my gosh, that's it! Let's get sexy stuff for them to wear on their wedding night. We gave Lizzie some cute things for her bridal shower, but you can never have too much."

"I like the way you think. But, babe, guys don't really wear *sexy stuff*."

She wrinkled her nose, and then her eyes brimmed with amusement. "True. She'll probably have Blue wearing nothing but his leather tool belt anyway."

"Tool belt?" He hauled her against him. "Are you thinking about my younger brother naked?"

"A tool belt isn't naked." She laughed, obviously enjoying torturing him. "It's hot. Like a stripper."

"That's wrong on *so* many levels."

"I'm only thinking of Lizzie, the same way you thought of lingerie for Blue." She slid her finger into the waist of his jeans and fluttered her lashes. "Don't you want to know what I think about *you* wearing?"

"I'm still trying to get the thought of you lusting over Blue out of my mind."

She pressed her body against him and said, "I promise, I've got no interest in Blue beyond friendship. But I do love to see your jealous side come out."

"You do, do you?" He wrapped his arms around her.

"Mm-hm." She put her lips beside his ear and whispered, "The only man I want to see strip is you. But only for me. A private show."

He laughed, but her pinked-up cheeks told him she wasn't kidding. She was so adorable, all bundled up in her sweater, her hair cascading over her shoulders like spun gold, and those big blue eyes an alluring mix of sensuality and *did-I-really-say-that?*

There wasn't a thing he wouldn't do for her. "You're serious?"

She lifted one shoulder with a shy smile. "I've never actually seen a stripper. And I don't have an interest in seeing a stranger do it."

"Damn, baby. What other secret desires are you hiding?"

"I never knew I wanted to see that until right this second."

Just the idea of stripping for Sally made him hot and bothered. "I'll make you a deal. The day I'm allowed to tell the world we're married, I'll strip for you."

"Really?" Her eyes widened—and heated. "That's a lot of incentive to offer a girl who's small on experience and big on wanting you."

"Just the way I like you."

They shopped for a while longer. Coming up empty on a gift idea for Blue and Lizzie, they stopped at a baby store to pick something up for Blake and Danica's baby shower.

"Isn't this gorgeous?" She admired a mosaic bowl that had designs of baby's feet in the center.

"Didn't you and your mom do mosaics together when you were young?"

"Yes. When we traveled she always found an artist who would let us work in their studio." She looked at him thoughtfully. "I can't believe you remembered. I haven't thought about that since..."

"Since we went to that little shop in the Village, Jewels of the Past, when we bought Danica and Blake their wedding gift." A day he'd never forget because it was the first time she'd opened up to him about her parents.

"That was so long ago. How on earth did you remember?" She set the bowl down.

"It'd be hard to forget. You got this look in your eyes like you missed it, and you went into so much detail about how connected you'd felt to your mother during those times."

"I do miss it." She looked at her hands as if she were remembering how it felt to work with clay. "That time with my mom was special."

"Then you should do it again. Find a studio and invite your mom to go with you next time she's in town."

She rolled her eyes. "She's never in town. You know that. They travel all the time now that they're retired. But maybe I will try it again." She lifted a tiny pink dress from a rack and her gaze softened. "Aw, look at this. I remember when I was pregnant with Rusty, I'd go through stores looking at all the infant clothes, dreaming of what it would be like to finally meet my baby. I didn't want to know if he was a boy or a girl until he was born, so the poor guy was dressed in mint green and yellow for most of his infancy. I wish we knew if Danica was having a boy or a girl."

Gage drew her in close, looking forward to one day shopping for their own baby's clothing. "I bet you were the prettiest pregnant woman there ever was."

"Hardly, and I wasn't a woman. I was barely done being a girl when I became a mom." She smiled and added, "But I remember when they put Rusty in my arms for the first time. He was so tiny and vulnerable and perfect. I couldn't get over that he was part of me. To actually see this little person we'd created was overwhelming. I don't know how I got anything else done the first six months after he was born. I swear I stared at him every second, marveling at how beautiful he was."

"I want that with you, Sal. Not now. I know we have a while before we're there. But I look forward to seeing your belly round with our babies and being right beside you when you give birth."

She set the dress back on the rack and wound her arms around his neck. "Gage, you know there are risks involved with having babies after age thirty-five, right? Premature birth, birth defects, getting pregnant with multiples..."

"I know all about that. I've been in love with a cougar long enough to have thought it through."

She swatted him. "I am *not* a cougar."

He chuckled as they meandered through the store.

"Don't you know you're not supposed to talk about a woman's age?"

He grabbed her around the waist and ducked into an aisle, out of view from the employees. "I like being your boy toy." He began kissing her neck.

"You sure you don't want someone younger? With *years* of possibilities ahead of them? Someone who could give you a baby a year for five years?"

He bit her lower neck.

"Hey!" She scowled.

"Don't even start that with me, Sally Tuft—*Ryder*." *Holy shit.* How did he not put that together earlier? By the look on Sally's face, she hadn't put two and two together either. "What do we have to do to change your name?"

"Um..."

"What? Not this second. After we tell Rusty."

"But Rusty's last name is Tuft. And he's my son."

"And I'm your husband. I'm not asking you to forget Tuft. But I think Sally Tuft-Ryder has a nice ring to it."

"If Rusty freaks out—"

He silenced her with a kiss, unwilling to entertain the idea of not being married, much less of Sally not taking his name.

Maybe that made him too possessive or old-fashioned, but he didn't care. He was proud to be with her, and he wanted the world to know it.

When their lips parted, he touched his forehead to hers and said, "I love you, Sally. Please tell me you're not going to walk away from us."

"Never," she said quickly.

"Thank God. Then what…?"

"I'm just thinking about the best way to handle Rusty. Does it make more sense to ease him into it? Tell him we're dating and eventually move on to being engaged and *then* married?"

"Not unless you're talking speed dating, an hour engagement, and immediate elopement."

AFTER BUYING BABY gifts and a special doll for Chessie, Gage and Sally grabbed dinner in the food court. On their way back toward the exit where they'd parked, Sally stopped to admire a long red dress in the window of a clothing store. It was the most gorgeous shade of crimson she'd ever seen. Lace-capped sleeves decorated with rose and pearl appliqué gave the dress an air of elegance. The sweetheart neckline and empire waist would be slimming and comfortable, and the crinkled chiffon gave it a hint of shine.

Gage took Sally's hand and dragged her into the store. "You need that dress."

"No, I don't," she insisted as he made a beeline for a rack where several sizes of the gorgeous dress were displayed.

"Then *I* need you to have it. I need to see you in that dress." He fished through them and his shoulders slumped. "What is this? A children's store? Six? Ten? Twelve?"

She laughed. "That's how women's sizes run. I have no place to wear a dress like that, Gage. It's too glamorous. Let's just go."

He pulled every dress off the rack and flagged down the salesgirl. "She needs to try these on."

The salesgirl couldn't have been more than twenty years old. She smiled at Sally, laughing softly. "All of them?"

"Just sizes eight and ten, please," Sally said, glaring at Gage as he sifted through the sizes of the seven dresses in his arms. She lowered her voice as the salesgirl unlocked the dressing room. "Gage, I really can't wear it anywhere. This is silly."

He held up two dresses, victory written in his beaming smile. "It's perfect for Christmas, bird." He shooed her into the dressing room and stepped in with her. "I can't wait to see you in it." He was like a kid in a candy store, unzipping the back of the dress as quickly as he could. His enthusiasm was contagious. Sally wanted the dress to look as good on her as it did on the rack just to see his reaction.

The salesgirl's face was pinched. She opened her mouth to speak, then closed it again, like she was trying to work out how to tell him that he couldn't stay in the dressing room.

"Um, Gage?" Sally touched his arm as he slipped the dress from the hanger.

"Yeah?" His gaze moved from Sally to the salesgirl, who pointed to a plush armchair meant for waiting customers. "Oh. Right. Sorry."

He handed Sally the dress, gave her a chaste kiss, and plunked himself down in the chair, anxiously tapping his fingers.

As Sally closed the dressing room door, she heard the salesgirl say, "That's the prettiest dress in the store."

Sally stripped off her top and heard Gage say, "The perfect dress for the perfect wife."

She reveled in his admiration as she changed into the dress. The length was ideal for a pair of low heels, and the satin lining felt heavenly against her skin. She turned to look in the mirror, momentarily awed by her reflection. She'd never owned anything so glamorous. The crisscross bodice and empire waist were flattering. It was the type of dress that belonged on a red carpet, not a holiday dinner. As she turned to open the dressing room door, she was suddenly nervous again.

She peeked out of the dressing area, and Gage leapt to his feet, adoring eyes drinking her in as she turned for him to zip the back.

He zipped the dress and turned her by the waist, his gaze remaining on her face. "Jesus, Sal. You're stunning. Beyond stunning. *Exquisite.* That dress was made for you. We're getting it."

She flipped up the price tag and gasped. "Gage, it's four *hundred* dollars." She headed for the dressing room.

He caught her around the waist, turning her in his arms again. "You're worth a hell of a lot more than that. It's the perfect dress for the holidays, and I'm buying it, so be careful when you take it off."

"Gage, you don't need—"

He silenced her with a kiss.

"You can't keep shutting me up with kisses."

"Try me."

Chapter Nine

FRIDAY MORNING SALLY awoke to the feel of Gage's lips working their way down her belly. She closed her eyes, wishing they didn't have to leave later today, and reveling in the memories of the date they'd gone on Wednesday night, and the delight in Gage's eyes when he'd seen her in that gorgeous dress. She'd never felt prettier than she had the moment he'd seen her wearing it. Thursday had passed in a blur of interviews and other preparations for the new center. Sally had silently mourned the end of their time away, which was fast approaching, and when five o'clock hit, she savored every minute of the rest of the night. They had gone to the movies and for a long walk through town, holding hands and kissing under the stars. It had been bitter cold, but they'd heated up in the elevator, and when they'd gotten back to their room, they'd barely made it inside before tearing off each other's clothes.

Now, Gage's hands skimmed her legs with featherlight touches, bringing her mind back to the present. He kissed her inner thighs, making her squirm with anticipation. The first slick of his tongue sent shivers racing through her. He kept up a slow, torturous rhythm, licking her center, then kissing her thigh repeatedly. He splayed his hands over her hips, holding her down as he lowered his mouth to her sex. She loved the way he forced her to endure his torturous teasing, refusing to let her hurry things along. She widened her legs, lost in his scintillating tease. His hands pushed beneath her bottom, lifting her hips, and he did something with his tongue that sent spirals of ecstasy shooting through her. She fisted her hands, her heels digging into the sheets.

"You need to"—*pant, pant*—"patent your tongue. Good Lord." She writhed against his mouth. "You should have told me how good you were at this years ago."

He lifted his head, smiling.

"Don't stop," she urged.

"Baby, I could feast on you all day long."

His teeth grazed, his tongue plunged, and those fingers…Gage never held back with his words or his touch, and the combination took her up, up, *up*, rousing her passion to levels she'd never imagined. She stole a look at him, and he must have felt her shift, because his eyes opened and caught on hers, electrifying the air around them. It felt so naughty, watching him devour her, and when he licked along her center, holding her gaze with a dark, erotic look in his eyes, she nearly lost it. An orgasm clawed at her core, but she struggled against it, enjoying the overwhelming sensations bursting inside her. She lay back, eyes slammed shut, trying desperately to stave off her orgasm. He did something magical with his fingers and her hips bolted off the bed. A cry of pleasure flew from her lungs. "*Gage!*"

He had already become a master at catching her on the way down and sent her soaring again. Scintillating sensations filled her, one after another, until she was hanging on to her sanity by a thread.

"Too much," she pleaded. "It's too much."

He moved up her body, slowing to seal his mouth over one

nipple and tweaking the other between his finger and thumb, doling out more sensual torture. He rocked against her center, creating the most delicious friction.

"*Ohmygod,*" fell from her lips like a plea. "*Gaaaage—*"

He clamped down harder, sending her spiraling into oblivion again, and captured her mouth midorgasm. His tongue swept passionately over hers, and his hands took over where his cock had started. Flashes of heat flamed inside her, burning hotter with every tantalizing touch, until she came in a shuddering quake, gasping and clinging to the mattress.

When she finally fell back, spent and sated, he lavished her with several tender, loving kisses, whispering sweetnesses in between. "Love you. You're so beautiful. I can't believe you're finally *mine*."

She smiled at his words, and when he reached for a condom, she pushed him onto his back, wanting to bring him just as much pleasure as he'd given her. "Oh no you don't."

"What do you have in mind, sexy girl?"

"Something like this." She kissed his abs and wrapped her fingers around his shaft, earning a guttural, insanely sexy sound from Gage. Holding his gaze, she dragged her tongue from base to tip, circling the broad head. The heated look in his eyes made her feel empowered and seductive.

"Christ, baby. You feel *good*."

She lowered her mouth around him, taking him to the back of her throat. He wound his fingers into her hair, holding so tight her scalp stung. The sharp sting spiked through her body all the way to her core, igniting her all over again. She moaned around his shaft, and he uttered something indiscernible but so damn hot she couldn't resist moaning again. His hips bucked off the mattress, and she quickened her pace, chasing her mouth with her hand in tight, fast strokes.

"*Babybabybaby—*"

She kept up the maddening pace, loving the way he squirmed and clung to her hair. When he let out a long, surrendering groan, she eased up. *Torture* was the name of the game this morning. She loved it when he took her to the edge, then backed off, making her so desperate she begged. She wanted him to feel the same excruciating pleasure. She got up on her hands and knees so she could take him deeper, and his hand moved to her ass, caressing and groping as she teased and taunted him.

"I love your ass, baby."

His fingers pushed into her sex, and she released his cock, rocking as his fingers stroked that magical spot inside her.

He guided her mouth back to his shaft. "Suck me, baby. Come with me."

His words alone could make her come. *God*, she loved him. His dirty talk was addicting, and his wicked mouth and hands made her head spin and his rock-hard cock…Lord, she loved every inch of him. His fingers moved faster, and she followed his lead, speeding up her efforts. But concentrating on her rhythm while waves of pleasure swamped her was impossible. She must have stopped moving completely, because he took over, helping her find their tempo.

"Baby," he ground out. "I'm gonna come."

He tried to pull her head back, but she continued sucking and loving and stroking. She wanted *all* of him.

"Bird," he pleaded.

She was consumed by the tingling sensations climbing up her legs and the mounting pressure in her core. His fist tightened in her hair, and his hips bucked at the same moment her orgasm crashed over her. Her inner muscles pulsed around his fingers as warm jets of his release hit the back of her throat.

"Good Lord, bird," he panted out, pulling her up beside him.

"Good morning," she said cheekily.

"Good? How about spectacular?"

His mouth came down over hers in a kiss that told her he was as reluctant to get out of bed as she was. Getting out of bed would bring them one step closer to leaving their solitude behind.

AFTER A LONG, steamy shower, during which they drove each other mad *again*, they packed their bags in silence. Sally couldn't believe their time alone was almost over. She watched Gage through the adjoining door, remembering how elated he'd been from the moment they'd realized they were married. Had it really been only six days since they'd woken up married in Vegas?

She was still getting used to the idea that they were actually married. She'd never had a real wedding with Dave, and they'd never even gone on a honeymoon. When she'd lost him, she never thought she'd marry again, but even just a few months into her friendship with Gage, she'd been imagining more. She'd give anything to remember their wedding night, though every night since had been nothing short of amazing.

Gage glanced over, catching her staring, and blew her a kiss. He mouthed, *You okay?*

She nodded, remembering how hard he'd pushed for them to share the honeymoon suite when they'd checked in, and how worried she'd been about whether this marriage would be the start of their lives together or the beginning of the end. Now going home felt like the same quandary. She was already used to sleeping in Gage's arms, waking up in middle of the night to the feel of his body, the sound of his breathing. How would she keep her hands to herself in the office? How could they be together as a couple without everyone knowing? She couldn't risk Rusty feeling like he was the last to know. And to top it all off, even though she'd fallen in love with Gage a long time ago, they'd come together and their love had become real and *alive* here at this hotel. She hated leaving it behind.

Running late, they checked out and grabbed breakfast to go. When they arrived at the youth center, their overanxious applicants were waiting by the door. Sally had been on a dead run ever since. Unfortunately, every time she had a break, Gage was tied up, and she barely had a minute to connect with him. She was used to him being on her mind, but how could things change so much that she actually *missed* him when they were apart for only a few hours?

Later that afternoon, Sally was wrapping up her interview with Haylie Hudson, a petite blonde with serious blue eyes and a wealth of experience. She had been the administrator for a recreation center and had also run an elite travel agency. She was by far the strongest candidate for the administrator position, and she had the take-charge personality needed to run the facility.

"What do you think is the greatest asset you'll bring to the position?" Sally asked.

"In addition to my administrative experience, handling off-site events has given me firsthand knowledge of the flip side of the business. I know what complications can occur for customers who are renting space or holding events at the center, and I will be able to anticipate and work around them before they occur." She smiled and added, "Personally speaking, I think being a single parent is my biggest asset."

That piqued Sally's interest. "Why is that?"

"Because as a single parent, work is a priority and a necessity, but I also really enjoy being productive. Working makes me a stronger parent, and caring for my son has made me even more efficient and organized, which carries over to the workplace. I don't know if you have kids, but once you've stayed up all night with a colicky baby and had to function the next day, you learn what you're made of."

Sally laughed. "I remember those days."

"Excuses don't cut the muster for kids or for clients. I've become a master at multitasking, sifting through nonsense to get to the heart of the matter and find solutions to problems before they escalate. And"—she held up her index finger—"I have a backup sitter for my backup sitter and a wonderfully supportive family who is always willing to pitch in if I need to work late."

She reminded Sally of herself, even though she'd been married to Dave when Rusty was younger. Dave had worked seventy hours a week to get his business off the ground, and she'd often felt like a single parent.

"And why do you want to leave the company you're currently working for?" Sally asked. "I have to be honest, the salary potential here probably won't be as high as you might receive there in the long run."

Haylie's gaze softened. "Because while I need financial security, I also need to love what I'm doing for eight hours a day, or what I said about work making me a stronger parent will no longer be true. Working for the travel agency is interesting, but if I can be honest with you…?"

"Yes, please. Whatever you say here will remain confidential."

"Thank you. Working with wealthy clients has many advantages, but it's not as fulfilling as working with the rec center was. I love the look on people's faces when they find a place, and people, that resonate with them and make them feel like they belong. In the rec center, I felt fulfilled every day. Nothing compares to the gratification that comes from a child learning to play basketball, or dance, or find a tutor that *gets* them. I've read up on No Limitz in Allure, Colorado, and I know these are things you hope to do with this location. It would be an honor to be considered for the position. Money isn't my top priority. I've learned that sometimes you have to follow your heart and trust that the rest will fall into place."

She could have been speaking about Sally's situation with Gage and Rusty. "Yes, I think there's truth in that statement."

Gage knocked on the door and poked his head into the office. "Sorry to interrupt—"

"That's okay. Come in, please." Sally rose to her feet. "Haylie Hudson, this is Gage Ryder, the sports director for our Allure location." *And my incredible husband.* It surprised her how easily that thought followed, and it must have shone in her expression, because Gage had a warm look in his eyes, like he noticed the change, too. "Haylie is interviewing for the administrator position." *And opening my eyes to what's right in front of me.*

AFTER HAYLIE LEFT, Gage and Sally locked up and headed for the gym to clean up their decorations. Sally was in a great mood, smiling endlessly and talking nonstop about Haylie, and Gage couldn't help stealing kisses as she spoke.

"She's experienced, professional, and smart, and definitely my number one candidate," she said as he kissed her cheek, but she refused to be distracted. "How did your interviews go?"

"I made an offer to Sin, and he's accepted it." He touched his lips to hers.

"We're on a timeline here, Mr. Kissy Face."

"I'll try to behave, but that's asking a lot." He chuckled. "You won't believe the stories I heard today. I never knew so many people overinflated their experience. One guy said he had four years of sports-team management. It turned out it was with fantasy football leagues."

Sally rolled her eyes. "At least I don't have to deal with that. I get the, 'Sure, I managed the office. I made the coffee and ensured there was ample creamer in the fridge.'"

"Maybe it's a generational thing. We'll have to give Rusty lessons in interviewing before he graduates." Gage reached for the gym door, and Sally touched his arm, stopping him with a thoughtful expression.

"Thank you for thinking of him. I know I've been on the fence because of Rusty, but that's not because I don't love you. I'm just scared of handling things in the wrong way."

"I know, babe. I'm worried, too, but I have faith in all of us."

"I think we should tell him the night he comes home and explain everything at once. You're right, he's not a moody teenager anymore. Hopefully he'll understand and be happy for us."

Her beautiful eyes brimmed with love and hope. "The only thing that will make me happier than hearing you say that is when Rusty knows about us and that shadow of worry that's following you around disappears."

"I'm hoping for the best. I don't want to hurt him, but I can't imagine not being with you this way every day. I still don't know how to handle it all, but I don't think we should tell anyone before Rusty hears it from us in person."

"I agree with you."

She glanced at the door to the gym. "And I *really* don't want to clean up the lovely decorations you put up for us, *or* leave Oak Falls. This time alone with you has been life changing. We're married, Gage. *Married!* I can say that now without totally flipping out, and I don't want to go back to our real lives where we have to be careful about what we say and do."

"I promise, bird, every day of the rest of our lives will be just as wonderful. With the exception of the times I irritate you, or leave the toilet seat up, or forget to bring home milk, or—"

Her arms circled his neck and she pressed her lips to his in a sweet kiss that quickly turned fierce and demanding. He lifted her into his arms and her legs wound around his hips. Her effervescent smile cut straight to his heart.

"I want all of that with you. Except maybe the toilet seat thing." She tightened her legs around his waist. "What are you going to do now that you have complete control of me?"

"What I should have done the first night we were here."

He pulled open the door to the gym, kicking the partially deflating balloons out of his way as they kissed.

"Oh, no, you're not," she said with a laugh. "We're traveling all evening, and I don't have time to shower."

"See? You'll do great having more kids. You've got the practical mommy thing down pat." He stole another kiss and set her on her feet. "Why do I find that so hot?"

She began picking up balloons and shoving them into a garbage bag. "Because of that steel rod in your pants. You're thinking about making babies." She narrowed her eyes, giving him the challenging look he loved so much—the one that made him want to test her resolve about no sex before traveling.

He shook his head, chuckling. "That's your fault, baby doll."

"Good. I like having that power over you."

They gathered the balloons, and he copped a few feels and stole a few kisses while Sally futilely tried to pretend she wasn't affected. The flush on her skin and the hitch in her breathing gave her away.

"You know you want me," he teased as he unwound the peach and white silk drapes from the canopy.

"How do you carry around that ego without hurting your back?"

He twisted the drape and snapped her ass with it, reveling in her wild laughter. "I'll lay you down on this floor and show you what a hurt back feels like."

"Sorry, horny husband, but you'll have to wait. Two hours to flight time." She bent down and picked up a bunch of balloons.

"You keep flashing that gorgeous ass of yours and I'll *take* what I want."

Crimson crawled up her cheeks.

After dismantling and stowing their decorations in the storage room, they went to work picking up the remaining balloons.

Gage rubbed against Sally like a cat and whispered, "We have showers here."

She wiggled her butt and he smacked it.

"Hey!" She spun around with an armful of balloons.

He took a step toward her and she squealed and ran, sending balloons flying in all directions. He caught her from behind and let his hands wander.

"You can't run from me, wifey." He sank his teeth into her neck, earning a lusty whimper.

"Gage," came out with a laugh. "I can't be the skanky ho who smells like sex on the plane."

"You couldn't be a skanky ho if you tried." He dragged his tongue over the frantic pulse at the base of her neck. "Does that mean joining the mile-high club is out?"

She rested her head against his chest, sighing wantonly, and he snuck a few more delicious kisses.

"Do people really do that?" she asked. "In those tiny bathrooms?"

"We could do our own research. See if it can be done?"

She turned toward him, pressing her hands flat against his chest. Did she know how much he loved when she touched him like that? He covered one hand with his own and heat filled her baby blues.

"God, baby. That look..."

He lowered his mouth to hers, tasting the sugary drink she'd had earlier. He delved deeper, unable to tamp down the desire that had been building every time he heard the heels of her boots outside his office door, her laughter floating down the hall, and when he caught sight of her walking an applicant into her office. Maybe she was right to worry about their relationship having an impact on their jobs. How would he ever hold back when all he wanted was more of her? His hands were unstoppable, groping her ass, her breasts, tangling in her silky hair.

"Gage," she said breathlessly. "I want you, but I don't want to be uncomfortable on the plane."

"So, no skanky ho?" he teased, and she shook her head, flashing the shy smile that made him hold her tighter. "How would you feel about being the gorgeous wife in a car, on the way to her honeymoon?"

Her brow furrowed. "Honeymoon?"

"I can't take my new wife home without first treating her to a proper cheesy honeymoon."

"But…? Danica expects us back."

"No *buts*, baby. We'll be back in time for work Monday morning. I didn't have much time to plan, and I promise, when we have our real wedding, I'll take you on the honeymoon of your dreams."

Her eyes teared up. "I've never had a honeymoon."

"What a coincidence. Neither have I. But I have to warn you. I literally looked for the cheesiest place to match our cheesy Elvis wedding."

She laughed, and a single tear slipped down her cheek. "I don't care if it's cheesy or extravagant, or if we spend the night in a tent. Just knowing you went to the effort to plan a honeymoon is more than I could have ever hoped for."

Chapter Ten

IT STARTED SNOWING four hours into Gage and Sally's drive to the Poconos, reminding Sally of last year at this time, when they were at the Christmas tree lighting in Allure and it had snowed like crazy. She realized they were going to miss the tree lighting this year. She and Gage had gone together every year since they'd met. Maybe it was time for new traditions. She felt a pang of longing at the idea of missing it but pushed those thoughts aside and focused on the wonderful man driving her oh so carefully to their secret destination. *Our cheesy honeymoon.*

She felt herself smiling and rested her head back, watching her hubby. Two big hands gripped the steering wheel, and his serious eyes concentrated on the road. When the snow had started, he'd checked her seat belt and told her not to worry; he'd checked the weather before they left and had anticipated snow. He had extra blankets and other provisions in the trunk just in case they got stuck on the side of the road. She wondered what those other provisions were. His brother Cash would be proud of Gage's preparations. Cash was a firefighter and was always harassing everyone about being prepared for anything. It dawned on her that Cash was now her brother-in-law. In fact, she had several brothers-in-law and a sister-in-law.

And a mother- and father-in-law.

A flurry of emotions swamped her. She was close to Gage's

family, but to actually become a part of it? She gazed out the window, warming with the idea of his loving parents welcoming her and Rusty into their family. She was gaining an entire family, every member of which she already loved. Rusty would have even more people to watch over him if anything ever happened to her. She worried about that, though she knew Gage would always be there for him, as would Danica and Blake, and likely, Gage's whole family whether they were married or not. Dave's parents had moved away after his death, and they'd made only one attempt to see Sally and Rusty since. Knowing Rusty would be part of a larger family comforted her.

By the time they pulled up in front of the resort, there were at least six inches of fresh snow on the ground, but Sally was toasty warm with loving thoughts. The cedar lodge stood three stories tall, with a turret anchoring the left side and balconies on the upper two floors. Twinkling holiday lights lined the railings and hung around enormous windows in a scalloped pattern. Against the backdrop of the illuminated ski slopes, the lodge looked enchanting, as if they'd driven into a dream. She'd lived in Colorado her whole life, had seen snow thousands of times, but somehow it has never looked quite as beautiful as this.

Gage reached across the console and slid his hand to the nape of her neck. "What do you think, bird?"

"I thought you said it was *cheesy*. This is magnificent. It's more beautiful than the resorts back home, and we live in a resort town."

"Ah, don't underestimate my ability to seek out cheesiness. 'Welcome to Lovers' Lodge, where customers come often and leave happy.'"

She laughed. "Did you just make that up?"

"I'm not that clever. That's their tagline. It's right across the middle of their website in big red letters." He leaned in and kissed her. "As much as I'd like to sit here and make out with you, the snow slowed us down and we'll miss the Christmas tree lighting if we don't hurry."

"Christmas tree lighting?" she said excitedly, but he was already out of the car, retrieving their bags from the trunk.

Gage opened her door and helped her out. "You didn't think I'd let you miss this year's tree lighting, did you? Priorities, little bird."

She melted at his thoughtfulness. "I was a little bummed that we were going to miss it." She tugged him down by his collar and kissed him again. "Thank you."

"Man, I love your kisses. Come on, sweet one, before I decide to forgo the tree lighting and light *you* up instead."

That didn't sound like a bad idea to her.

The inside of the lodge was just as gorgeous as the outside, with roaring fires in stone fireplaces at either end of the luxurious lobby, plush leather sofas, soft-looking recliners, and crystal chandeliers. Beyond the large reception desk was a wall of glass overlooking a patio with a fire pit. Red and orange flames danced against boulders that lined the pit like rebellious taunts to the cold, and the mountains stood sentinel in the distance.

Sally snuggled in close as they waited to check in. "This is gorgeous. Maybe after the tree lighting we could sit out by the fire?"

"Baby, we have two nights to do whatever you'd like." Gage stepped up to the desk. "Hi. We have a reservation for Mr. and Mrs. Ryder."

Hearing him introduce them that way made Sally's head spin. *Mr. and Mrs. Ryder. Sally Tuft-Ryder.* She *really* liked the sound of that.

The blonde behind the desk took care of the paperwork and handed Gage a keycard hanging from a heart-shaped key ring. “You’re in our best honeymoon suite.” She smiled brightly, tapped a little bell on the desk, and said, “The Boom-chicawowow Suite.”

Two muscular, tanned men wearing loincloths appeared out of nowhere, beating drums, and two gorgeous women wearing slinky sparkly outfits danced their way out of a door to their right singing, “Boomchica, boomchica, boomchicawowow—”

Gage put his arm around Sally, eyes wide, as the foursome danced around them singing a song about bumps in the night and fireworks going off. The women twirled and the men flexed, circling Sally and Gage like they were ready to pounce, or give lap dances. Sally covered her mouth to hide her laughter as one of the men did a dramatic pelvic thrust in front of her. Gage tightened his hold on her, glowering at the man. Oh, how she loved his jealous side!

She leaned closer and whispered, “I love our honeymoon so far. Are they part of the package?” She swore he growled.

One final twirl, another round of the chorus, and a drum roll earned applause from other guests who had gathered around to watch. One of the Tarzan-looking men removed the top of his drum and withdrew a basket wrapped with a big red velvet bow. He got down on one knee and presented it to them. “The essentials, for our newlyweds.”

“Thank you.” Sally took the basket and peeked inside. Red rose petals were sprinkled around a bottle of edible strawberry massage oil, candles, champagne glasses and a bottle of champagne, a box of condoms, a booklet called the *Naughty Sex Guide*, a bottle of lube—*Oh God, really?*—and an assortment of chocolates.

Gage thanked the dancers, and they headed toward the elevators. Once they were inside, he set the luggage and the basket aside and said, "Welcome to our cheesy honeymoon."

"Lube!" Laughter burst from her lips. "What if their guests get offended? Can you imagine?"

"Are *you* offended?" he asked in a seductive voice that made Sally's heart race.

She must have waited a beat too long to answer, because he trapped her against the elevator wall with his scrumptious body and began kissing her neck. He knew that did her in every time!

"Well, bird?"

Threads of desire weaved around them, binding them together as he tiptoed around her boundaries. It was so much easier to get carried away in a dark bedroom and allow their bodies and hearts to take over than it was to admit her thoughts out loud in a bright elevator. But the hungry look in his eyes shattered her inhibitions.

"No," she said confidently.

The edge of his lips curved up in a sinful smile, and when those lips met hers, his fingers tightened in her hair. He kissed her slow and deep, and so sensually, she felt herself floating away on a tide of pleasure so enticing, she went up on her toes, trying to take more, but he drew back, leaving her panting and needy.

His thumb brushed over her lips, and when he spoke, his voice was hot as fire. "I will never get enough of you, and rest assured, baby, I'm never going to stop taking *and* giving."

The elevator doors opened, but she was frozen in place. Gage took far too much pleasure in her wobbly legs and lust-addled brain, chuckling as she struggled to swim to the surface.

She didn't know how she managed to walk, much less carry the basket down the hall.

He pushed open the door to their room and took the basket from her hands. He set it on the floor and swept her into his arms.

"My bride is *not* going to walk over the threshold on her honeymoon."

God, she loved this man! His handsome face grinned down at her as he carried her inside. She felt weightless and sexy, and so happy, laughter bubbled out as she kissed him. People didn't get second chances like this, did they? How did she get so lucky?

A SENSE OF pride and happiness filled Gage as he carried his bride into the room. The light in Sally's eyes made him want to do things like this every day just to experience her elation. He set her feet beside the heart-shaped bed, wondering what she'd think of the lighted, mirrored headboard, red rose petals strewn across the blanket, and twelve dozen roses he'd had delivered. He brought the luggage and basket inside and closed the door behind them.

"Oh my goodness!" she said. "Look at this room! Did you do this? The roses?" She turned in a slow circle, taking in the mirrors on the ceiling and walls, the heart-shaped bathtub on the other side of the room, and the roses on nearly every surface.

"All but the ones on the bed. Wish I'd thought of those, too, but…" He shrugged, and she threw her arms around his neck and kissed him.

"It's not cheesy. It's perfect for us."

Music to his ears. "It's definitely cheesy, but how can you

top Elvis, if not with lights and mirrors?"

He unzipped his suitcase and set their wedding picture on the dresser.

Sally picked it up with an awed expression. "You framed it?"

"It's our wedding picture. Of course I did. I won't let Rusty see it until we tell him, but I don't want you to forget."

"Forget who I'm married to? Like that could ever happen? I wake up in your arms, remember?" She set the frame down. "I still don't know how I missed picking up on the fact that you're a die-hard romantic."

"I think it's because I wasn't," he admitted. He grabbed the scarf, hat, and gloves he'd bought for her while they were in Virginia and wound the light blue scarf around her neck. "Until you came along."

"You bought me all of this? You really planned ahead." She rubbed the cashmere scarf on her cheek. "It's so soft. Thank you."

"And it brings out your baby blues." He put on his own gloves and scarf and reached for her hand. "Come on, beautiful. We have a tree lighting to get to."

They followed other guests down a wide path around the resort. The snowy night smelled of hopes and dreams sprinkled with lust and love. A crowd formed around an enormous Christmas tree that must have stood thirty feet tall. Festive music hung in the air, and a white tent sat off to one side, where the staff was dressed as elves, serving champagne and snacks.

A heavy hand landed on Gage's shoulder, and he tightened his grip on Sally, turning to find a man dressed up like Santa Claus. Sally cuddled up to Gage, her cheeks pink from the cold.

"Ho, ho, ho! Happy holidays!" the round, bearded man sang out.

"Happy holidays," Gage and Sally said in unison.

Santa handed them two ornaments. "One for the tree, one to take home." As quickly as he'd appeared, he moved on to greet another couple.

Sally held up the ornament, a miniature replica of the lodge that had the year etched into it. "Our first ornament."

"Merry almost Christmas, sweetheart."

"Merry almost Christmas. I love our cheesy honeymoon."

A group of elves began singing Christmas carols, and the crowd moved forward, each couple hanging their ornament. A handful of photographers moved around them, capturing the moments. When it was Sally and Gage's turn, Gage stole a kiss just as the photographer snapped the picture. He knew when they returned home, he'd have to rein in his desires in public, but until then, he wasn't even going to try. The photographer handed Gage a card with instructions for claiming the picture online so it would be printed and ready for them when they left on Sunday.

They sang along with the crowd, huddled together for warmth, enjoying a glass of champagne and a few hors d'oeuvres as the rest of the guests hung their ornaments. A long while later, the music silenced, and the air itself seemed to still in anticipation of the tree lighting.

Gage leaned in close, speaking directly into Sally's ear. "I love you, Mrs. Ryder."

She turned in his arms and said something at the same moment the crowd cheered, drowning out her voice. He dipped her over his arm in a celebratory kiss. The lights of the tree sparkled in her eyes, and he knew he'd never forget this night, this *moment*, or the look in his wife's eyes as she tugged him down for a repeat performance.

It stopped snowing as the evening wore on, and Gage and Sally made their way to the patio, claiming one of the lounge chairs by the fire. Sally lay with her head on Gage's shoulder, their hands entwined. Around them, couples danced, snuggled, and mingled. He couldn't imagine a more perfect evening.

"Gage?"

"Hm?"

"I haven't skied since Dave's accident."

"I know, babe. It's fine. I didn't think we'd go skiing." She'd told him years ago that she didn't want to think about skiing ever again. He respected her feelings and had accepted that there were going to be things in their life they avoided because of Dave's death.

She rested her chin on his chest, looking gorgeous in the evening light. "Would you mind if we did?"

Surprised, he took a moment to process what she'd said. "No, babe. Whatever you'd like to do, I'm with you. But don't feel like you have to because we're here."

"I don't. It's time." Her lips curved up in a sweet smile. "I couldn't do it before, but I'm ready to move forward. I don't know if Rusty will ever be, but I sometimes wonder if his hesitation is somehow driven by mine."

He leaned forward and kissed her, marveling at her strength. "I'll be right there by your side, and when Rusty's ready, I'll be there for him, too."

Chapter Eleven

SALLY AWOKE TO Gage whispering, "Good morning, Mrs. Ryder. How's my beautiful wife?" followed by his loving hands and mouth all over her body. After enjoying each other, they had a leisurely breakfast in the hotel restaurant. Then they purchased ski pants at the shop in the resort, rented skis, and sat on a bench outside the equipment building to put them on. Sunshine brought warmer temperatures, but that wasn't the cause of Sally's perspiration. As she secured her bindings, the sights and sounds of skiers brought an onslaught of emotions. Dave had been skiing with Blake when he'd gone off alone to ski Little Hellion, one of the most dangerous slopes in Allure. Although Dave had been an expert freestyle skier, visibility was low on that fateful snowy night. He must have misjudged the angle and distance of his jump and landed in the trees. His neck was broken on impact, and he was killed instantly.

Gage squeezed her hand. His compassionate eyes searched hers. "Babe, we don't have to do this. I don't care if I never go skiing again."

She inhaled a ragged breath and gazed out at the mountains, remembering how she and Dave had taught Rusty to ski when he was four years old. Skiing had always been a part of their lives, at least until Rusty hit his teenage years and decided doing anything with his parents was uncool.

"*I* care," she admitted. "I used to love skiing, and even though I'm so nervous I feel like I might pass out, I need to do this and put this fear behind me. Don't take this the wrong way, but I need to do it for Dave and Rusty as much as for me and you. Once I get past this, it'll open a door for Rusty that I think he needs. Even if he doesn't ever want to ski again, at least he'll know it won't make his mother sad if he decides to follow in his father's footsteps. That's the whole reason I've held on to Dave's share of the business. It's all for Rusty."

"Babe, don't ever worry about me taking things wrong. You had a whole life before me with a man who loved you, and you had a child together. If Stacy hadn't done what she'd done, I might have had the same thing—with a woman, that is—and probably the baggage of divorce. I'm glad you were loved, and I'm glad Rusty is in my life. I'll never see him as anything less than however much of a son he'll allow himself to be to me. I want to be with you, and that means accepting your love for Dave, being by your side, and doing whatever it takes to keep you and Rusty safe and happy."

She hurt knowing he had to even think about her loving anyone else, but starting over was complicated, and she was glad he understood. She finished securing her bindings. The feel of the skis beneath her feet brought an unexpected sense of euphoria. She'd forgotten how skiing had that effect on her. She wanted the freedom to enjoy doing this again without Dave's death overshadowing her.

Overshadowing us.

"I appreciate that, Gage. I *am* happy. I'm just nervous. It's not like I think I'm going to ski off the mountain or get hurt. It's just that when I look at the slopes, it all comes back to me. But I don't want to spend the rest of our lives with skiing being mine and Dave's thing, and honestly, I don't want memories of Dave always living between us. I'm glad we're doing this, and talking about it, and I know we'll have times that Dave will be brought up when Rusty's around and even when he's not. That part of my life will always be special, but it's been more than five years. I want to find what's yours and mine. There's a big mountain in front of us. I think we should take one final goodbye run down the slopes and then create our own memories."

"You can't imagine how much I love you right this second." Gage embraced her.

"I have a great imagination," she teased. "I bet if I climb into your lap I won't have to *imagine* anything."

"Hell, baby. Thinking about you on my lap turns me on. What did you have in mind for creating our memories, sexy Sally?"

Laughter fell from her lips. "Gee, I don't know, *gorgeous Gage.*"

"We could find a cave and test out our body heat."

"That sounds cold, and you know…" She lowered her voice and arched a brow. "You might experience shrinkage."

He scoffed and took her in a passionate kiss that heated her up all over again.

"Baby, Alaska isn't cold enough to make that happen when I'm with you. Hell, no place is."

"I think we should go to Alaska one day. Just to test your theory, of course."

"Ah. My girl still wants to travel." He brushed his lips over her cheek and said, "I knew I saw that in your eyes."

"Not for weeks on end or anything. Just…" She shrugged. "To see what's out there. Now that Rusty's older, I can actually go away like this without worrying so much. Wouldn't you like to travel a little more?"

"With you? Absolutely. But for today, how about that cave?"

"I was thinking of something *clothed.* Like toboggans or snowboards. Something where I can dominate you."

His eyes turned volcanic. "You can dominate me anytime you want. Tie me up. Make me your sex slave."

She rose to her feet and grabbed him by the hand, pulling him up beside her. "Let's do this, Romeo."

They waited in line for the chair lift, joking about various forms of domination. When the lift hit the back of Sally's legs, she settled onto the seat and Gage put his arm around her, pulling her close.

Crisp mountain air filled her lungs and stung her cheeks. She was proud of herself for finally taking this step. She thought about Dave as the lift climbed the mountain. Nothing had made him happier than skiing. If she were honest with herself, she might admit that sometimes even she didn't quite measure up, and that was okay. Sally had never felt the need to be his entire world the way some other women wanted to be with their spouses. She'd been happy with Dave, and she was happy with Gage. *Happier?*

She glanced at him, knowing she couldn't begin to compare being married so young after six months of dating and thrust into the responsibility of child-rearing to being married accidentally with a world of experience and years of loving Gage behind her.

"You okay, bird?" Gage asked.

"Yes. I am. I'm glad we're doing this together."

When they reached the top of the mountain, the slope lay

before them like a magic carpet, and a familiar adrenaline rush kicked in.

"You've got this, bird," Gage called over to her.

She squinted against the sun, looking at him and thinking about how lucky she was. Her pulse quickened for a whole different—*and better*—reason. She knew she could do anything with him by her side. As she skied down the mountain, a sense of releasing the past exploded inside her, and when Gage sped past her, she raced him toward their future.

"*BRR.*" SALLY RUBBED her hands together as Gage opened the door to their room several hours later.

"Come here, baby." He reached for her, rubbing her icy hands between his. "Why didn't you tell me you were so cold?"

"I was having too much fun."

They'd learned to snowboard, enjoyed a late lunch at the café, and spent hours practicing, taking silly pictures, and trying to learn tricks from a group of teenagers. They'd spent the afternoon making memories. Sally had been adorable, refusing to give up until she *almost* mastered the ollie and the nollie, which involved jumping off ramps. She blew him away with her agility and her determination.

"Let's take a hot bath," Gage suggested as he helped her off with her coat. "That'll warm you right up."

Sally disappeared into the bathroom and he filled the tub, adding vanilla-scented bubble bath and setting the champagne and glasses within reach. They'd been on a dead run since attending the conference in Vegas. A quiet evening was just what they needed. He grabbed a few condoms and set them by the tub, not altogether sure how well that idea was going to work in the tub, but hell, he was looking forward to figuring it out. He gathered candles from around the room and lit them along the windowsill. *Perfect.* As an afterthought, he snagged the *Naughty Sex Guide* and set it by the tub, and stripped down to his briefs, taking a last look at their little love nest. Something was missing.

My wife.

He saw himself smiling in his reflection in the window and had a feeling the happiness of being married to his best friend would never wear off. He gazed out at the sun skimming the horizon. He felt like a new man, with renewed purpose, since marrying Sally, and although he played it off well, he was also a man with new worries.

When he'd told his father about Stacy, his father had given him the standard lines parents doled out in painful situations. *It wasn't meant to be. It hurts now, but with time you'll heal.* And then Ned Ryder had set his large, strong hands on Gage's shoulders, his eyes as serious as ever, and he'd said, "Son, I know you hurt more than anything right now, but do yourself a favor. Try to step back from that hurt long enough to see your years with Stacy for what they were."

Gage hadn't accepted what his father had wanted him to see until last night when Sally had asked him to be there with her when she skied for the first time since losing Dave. There was a world of difference between building a life with a woman who wanted you to be part of it and spending time with a woman who wanted to experience the world without any ties to bind her. It wasn't the act of skiing, or learning to snowboard, or the way they'd cheered each other on and tumbled into the snow in a tangle of limbs and laughter. It was five years' worth of moments culminating in a love so deep he couldn't imagine a life without her. It was helping Sally as a friend to deal with her pain over losing her husband, trying new restaurants together, and the silly stuff, like grocery shopping and calling each other when they'd had a bad or funny dream, just to share it with the person who meant the most to them. It was shopping for presents, even if they found none, and watching movies in their comfy sweats while eating ice cream. It was working together at the center for so many years, building programs and changing lives. It was evenings spent dancing together at their friends' and his siblings' weddings knowing he wasn't going to be taking her to bed that night, no matter how much he'd wanted to. Those moments had built a foundation that he and Stacy never could have had. And he knew in his heart there was no other woman on earth he could build such a remarkable future with.

CHAPTER TWELVE

SALLY TOOK ONE last look in the bathroom mirror, wondering why she was so nervous. It wasn't like this was the first time Gage would see her naked, but for some reason her insides were doing backflips. She put on her robe, opened the bathroom door, and hoped she could hide her nerves. A hint of vanilla hung in the air, soothing and enticing. She found Gage gazing out the windows. His broad back tapered deliciously down to a pair of tight black briefs. His muscular thighs and perfect butt were almost too much to take. *No wonder I'm nervous.* It wasn't that Sally had body issues. The fluttering in her stomach and the quickening of her pulse was that of a woman on one of her first dates with a man she couldn't get enough of. Sharing rooms, *baths*, making decisions like *should we make love or watch television*? were *couple* decisions. And even though they'd done so much together, they were still new to coupledom.

"I see you drooling over me in the mirror," he said, turning slowly. A sexy smile lifted his lips. "Nervous, baby?"

He raked a hand through his short hair, and the tattoo on his arm caught her eyes. She'd seen it so many times, she never thought about it. Maybe it was the lights and mirrors, the candles and bath, or maybe it was just that she loved him so much it magnified her attraction to him. But suddenly the tattoo made him look edgy and mysterious.

"I'll take that finger twirling in your hair as a yes," he said with a dark look in his eyes.

The nervous habit had followed her from the time she was a little girl. She'd tried to break it when she was a teenager, feeling like it made her look ditzy. But it had been a futile effort and had made her even more anxious trying to fight the outlet.

"I'd say sorry," she said as he took slow, determined steps toward her, ratcheting up her pulse with each one. "But I like looking at you."

She was getting bolder with her sexuality. Saying things she had only imagined saying. As Gage began untying her robe, she knew it was because of the way he looked at and spoke to her. He made her feel desired.

"That's a good thing, bird, because I will never get enough of looking at you."

Her robe fell open, revealing a path of flesh down the center of her body, and Gage took in every inch. *Okay, this is why I'm nervous.* He never hid his desires, and seeing the heat in his eyes, the way he licked his lips as he drank her in, made her body hum with anticipation.

He took her chin between his finger and thumb, tipping her face up. "Will you be nervous when we're old and gray and I want to look at and touch you?"

"Probably, but by then you may feel differently."

"Not a chance, my love." He lowered his soft lips to hers, kissing away her worries as he pushed the robe from her body.

He stepped back, his piercing stare never wavering from hers as he removed his briefs. She could see her chest rising with each heavy breath, and she had absolutely no hope of not lowering her gaze to his thick erection.

"See something you want, sweetheart?"

His voice was calm as a summer breeze as his arm circled her waist, drawing her against him. Heat rushed from her head to her core, gathering speed and temperature until it pooled between her legs, turning every inch in between to liquid fire. Lost in the sensations, she couldn't form a response, and she didn't need to. Gage claimed her mouth again, devouring her with fervor, sending electrical currents arcing through her. His hands were everywhere. On her ass, back, shoulders, neck, and finally, tangling in her hair the way they always did. She was hypnotized by the rough, strong feel of him possessing all of her. It was all she could do to hang on as their hips began an urgent, sensual grind. His erection moved against her belly, thick, firm, and beyond tempting. He moaned into the kiss, his arousal taking her even higher.

"Love you so much," he ground out.

And then his mouth was on her breast, sucking so hard she went up on her toes and cried out with his divine ravishment. His fingers thrust into her slick heat, and her thoughts shut down. There was only the feel of his mouth, the lingering taste of his sweetness, and the earnest thrust of his hard length against her belly, matching the rhythm of his hand as he fucked her. Her hand circled his arousal, earning a heady groan, but she couldn't keep a rhythm when her legs were turning to jelly. She grabbed his arms as her orgasm claimed her, pulling long, lust-filled moans from her lungs.

"I *love* hearing you lose control," he said in a gravelly voice.

She clung to him, trying to catch her breath. "When you say stuff like that it makes it harder to regain control."

"I'm definitely using that to my advantage from now on." He nuzzled her neck. "Tell me more of your sexy secrets."

"I have a feeling you'll discover them all on your own."

With an arm around her waist, which was necessary since her legs decided they no longer needed to function, he led her to the tub and helped her in.

Too revved up to sit and wait patiently, she straddled him, rubbing her hands over the hard ridges of his pecs, teasing over his nipples, and kissing his shoulders. Gage leaned back, his eyes as dark and wild as a summer storm. His eager arousal twitched enticingly against her bottom. She shifted her weight so she was half on his hip, half off, and lowered her mouth to his as she fisted his shaft, giving it a long, tight stroke and earning a heady groan from Gage. He grabbed her wrist and tore his mouth away.

"You'll make me come."

Sally grinned and reached for a condom, eyeing the *Naughty Sex Guide*. "My, my, what did my naughty husband have in mind?"

"Fuck, baby. What *don't* I have in mind?" He ripped the condom package open with his teeth.

She picked up the *Naughty Sex Guide* and flipped to a page. *Reverse Cowgirl. Hm. Now, there's an idea.* "I might need to study that later." She tossed it away.

He rose onto his knees, watching her every move, as she lowered her mouth to his cock, giving him a few deep sucks. His body shuddered, and when he tangled his hands in her hair, she couldn't stifle a moan. She gave in to the wild girl inside her, loving him with her mouth and hands. When he tugged her hair, making her release him, and crashed his mouth over hers, she opened her mouth wider, rising taller on her knees to meet his height as his slippery hands moved over her heated flesh. She had no idea where the condom ended up, but his hands were definitely empty save for various parts of her body. His magical mouth came down over her breast again, and she arched against him, cupping his balls.

"*Christ,* Sally," he panted out. "You drive me insane."

She grabbed another condom with a shaky hand and he tore it open, rolling it on quickly. He sank down in the tub, holding the condom in place, and when he tried to guide her, she shook her head and turned around, facing away from him, and lowered herself onto his shaft. His breath left his lungs in a hiss.

Okay, Reverse Cowgirl. Let's see what you've got.

She moved slowly at first, getting used to the position, and *holy cow,* it was a good one! He hit the perfect spot with every thrust, and when he rose behind her, cupping her breasts and squeezing her nipples, lightning raced through her veins, exploding in a flood tide of sensations. She arched her back, deepening their lovemaking, clinging to Gage's arms for balance as one pleasurable assault after another soared through her, until she was shaking all over, even while she tried to remain still.

"Guess my baby likes this position."

Her chin fell to her chest. "Ohmygod," she said breathlessly. "Help me turn around?"

"Sure you don't want to come again like this?"

Oh Lord. Hearing him say *come* made her insides burn. She shook her head.

He held the condom in place and helped her turn. She straddled him, taking all of him inside her again, and his arms circled her, steadying her spinning world.

"This is so much better," she whispered. "Nothing compares to being in your arms."

He poured bubbles over her shoulders, drawing her close again. "Better than that raging orgasm you just had?"

"*Much*. That was intense, but I'd rather see your face."

"Me too, baby."

He ran his hands through her hair, drawing her into a steamy kiss and sending her senses reeling. His hands spread over her butt, guiding their speed. She tried to continue kissing him, but their bodies moved too fast and the incredible friction between them made every ounce of her pulse. Her breasts grazed his chest in a dizzying rhythm. The candle flames danced as their lovemaking created invisible breezes, and the bathwater sloshed around them. Gage feasted on her neck, murmuring sweet sentiments into her skin. She tried to concentrate on every word, but the feel of him loving her and the desire coursing through her were too much. She gasped in sweet agony, trying to capture the orgasm in her periphery, and Gage silenced her with a kiss. His fingers dug into her bottom, quickening their pace, taking her hard and rough and somehow also tender and loving. She felt his breathing stilt, his muscles cord tight, and with the next thrust, pure, explosive pleasure tore through her as they lost themselves in their mutual release.

CHAPTER THIRTEEN

"HURRY!" SALLY SAID the next morning as she and Gage rushed around the hotel room stuffing their belongings into their bags. They'd stayed up so late fooling around, they'd overslept and were in danger of missing their flight.

Gage threw the covers back, making a final sweep of the sheets. A wicked grin spread across his face as he snagged something from the bed, dangling her pink panties from his fingertips. "My favorites."

Sally rolled her eyes, and he stuffed them into his bag and grabbed the framed wedding photo. She took it from his hands and wrapped it in one of her sweaters, packing it carefully.

"Do you have the baby gifts we bought?"

He lifted his suitcase. "Right here."

"Then I think we're ready." Her eyes sailed over the room one last time. And she was once again hit by the magnitude of what he'd done for her. Planned their honeymoon, found a cheesy room with a lighted headboard, and even a Christmas tree lighting ceremony, while she'd been too caught up in their relations, their love—*everything*—to think ahead. She looked at her handsome husband, so patient and loving and loaded down with luggage, and she couldn't stop smiling. She took his face between her hands and kissed him.

"Thank you for an incredible honeymoon."

"You can thank me properly when we get home. *Twice.*" He gave her a quick kiss and headed for the door. "That is, if we make it to our plane on time."

"Wait!" Sally ran back to the chaise lounge, grabbed the *Naughty Sex Guide*, and stuffed it in her purse.

Gage chuckled.

"What? You know you want it." She hiked her purse over her shoulder as she reconsidered joining the mile-high club. "Do you have our ornament?"

"Yup. Let's go, my beautiful bird."

My beautiful bird. She looked forward to hearing that for the rest of her life. "This has been so fun," she said as they left the room. "Maybe *cheesy* should be our thing."

"*Everything* should be our thing."

Gage drove fast but carefully toward the airport, but there was an accident on the highway and they missed their flight. Neither of them minded the delay, because even time spent sitting in an airport was extra time together. Several hours later, they finally boarded the plane. Gage laced their hands together and pressed a kiss to the back of Sally's. She inhaled deeply, feeling as though she were breathing for the first time that day.

"You okay, bird?"

"Yeah." She rested her head on his shoulder. "So much has changed, but we're the only ones who know it."

"For now. That'll change in a few weeks when we see Rusty." He brushed his thumb over her ring finger. "What kind of engagement ring and wedding band do you want?"

"I don't know. I liked our inked rings."

"Tattooed rings work for me. I'm not picky. I just want rings on our fingers so the whole world knows we're all in." He kissed her ring finger and said, "I actually hope to wear my grandfather's ring."

"The one who taught you about sports?" Over the years, Gage had told her many stories about going to sporting events with his grandfather and learning all about scoring and positions and being a team player.

"The one and only Trenton Theodore Ryder. He taught me about sports, and before he died he told me that the only goal that really matters in life is loving a woman so completely that she can't wait to come home to you."

"That explains why your family is so loving. Good roots."

The plane taxied down the runway.

"I think I'll text Rusty real quick and let him know we're heading back home." She sent him a quick text. *Heading back to Colorado. Did you decide on the Jeep?*

Gage eyed her phone and took out his, showing her a text from Rusty. *Thanks for warning me about the inspection. The Jeep I wanted needed $1500 of repairs. I'm looking at another one next week. Taking the bus blows.*

"At least he's taking your advice." She put away her phone, wondering why Rusty hadn't texted her. "It's weird being a mother to a twenty-year-old. When he first went away to college, it seemed like he called me for everything."

"He did. I remember him calling to tell you about parties he'd gone to and you worrying about *whether* you should worry or not."

She smiled, remembering those calls. She did worry. "I still worry about whether I'm worrying enough. I'm just not used to finding out things about him secondhand, I guess. I know it's normal to ask a man about stuff like cars, but still. It's like I've passed an invisible baton I don't remember releasing."

"At least you're not passing it to a stranger."

Takeoff was uneventful and when they turned off the seat belt signs, Sally whispered in Gage's ear, "Your honeymoon present will be waiting for you in the bathroom." She rose to her feet, enjoying the shock rising in his eyes.

She headed down the aisle with her heart beating so hard she was sure everyone heard it—and knew exactly why she was so nervous. Could they see it on her face? Did she look guilty? She stepped into the tiny lavatory and surveyed the confined space. It smelled like urine and cleaning products. Not a sexy combination. She flipped the top of the toilet down with the toe of her shoe. The door opened behind her and she moved back, straddling the toilet, giving Gage room to step in. He closed the door behind him and hauled her against him.

Her anxiety tumbled out. "Did anyone see you? Do they know we're both in here?"

"I'm pretty sure everyone saw me walk past." He lowered his mouth to hers, their bodies mashed together in the tight quarters.

"Then they *know*?"

He grinned. "All they *know* is that I went into one of the bathrooms, but if you don't keep it down, they'll know the rest."

Their mouths came together, and she willed herself not to think about the rest of the passengers. Gage made it easy. His hands explored, bringing her every nerve to the surface, and he kissed her sensually as he worked the button on her jeans free. She backed into the counter, giving them more space as she fumbled with his zipper, and they both dropped their pants. Turbulence sent Sally flying into him, and he stumbled backward, falling onto his ass on the toilet lid with Sally leaning over him, laughing. He ground his teeth together.

"*Christ.*" He pushed to his feet, and in one quick move he lifted her up and set her on the sink. She braced herself with both hands, wondering why anyone would want to join this club in the first place. She had boots on, and there was no way they were coming off. With a look of fierce determination, he tugged her pants down to her ankles and pushed her knees apart.

"Condom," she whispered urgently.

"Fuck." He bent to grab his wallet from his pocket and hit his forehead on the edge of the sink. "Mother fu—"

"Are you okay?" came out with another laugh. She couldn't help it. The whole thing was preposterous. Why did she think this would be a gift? It was like the gift from hell for him.

"Fine." He tore open the condom and rolled it on.

She swallowed her laughter and cradled his face in her hands. "I'm so sorry. We don't have to do this."

"Oh, we *are* doing this. I will *not* let you down, beautiful girl."

His arm circled her waist and he aligned their bodies as his mouth descended on hers, and they came together. Sally wanted her legs around his waist, but they were trapped at the ankles, making their lovemaking rough and even more exciting because they had to angle their bodies and fight for deep penetration. When the plane lurched, Gage clung to Sally, bracing them both with one strong arm against the edge of the counter.

"You okay?" he asked quickly.

The plane bounced and lurched, and the seat belt light came on.

"Yeah. Hurry."

Gage picked up his pace, thrusting faster, holding her tight, using his powerful legs to steady them against the careening plane. Seconds later he was grunting out her name, his body shuddering as he came.

"Welcome to the mile-high club, sweetheart." His devilish grin made the whole thing worthwhile.

The plane lurched and tilted. A knock sounded at the door seconds before it swung open, hitting Gage in the ass. He used his body to block Sally from the intruder.

A gasp. "Sir!"

Sally peered over his shoulder at the flight attendant, who looked as mortified as she felt. She rested her forehead on Gage's shoulder and he put his hand on the back of her head.

"Shit." Gage used his foot to try to kick the door closed.

"This is not allowed," the attendant snapped, her eyes shielded by her hand. "You need to return to your seats immediately."

"Shut the door and we'll return to our seats," he growled.

She closed the door, and Sally's breath rushed from her lungs. "Did you forget to lock the door?"

"Shit. I don't know. I guess." He took care of the condom and helped her from the counter, both of them scrambling to get cleaned up and dressed, bumping shoulders and elbows while Miss Back to Your Seat was probably standing outside the door tapping her foot.

"Everyone knows!" Sally said as she buttoned her jeans.

"No one knows. Just be cool about it. Who cares what anyone else thinks anyway?" He lifted her chin and kissed her. "I adore you. That's all that should matter."

Maybe so, but when they left the bathroom, a twentysomething guy eyed her up and down with a knowing grin, and when Gage passed he said, "Welcome to the mile-high club, dude."

So much for acting cool…

THEY STOPPED FOR dinner on the way back to Allure, and as they walked back to the car, it dawned on Sally that this would be the last time they could be openly affectionate in public until they told Rusty about their relationship. The pit of her stomach knotted.

She stopped in the middle of the parking lot and said, "I need you to kiss me right here, right now."

In the next breath she was in his arms, melting against him as he made all the unsettled pieces of her come back together.

"I'm going to miss having the freedom to do that whenever I want."

"Me too, bird. But soon we'll be free to do it for the rest of our lives."

Only a few more weeks, played in Sally's head like a mantra as Gage drove through Allure traffic. Their small town was overwhelmed with tourists in the winter.

"I'm so glad I live in the mountains," Gage said. "I don't know how anyone stands this traffic on a daily basis."

Sally loved Gage's private mountaintop oasis. He lived on five wooded acres, with a big, gorgeous barn and a rustic four-bedroom stone and wood home that was built partially into a hill and looked like it had sprouted from the earth. The wide-planked hardwood floors, heavy wooden furniture, and stone fireplace made the house feel rugged and stable, like the man who owned it.

Gage squeezed her hand and turned off the main road toward her house. "Time away from this traffic is something to consider while we figure out where we should live."

"Where we should *live*? I'm still trying to figure out how to tell Rusty we're married. Have you thought any more about the idea of telling him we're dating?"

He turned down Sally's street and parked in front of her house, his expression serious. "For how long, Sal? Are we supposed to stay at separate houses until we're married? Do we tell him we're dating and then suddenly get married a week later? Isn't it better to tell him the truth and let him deal with it all at once?"

"I don't know. He lost his father, and he—"

"Baby," he said compassionately, although also with a bite of irritation. "That was *years* ago."

"Yes, but still." She looked at the modest ranch-style house she and Dave had rented when she was pregnant, and purchased a few years later. It was the only home Rusty had ever known and the place she'd lived since she was eighteen years old.

"I didn't think this through," she said more to herself than to Gage. "How will Rusty feel about you sleeping in the house? This is the only home he has ever known, and in his mind, it's..." She grasped for words that wouldn't minimize her relationship with Gage but would clearly describe how difficult this might be for Rusty.

"It's the house where he probably still sees his father walking in the door. I get it, Sal. Don't you think I have the same reservations about how *I'll* feel being with you in that house? How *you'll* feel? That's why I think we should live at my place, where the past won't be a problem."

"And just uproot Rusty's whole world like that?" She opened the car door, needing air. "That seems harsh, and would probably make things worse." She stepped from the car and paced.

He came around and reached for her, but she turned away. "Baby, he's twenty, not *five*. He's got a whole life, a job, an apartment, and friends out in Harborside. He's hardly ever here."

"But this is still his home, Gage, regardless of how often he comes back from school." Her heart was being pulled in two different directions.

"And what about you, baby?" Gage asked solemnly. "Where do you want your home to be?"

Blinking against tears of frustration, she looked up at the house, memories flooding her. She shifted her gaze to Gage, and the last few days came slamming into her. "I don't know. That's an unfair question. I want my home to be wherever you are and where Rusty is when he comes back, but…" She glanced at the house again. "It's also here, until I know it's okay for it not to be."

He pushed his hand through his hair, his jaw clenched tight. Without a word, he opened the trunk, unloaded her bags, and carried them to the front door.

"You're mad?" *Duh? Wouldn't I be?*

"No, Sal. I'm not mad. I'm just trying to figure out where we go from here. It sounds like we're on hold until we see Rusty. I'm tempted to get back on a fucking plane and head out to Harborside to get this over with."

She sank down to the front step with a heavy heart. "Why does it hurt to hear you say it that way? 'Get this over with.'"

"Because you're hearing my frustration. Do you think I want to spend one night apart from you? What if Rusty's not cool with this? Then what? Do we back off?" He sat beside her and pulled her close, pressing his lips to the side of her head.

"I'm sorry. I guess we're both realizing we have a lot to figure out."

Tears welled in her eyes. "I thought telling Rusty would be the hard part, but until we see him, what do we tell our friends? Where do we sleep? I honestly don't know how I'll feel sleeping with you here. Maybe I should have realized that before, but I was so swept up in us, half the time I couldn't think clearly. I still can't."

"I know, babe." He dried her tears with the pad of his thumb. "What do we tell our friends? Nothing. You said you don't want anyone to know until Rusty does, and I respect that."

"Doesn't that upset you?"

"I'm not a saint. Of course I'm upset, and a little hurt. But that makes me sound like a selfish pansy, so I'll never admit it again."

"No, it doesn't." She reached for his hand. "It makes you sound like a normal guy whose new wife is a head case."

"Then figuring out our living arrangements should be easy." A playful grin lifted his lips. "I can visit you at the insane asylum on a regular basis."

She nudged him with her shoulder. "Seriously, what should we do? How do we go from spending every night together to living separate lives?"

"You can stay at my place, bird. Rusty will never know, and if anyone stops by, they know we're close friends. It won't strike them as odd if you're there."

"Maybe. I feel…" *Scared to death.* How did a person just walk away from their home of twenty-plus years? "Out of sorts. I think I need to stay here tonight and get my bearings and a good night's sleep. Hopefully it will all be clearer in the morning."

GAGE KNEW COMING home wasn't going to be an easy transition, but he hadn't expected to see so much hurt in Sally's eyes when he suggested they consider living in his house. He drove straight to the gym to try to work off his frustrations, but a six-mile run on the indoor track barely took the edge off. Seeing an unfamiliar truck in his driveway and the lights on in his house brought his frustrations to the surface again. He jogged around to the back window and peered inside. His youngest brother, Jake, was sitting on his couch drinking a beer with his feet up on the coffee table. Jake stopped by unannounced so often, he had his own key. As relieved as Gage was not to have to beat the hell out of an intruder, he wasn't in the mood for company. He threw open the kitchen door and Jake rose to his feet.

"Bro!" Jake closed the distance between them, arms open. "How was your trip?"

Gage embraced him. "Pretty damn good." *Until we got home.* "What are you doing here?"

"Didn't you get my message? I got called on a mountain rescue about two hours from here yesterday. We found the woman and her son late last night." Jake had followed in their father's footsteps as a search and rescue professional. "I thought we could hang out before I go back home tomorrow."

"I'm glad the rescue was successful, but I never saw the message. How's Addy?" Jake's fiancée, Addison Dahl, worked for Duke's wife, Gabriella, as a paralegal, and she was also training to do search and rescue.

"As hot as ever," Jake said cockily.

"I'm glad you're here." *It'll keep me from driving over to Sally's.* "Let me grab my luggage. I'll be right back."

Outside, Gage sent a quick text to Sally. *Miss you already. You sure you don't want to come over?* He didn't care that Jake was there. Even if he couldn't own up to the relationship, just having her in the house would feel better than the empty miles between them.

He grabbed his bags and carried them inside. Jake followed him into the laundry room, where Gage began pulling out his dirty clothes. Jake reached into the suitcase and picked up Sally's underwear.

"Dude. You and Sally finally hooked up?"

Gage grabbed them from him and ground his teeth together. He wasn't about to breach Sally's trust and tell his no-filter brother about their relationship. "No."

"No? You have some random chick's underwear?" He watched Gage throw them in the washing machine. "And you're *washing* them?"

"Christ, Jake." He grabbed the panties and tossed them in the trash, then went back to tossing his dirty clothes into the washer.

"Dude," Jake said sternly. "You and Sally are meant to be together. What are you doing sleeping around?"

"Leave it alone, Jake." He threw another shirt into the washer.

"No, I won't leave it alone," Jake seethed. "What the hell is wrong with you? I get that you need to get laid, but you were traveling *with* Sally. Does she know? Because I'm pretty sure if she does, you've just blown any chance you had with her."

Shut the fuck up. "Says the guy who saw Addy all the time and still left bars with other women." He threw the rest of his laundry in the washer and grabbed the detergent bottle, wanting to throw it against the damn wall. He was *this close* to losing his shit.

Jake got right in his face, his eyes as angry as Gage had ever seen them. "I never hooked up with another woman once I knew it was Addy I wanted. You know it's Sally for you. She's it. Shit, it's been Sally for years."

"Back off, little brother. I'm not in the mood for this." Gage's chest constricted. Yeah, he'd known for years, and now she was his fucking wife, but here he was at a separate house feeling like he was second fiddle, which was really messed up. It was totally reasonable that she needed time to wrap her head around their situation and all that came with it. He had no business feeling anything but supportive. But hell if that came easily—especially when he had Jake breathing down his neck.

Jake held his ground. "I'm not going to *back off* and let you fuck up your life."

Gage didn't know what was worse, trying to keep a secret from his brother who was trying to protect the woman Gage loved, or the look in Sally's eyes when she said she needed to stay at her place and find her bearings. Hurt and anger tore at his gut. What if Sally decided she'd made a mistake? What if she'd thought she was over Dave, but now that she was facing reality—a bigger reality than just wanting another man—she couldn't make the break?

"I'm not kidding, Jake. I'm not in the mood for this bullshit."

"Bullshit? Gage, we're talking about *Sally*. How could you hurt her like that?"

Gage grabbed him by the collar and pushed him against the wall. All the emotions of the past week came racing forward. "It was *her*, you idiot. That underwear was hers. But goddamn it—" He released Jake and stalked out of the laundry room, rubbing the knot at the base of his neck. He grabbed a beer from the fridge and took a long swig. "I need you to keep this between the two of us. Sally doesn't want anyone to know until we have time to talk to Rusty."

Jake stood between the kitchen and living room, arms crossed against his broad chest, with a cocky, know-it-all grin on his face.

"Stop looking at me like that." Gage pushed past him and dropped to the couch.

"This grin is not going anywhere, bro." He sat in the leather recliner and leaned forward, elbows on knees. "So…?"

"If you think I'm dishing on Sally in bed, you've got another thing coming."

Jake laughed. "I don't want those details. I'm sure after all these years the sex was amazing, but what's got your nuts in a knot?"

Gage took another pull of his beer, unwilling to divulge their marriage or the complications that went along with it. He shouldn't have even told Jake they'd gotten together, but hell, it was too late now.

"Gage?"

The worried look in his brother's eyes took his anger down a notch.

"It's complicated," he finally said.

"Aren't all women? Shit, that's why we love them. If they were easy, we'd get bored, right?" Jake sat back and clasped his hands behind his head. "Addy's got me tied in knots half the time. She's got a goddamn stubborn streak a mile long. Sometimes it's all I can do to stare at her and wonder what's going on in that gorgeous head of hers, but *damn*, man. Those times are just as awesome as when we're in sync."

"I *know* what's going on in Sally's head." His phone vibrated and he pulled it from his pocket. *Sally*. Hope swelled inside him as he read her text. *I miss you, too, but I need to figure out how I feel about this house before we see Rusty. Danica called. I'm meeting her and the girls for breakfast before work tomorrow. Are you okay?*

"Is that from her?"

"Yeah." Gage read the text again. She didn't say anything about not being able to face her feelings. That had to be good. Wishing he could barrel into her house, sweep her off her feet like a caveman, and carry her back to his place, he sent her a reply. *Have fun with the girls. I'm fine. Jake came by after a rescue. He's here for the night. Otherwise I'd be on your doorstep. I'm here if you need me. Love you, bird. Always.*

"Want to tell me what's going on and why you're not with her right now?" Jake asked.

Gage's phone vibrated with Sally's reply. *Tell Jake I said hello and have fun with him. Love you too* was followed by an emoji of a kissy face and two hearts. He set his phone on the table and felt himself smiling.

"I guess that means all is well again?"

"Getting there, but it's going to take time." Gage had thought that once they told Rusty, they'd move forward as a married couple and begin their lives together. But now he wondered if he had it all wrong. Maybe it wasn't *Rusty* who needed Gage and Sally to date, then get engaged, and eventually get married. Maybe it was *Sally*.

"Why?" Jake pushed. "What's the holdup?"

"Remember what Dad said to you about Addy when you didn't want to let her go on that camping trip alone after you two got together?" Right after Jake and Addy had spent their first weekend together, Addy had gone on a camping trip in the mountains and Jake had just about lost his mind.

"How could I ever forget? He told me if I caged her in, I was liable to get bitten."

"I'm starting to wonder if that might be the case with Sally, too."

Chapter Fourteen

SALLY LAY AWAKE for most of the night trying to imagine what it would be like to no longer live in her house. She and Gage had been so removed from their real lives, and had gotten so close, when she'd walked inside last night she'd felt like she'd walked into someone else's life, or a life she used to live but no longer quite fit in. It had taken her most of the evening to shake the feeling of guilt that had accompanied those unfamiliar emotions. She'd even set her and Gage's wedding picture next to her bed, hoping it might hold together the pieces of her that were unraveling, but it felt wrong to have it displayed in the house where she and Dave had lived. She'd turned the frame upside down, and that, too, had made her feel guilty.

Monday morning she still couldn't shake the feeling of being a stranger in her own home, and that terrified her. What if Rusty felt that way if they moved into Gage's house? What if it was best for Rusty that they remain in their house, giving him a touchpoint for his memories of his father? If she was this uncomfortable in the house, how could she expect Gage to put up with it?

As if he knew she needed him, Gage called when she was on her way to the café.

"How's my favorite wife?"

She imagined the smile in his voice reaching his warm blue

eyes. And as quickly as that warmth enveloped her, a spear of guilt hit her. *Favorite wife.* If she returned that sentiment, what did that say about her marriage to Dave?

Where did all these complications come from?

"I'm okay, but I hated sleeping without you. How about you? Did you have fun with Jake?"

"He left this morning. It was good to see him, but I wouldn't call it fun. I'd have been happier spending the night with you. I missed you."

"I missed you, too. But I needed last night."

"Did you come to any decisions?"

She glanced in the rearview mirror. No makeup in the world could hide the worry in her eyes. "I don't know," she said honestly. "Think we can find some time to talk later?"

"You're my top priority, babe. I can meet you now and talk if you'd like."

She wished she wasn't meeting the girls. She'd be a nervous wreck until she and Gage had a chance to figure things out. "I can't. I'm pulling into the parking lot to meet the girls for breakfast. I have no idea how I'll keep our relationship from them. I hate secrets."

"About that…"

Something in the way he said it told her he'd already blown it. "You told Jake, didn't you?" She knew how pushy Jake was. Gage was as bad at lying as Jake was at keeping secrets. If Jake had noticed the slightest difference in Gage he'd probably forced the truth out of him.

"He found your underwear in my suitcase and accused me of sleeping around behind your back."

She smiled as she maneuvered into a parking spot and cut the engine. His brothers were all protective of their significant others, and even though she and Gage hadn't been a couple for all these years, they'd always been protective of her, too. "Why does that make me smile?"

"Because you know we should scream it from the rooftops."

Oh, how she wanted to do that! But Rusty had to come first. "Gage—"

"Don't worry. I told him to keep it between us and that we wanted to talk to Rusty first."

"*We*," she whispered.

"Always *we*, Sal. Unless you changed your mind and you want to talk to Rusty on your own first?"

"No. Maybe. I'm not sure yet." She couldn't keep putting that decision off either. She needed to figure out how to tell him. She'd thought telling Rusty together was best, but after her own reaction last night, she wasn't sure Gage's being there was the smartest way to handle it.

"We have time, babe. I just wanted to hear your voice. I won't keep you."

"Keep me, *please*." *Help me figure out what to do about the house and how to tell Rusty.*

"I don't plan on letting you go, bird," Gage said lovingly. "Not for anything in the world."

She reveled in that promise all the way into the café, where Danica and her younger sister, Kaylie, and their friend Max Braden, waved her over to a table by the window.

Danica rose to greet her. Her thick spiral curls were as dark as Kaylie's long wavy hair was blond.

"Welcome back." Danica angled her burgeoning baby belly to the side and hugged her. Her eyes lingered on Sally's for a beat too long. "Everything okay? You look tired."

"Traveling tires a person out," Kaylie said, rising to hug

Sally as Danica sat down. "When I'm on tour, I fall into bed and sleep like the dead. It's good to see you, Sal." Kaylie had young twins, Lexi and Trevor. Between her singing career and the kids, she was always on the run.

"You too," Sally said, and leaned in to embrace Max, who was also pregnant, though only four months. Max worked for Kaylie's husband and was married to Blake's cousin, Treat. "How do you feel these days, Max?"

Max lifted her dark ponytail from the nape of her neck with a how-do-you-think look in her hazel eyes. "I love being pregnant, but I could do without the morning sickness, and I'm already outnumbered with two kids. I'll be sporting a ponytail for the next five months."

"Ugh, I remember that feeling." Sally dug her wallet from her purse and set her purse on the chair. "I want to grab coffee and a muffin. Do you guys want something?"

"Only if they sell concealer." Kaylie pointed to a tiny red mark on her chin. "Too much chocolate lately."

"Don't look at me," Danica said. "I don't carry makeup anymore." She patted her cheeks. "Nothing can hide pregnancy puffiness."

"I have some in the zipper pocket in my purse. You can use it," Sally said, and headed up to the counter to get her breakfast.

When she returned to the table, she was suddenly ravenous, and bit into her muffin.

"Um, Sally?" Kaylie said in a singsong voice.

Sally looked up with a mouthful of muffin. "Hm?"

Kaylie leaned across the table and whispered, "Even *I* don't carry lube in my purse!"

Sally choked on her muffin, coughing and spewing it into a napkin. Danica patted her on her back as she tried to catch her breath. She gulped coffee in an effort to clear her throat. "Ouch! Hot! What are you talking about? I don't have *that* in my purse!"

Kaylie held up the bottle of lube that had come in the honeymoon basket. "I guess it wasn't the traveling that wore you out after all."

Sally snagged the bottle from her and shoved it back into her purse. "I'm going to kill Gage."

Danica's eyes widened.

"About time you rode that stallion." Kaylie smirked. "Danica, you'd better put a lock on the break room door."

"It's not what you think." *Liar, liar.* She was dying to tell them the truth and rave about how romantic Gage was and how her heart felt full for the first time in years. But the mother in her silenced that enthusiasm, reminding her how important it was that Rusty not feel like he was the last to know. Her friends would understand once she and Gage came clean about their relationship, but she needed to protect her son, regardless of how old he was.

"Are you sure?" Max waved the *Naughty Sex Guide*. "Because I don't remember you carrying this in your purse either."

Sally cringed. "I am never, ever, *ever* letting any of you in my purse again."

"Lube. *Naughty Sex Guide*." Kaylie narrowed her eyes. "Spill your guts or we are going to make up our own stories, and I've got a *wild* imagination. If it's not Gage, then who's been riding *Mustang Sally*?"

Sally's mind raced through possible explanations, but as she met the expectant faces of the women who had helped her through not only the loss of her husband, but her son's trials and tribulations, she couldn't outright lie. She drew in a calming breath and hoped she could pull off a partial truth.

"Gage must have stuffed those in my purse as a joke. We were playing pranks on each other the whole time we were away. I promise you, we did *not* use it." At least that much was true.

"Bummer." Kaylie looked truly disappointed.

Max dangled the guide and asked, "What about this? Some of these positions look crazy. Listen to this one. It's called the Bridge. The guy lays with his shoulders and head on an ottoman or something, and his lower legs are on a chair."

The girls huddled together to peek at the picture. Sally tried to imagine Gage in that position. She felt her cheeks burn, and focused on eating her muffin as Max continued her detailed explanation.

"Then you sit on him and turn, using your hands to steady yourself. You lift one leg over his, give a few thrusts, then turn again, like a corkscrew." Laughter burst from Max's lips. "Can you imagine doing this and the guy falls between the ottoman and chair? I mean, really? Who could manage this? If I ever asked Treat to try this he'd think I was crazy."

"Treat would do anything you ask," Danica said. "Including *that*."

Treat had pursued Max relentlessly before they married, and he'd put her on a pedestal ever since. He doted on her and their two beautiful children, Adriana and Dylan, and Sally doubted there was anything he wouldn't do for her.

"I have to agree with Max on this one, Dan," Kaylie said. "I mean, I've done some crazy shit, but that? I can't even imagine asking Chaz to try that, and Treat? He's so tall. There's no way..." Her brows lifted. "Who knew Sally was wilder than me? And *damn*. Gage must be really fit."

"Gage is very fit, but we did *not* do that." *We did the Reverse Cowgirl.* Sally grabbed the booklet and put it in her purse, wishing she could disappear.

"I knew she used the lube," Kaylie chimed in.

Danica swatted her arm. "Hush."

"We did *not* use it," Sally insisted.

"Hey, I'm not judging you if you did," Kaylie said. "I mean, *hello.* Who wants to answer a knock at the back door without it?"

"Kaylie Crew!" Danica chastised.

"What?" Kaylie laughed. "You said you and Blake—"

"Okay, enough!" Danica put her hands up. "Time for a safer subject. Max, have you and Treat thought about baby names yet?"

Sally breathed a sigh of relief and made a mental note to clean out her purse—and give Gage hell for putting the lube in there. Although…it did give her a few ideas.

NO LIMITZ SEEMED to have a revolving door for most of the morning, and every time Gage went to talk with Sally she was either on the phone or dealing with an issue. He hadn't spent any time with her besides the hour-long conference call they'd had with Danica and the new hires for the Oak Falls location. Sin and Haylie were ready to take charge and get things organized, and they all looked forward to seeing the grand opening come to fruition.

Gage headed down the hall for coffee, relieved to find Sally standing at the counter pouring herself a cup. He wrapped his arms around her from behind, his body cocooning hers. Her feminine scent awakened the desires he'd been tamping down while they were apart.

"How's my girl?" he whispered beside her ear. She leaned her head back against his chest. The tension easing from her body underscored how right they were together.

"Better now. Last night was eye opening." She turned in his arms, and he ran his fingers through her hair.

"Listen, maybe I overreacted. If you need us to go a more traditional route and date, then get engaged, and eventually get married, that's fine with me. It's not my preference, but I've waited five years. I can wait another one if you need me to."

"I don't," she said quickly. "After last night, I know I don't want to stay at separate houses. It's just hard to think about giving up my house after living there for my entire adult life."

"I know, and we don't have to make the decision on what to do with your house anytime soon. Are you comfortable staying with me at my house? I don't want to go another night without you, but I don't want to pressure you, either." That wasn't exactly true. He wanted to pressure her, but he knew better.

Desire sparked in her eyes. "I want to be with you, whatever it takes, wherever we can manage."

They both leaned in, and their mouths came together gently, but their tenderness quickly turned heated. All the frustration and hurt from last night disappeared, replaced with desire as strong as rolling thunder. He wedged himself between her legs in an effort to get even closer, and deepened the kiss. His hands traveled up her ribs, brushing the sides of her breasts. His blood burned hotter with every touch. A wanton sound escaped her lips, and the enticing noise surged through him.

"Missed you so much," he said between kisses. He took her face between his hands, and the lascivious look in her eyes nearly did him in. "Tell me you'll stay with me tonight, bird. Don't make me wait."

Her gaze turned even more sinful, and she pulled him into another mind-numbing kiss. He was already hard, and she was rocking her hips, grabbing his ass, giving him all the "go" signals.

"Can't do this here," she said heatedly. Then her luscious mouth was on *his* neck, and he felt every suck as if she were on her knees.

"*Fuck*, bird," he ground out.

That only made her suck harder.

He grabbed her hair and tugged her mouth away. "I *need* you, and if you keep doing that, I'm going to *take* you right here."

Her gaze darted to the supply room door, and she pushed away from the counter. In three seconds flat they were on the other side of that door, frantically tearing at each other's clothes. He was blinded by lust and love, and being closer to Sally was all that mattered. She stepped out of her panties and lifted her skirt as he dug out a condom and rolled it on. He lifted her into his arms and groaned through gritted teeth as her body swallowed every inch of him.

"Shh," she said breathlessly.

Their mouths crashed together in a rough kiss, as urgent as the heat throbbing through him. Her back hit the wall with a *thud* as he pounded into her. He could barely see in the dark room, but he could *feel*. Damn, could he feel—her hot breath on his cheek, her thundering heart, and the pulse of her sex as she clung to his shoulders, her legs squeezing tight around his waist.

"Faster," she pleaded in a demanding whisper. "Oh God,

Gage—"

He could barely comprehend her words as blinding heat seared down his spine. Sally's breathing shallowed, and her nails dug into his neck. He needed an anchor in his spinning world as he thrust faster, loved her harder. Her sex pulsed tight and hot around him, and her nails dug deeper. The pierce of pain tangled with the pleasure blazing through him, and he captured her mouth, silencing their sounds as they both spiraled over the edge of ecstasy.

Gage leaned his back against the wall, holding her close as their kisses turned languid and sensual. When their breathing calmed, he lowered her to the floor and rid himself of the condom, feeling mildly guilty for taking her in the frigging supply room. But she was hot as fuck.

They dressed quickly, and he took her face in his hands and kissed her. Her hair was tousled with that just-been-fucked look, and when she blinked up at him through her impossibly long lashes, his heart swelled at the love looking back at him.

"I'm sorry, baby. I didn't mean for this to happen here. I just can't keep my hands off you."

"It's not like you forced me. I wanted you just as badly, and I loved every second of our sneaky closet sex."

He brushed his lips over hers. "Ah, you like sneaky sex?"

Her arms circled his neck as the door swung open, and they both jumped back. Danica stood before them with a confused look in her eyes. She opened her mouth to speak, then snapped it closed, her cheeks flushing as understanding dawned on her. "Sorry," she mumbled, and hurried out of the room.

CHAPTER FIFTEEN

"SHIT!" SALLY RAN after Danica. She never should have let herself get so carried away. What was she thinking? She wasn't thinking, *period.* The administrative area of the community center was far away from where kids were allowed to wander, but still. Anyone could have walked in on them.

"It's okay, Sally," Gage reassured her as they headed for Danica's office. "I'll handle it." His hair was messed up, and he had lipstick around his mouth.

Her stomach pitched. She was sure she looked like she'd wrestled with a tube of lipstick, just as he did, but there wasn't anything she could do about it right that second.

"This is *not* okay." She huffed out a breath and walked into Danica's office. Danica was pacing with a pinched look on her face, which made Sally even more upset.

"I'm sorry," she pleaded. "I should have told you the truth this morning."

"It's my fault, Danica." Gage stepped forward, forming a protective barrier between the two women.

"That's not true. It's my fault," Sally insisted. "Are you going to fire me? You should fire me. I lied to you this morning. Wait, not about the lube or the Bridge or any of that, but about me and Gage. And I know I'm going to kiss him again in the office. I just know it, because"—she waved at Gage, who looked confused—"look at him. How can we work together when I can't even keep my hands off him?"

"Lube?" Gage asked.

"Yes, *lube*," Sally snapped. "I have a bone to pick with you about putting it in my purse."

He chuckled, then quickly schooled his expression. "It was my fault, Salbird. I should have stopped us. If anyone's leaving the company, it'll be me."

"Would you guys both be quiet for a second?" Danica grabbed Kleenex from a box on her desk and handed some to each of them. "Clean the lipstick off your faces. No one is getting fired or leaving the company. I'm just a little shocked, and embarrassed for walking in on you, and thankful it was only *me* and not some kid."

If you only knew what you could have walked in on. Sally wiped her mouth. "I'm really sorry, Danica."

Gage put a hand on the small of her back, drawing her closer. And hell if she didn't snuggle right up, despite knowing she should keep a modicum of space between them. What was wrong with her?

"See?" she whispered to Gage. "I can't even stay away from you *right now*. This is bad."

"This is *beautiful*, baby."

Danica pointed to the couch. "Sit, lovebirds."

They sank down to the couch, Gage's arm around Sally's shoulder. The gig was up. No use fighting it now. She moved closer to him.

Danica sat in an armchair, one hand on her belly, a smile playing at the edge of her lips. "You don't have to tell me, but how long have you two been together as a couple? Have I been missing signals?"

"Since the conference," Sally said.

"Vegas," Gage reiterated.

"This is good news, right?" Danica said. "Why are you hiding it?"

"Because after all Rusty's been through, I don't want him to be the last to find out."

Gage gently removed her fingers from the ends of her hair and set her hand on his leg, covering it with his own. "We're going to tell him in person, when he's home for the holidays."

"Why would he mind if he wasn't the first to know that you two are going out?" Danica asked.

Because we're really married.

Gage squeezed her hand. "After finding out about Chase, Sally thought it was best not to take any chances. We don't know how he'll react."

"I don't want Rusty to worry that if this doesn't work out between us, he'll lose Gage," Sally explained.

"He will *not* lose me," Gage insisted. "Nothing is going to go wrong between us."

"We don't know that! People get divorced all the time, and Rusty doesn't need to go through that."

"Divorced?" Danica's gaze darted between the two of them.

Sally pushed to her feet, pacing again.

"Break up," Gage said. "She meant *break up*."

"Sally, even if you two broke up, why would he lose Gage?"

"I don't know!" All the love she felt for Gage came rushing forward, pushed by the fear and confusion of doing right by her son. She threw her hands up in the air, unable to keep their secret any longer. "Maybe because we're *married*. You're the ex-therapist. You tell me what to do. We got drunk and ended up married in Vegas. It was an accident. Or maybe it wasn't." She looked at Gage, her heart aching, tears welling in her eyes, and her heart tumbled out too fast to stop it. "What if this is what we've wanted for so long, we just did it? Could it have been a moment of sanity in a night of debauchery? I don't know what we were thinking that night, and even though I love Gage with all my heart, once Rusty finds out, he'll never trust me or listen to me again. How can he? His own mother got rip-roaring drunk and married her best friend. It was selfish of me. And once he realizes that I put myself before him and that trust is broken, how can it ever be repaired? What kind of mother does that? And what if we *do* get divorced? Then I've screwed Rusty out of the best thing that has ever happened to him."

"Slow down, baby." Gage rose to his feet and wrapped his arms around her. "That won't happen. I promise you. We're too good together. We're happy. We love each other. What else is there to overcome?"

"I don't know," she said through her tears. "Maybe the fact that I feel like a stranger in my own house—the house Rusty may never want me to get rid of."

"We'll figure that out," he reassured her. "We can keep the house. We don't have to sell it. You're shaking all over, baby. Sit down."

She moved in a fog, relieved to be free of her secret and petrified of the aftermath. "I'm sorry to blurt it all out like that."

"It's okay," Gage said. "It's better this way."

Danica's eyes were wide with surprise. "You're *married*?"

Gage handed Sally more tissues and said, "Yes, and we *want* to be married. But not at the expense of Rusty. If you have any advice on how best to handle this, please, we'd love to hear it."

"Married?" Danica shook her head. "I'm sorry. I can see

Kaylie doing this, but you're the careful ones. I think you both must have wanted this for it to happen."

"Great." Sally sank back against the cushions. "How messed up do I have to be to need to get drunk to be with the man I love?"

"You're not messed up," Danica said. "You've put motherhood above all else since you were eighteen years old. Why does this surprise you? I'm just taking a wild, unfounded guess, but you probably needed to be drunk to allow yourself to take what you wanted. And the harder you fight it, the more you'll want each other."

Sally waved a hand. "Obviously, since we had sex in the supply room."

"You had *sex* in the supply room?" Danica laughed. "I thought you were just making out."

Sally buried her face in Gage's chest. "Go ahead. Fire me. I deserve it."

"I'm *not* firing you! I'm tickled that you two are together. But we do have children in the building, so—"

"We won't," Sally said at the same time Gage said, "Never again."

"Danica, what should we do?" Sally asked. "I can't tell Rusty about us over the phone. And I don't know how to tell him we're married. And what about Kaylie, and Max? I feel terrible for leading them to believe that Gage and I aren't together."

"Kaylie and Max are the easy part." Danica handed Sally the phone. "You can conference them both in on the same call and tell them so you don't stress all night about it. But maybe leave out the part about being married. I think you're right to want Rusty to be the first—*second*—to hear that. And when you see him, you'll know what to say. You don't need me for that part. You have each other, and you'll figure it out together."

Sally looked down at the phone and lifted a questioning gaze to Gage.

"I'm behind whatever you want to do, babe. If you want to tell the girls or if you want to wait. It's up to you."

He was willing to continue keeping their secret to protect her son *and* her heart, despite how badly she knew he wanted to tell the world about their relationship. She felt her love for him grow, like a living, breathing being inside her, and as she called the girls and explained the truth, it was Gage's unrelenting support that settled her worries, carrying them another step forward.

LATER THAT EVENING, Gage grilled steak while Sally prepared a salad, and they ate by the roaring fire in his house. They'd decided to give staying there a try. They washed the dishes and shared half a bottle of wine. It was nice not to be stuck in a hotel or in separate houses. After dinner Gage emptied several of his dresser drawers and cleared space in his closet for the bag of clothes Sally had brought over. Seeing her clothes beside his filled a void inside him he hadn't realized existed.

She set the last of her shirts in a drawer and closed it carefully. Her gaze swept over the heavy wooden dresser, where her hairbrush and mirror lay beside a bottle of her perfume. "I've been in your house so many times, but it's never felt like this."

He pulled her into his arms. "Is that bad or good?"

"Good. But different. Last night when I went inside my

house, I felt like I'd walked into someone else's life. It was weird after being with you every second of the day. I know things about you now that I didn't used to, like that you wash out the sink after you brush your teeth and you always hang your towel after using it. You made the bed while I dressed *every* morning, and when you used a pen, you put it back where you got it, even if it was across the room. As I walked around my house last night, it felt like a part of me was missing. I missed all the little things about you. But at the same time, I tried to imagine not living in the house where all my memories of Rusty growing up were practically ingrained in the hardwood, and it hurt. It was confusing and it brought up so many worries. And now I'm here, and it feels *good*, and *right*, to be together again. And that makes me feel guilty." Her shoulders slumped. "I told you I'm a head case."

"No, babe. You're not a head case. That would be confusing for anyone. I was an idiot to try to overlook all those things in the first place. I don't want anything about our relationship to make you feel bad. Would it help to try staying at both houses and see which one you feel better in when we're together? I want this to work, Sal, whatever it takes."

"Maybe. But I'm not sure I can sleep with you there. For now I'd rather settle in here where it feels like we both belong."

"I think that's a great idea. And since you've had such a stressful day, getting caught having sex and all." He waggled his brows, and she laughed. "How about letting me give you a back rub?"

He opened the drawer beside the bed and withdrew the flavored massage oil they'd received in the honeymoon basket.

"I still can't believe you put that lube in my purse. Talk about embarrassing."

"I'm sorry about that. I thought you'd see it last night and get a kick out of it." He put the bottle in his pocket and stepped closer. "Now, how about you take off that pretty little sweater and let me redeem myself for all the awful embarrassment I've caused you. I'll make you a comfy bed by the fire and make you feel good all over."

She raised her arms as he lifted her sweater over her head. "You're not even being subtle about this seduction—you realize that, right?"

He kissed the swell of her breast. "This isn't subtle?" He unhooked her bra and gently pushed it off her shoulders.

"No," she said breathily.

"Shame on me." He lowered his mouth to her breast, teasing her nipple. "I should learn some tact."

Her sexy murmurs brought his mouth to hers, and he kissed her deeply.

"Let me love you like you deserve to be loved." He led her into the living room and laid blankets and pillows out by the fire. "Let's take off your pretty skirt so it doesn't get oily."

She wiggled out of her skirt with a playful look in her eyes. "Shouldn't you take off your clothes? To keep them from getting oily, of course."

"Ah," he said as he unzipped his jeans. "Tact. I like it."

She stood before him naked, save for a pair of panties, twirling her hair and watching him strip down to his briefs. Her eyes darkened and her lips parted.

"Maybe this wasn't a good idea." He stepped closer, loving the hungry look in her eyes. He unwound her hair from her finger and put her hand on his chest. "Do I really get to put my hands all over you?"

"Mm-hm." She licked her lips, moving her fingers in slow

circles on his chest. "How do you want me? On my stomach or my back?"

He pictured her lying on her stomach naked, and his cock twitched, eager to make his dirty thoughts a reality. "Jesus, baby. That's a loaded question."

She bit her lower lip and sank down to the blanket, lying on her stomach. He tried to tell himself it wasn't an invitation, but hell, his body had already sent the RSVP.

He retrieved the massage oil from his jeans and gave himself a pep talk, like he was readying himself for a big game as he straddled her hips and poured the edible massage oil into his hand. *You're here to give her a massage, not to tear those panties off and devour her. Do not rush her! You can do this. Willpower, man. You've got this.*

He fucking hated that voice in his head.

Willpower? Who was he kidding? A man would need balls of steel to be able to resist Sally's sweet, supple body. He began with her shoulders, feeling the knots ease beneath his fingers. Her skin was warm from the fire and grew warmer with every touch.

"Mm. That feels *so* good."

Fuck yeah, it feels good. You feel good.

He massaged each arm from shoulder to wrist and back up again, earning more appreciative sounds. Her seductive murmurs made it hard for him to think. He moved lower, perched on his knees as he straddled her thighs, careful not to put his weight on them, and worked his way down her back, massaging away from her spine. The scent of strawberries and lust hung in the air as his hands slid up her sides. His fingers grazed her breasts, lingering there as he kissed each vertebra.

"Mm," slipped from her lips.

He kissed each vertebra, his hands playing over every inch of her skin in slow, deep massages. Seeing her hair fanned out around her and her beautiful body laid out before him filled him with as much desire as it did love. He placed openmouthed kisses along the dip of her waist, the back of each hip, massaging as he went. He moved lower on his knees and shifted so he was between her legs. Her panties rose high on the curve of her ass, revealing the tender skin where each cheek met her thigh. He couldn't keep from running his tongue along the creases. Her hips rose off the blanket, and her long, delicate fingers curled into fists. *Damn*, she had no idea how torturous this was.

He dribbled oil onto her hamstrings, rubbing it in with slow strokes, one hand on each leg. His mind ran through so many dirty thoughts, they spilled from his lips, hot as lava. "Baby, I want to tear those panties off and touch you, taste you. I want to rub my body all over yours. I want to feel your oiled-up ass against me while I take you from behind."

She bit her lower lip, hunger radiating from her eyes as she gazed over her shoulder.

He moved both hands to one leg, massaging deep and sensually from the back of her knee to the curve of her ass, and once again couldn't resist tasting her sweet tempting flesh. She rocked her hips, moaning with each slick of his tongue. *Aw fuck.* This was too much. He splayed his hands over her hamstrings, squeezing too hard, and brushed his thumbs along her inner thighs, struggling to keep himself from taking what he wanted. Her hips gyrated, bringing his thumbs against her damp panties. A guttural sound crawled up his throat as he lowered his mouth and nipped at her bottom, making her squirm.

He inhaled the alluring scent of her arousal and licked her through her panties, his thumbs pressing along the sensitive nerves at the top of each inner thigh. Her bottom lifted higher, and her legs spread wider. He wasn't about to pass up this invitation. He slid a finger beneath her panties and tugged them aside, baring her ripe sex. There was no finesse, no holding back, as he greedily ate at her. She moaned and writhed, lowering her chest to the blanket. *Fuuuck*.

Where the hell were the scissors when he needed them? Forget willpower. He tugged her panties down to her knees, palming the soft globes of her ass with his slick, oily hands, and covered her sex with his mouth again, devouring her. She mewled and panted as he dipped his fingers inside her. He needed to taste her again. All of her. He licked around her entrance. The sight of his fingers inside her, her sweet, perfect body waiting to be taken, nearly did him in. He brought his mouth to one silky globe, licking and grazing his teeth over her sensitive flesh as his fingers stroked over the spot that made her moan. She thrust her hips back, giving him the green light, and he sped through without looking back, loving her with his mouth, fucking her with his fingers, making her body shake and shudder as she came apart.

One arm circled her waist, and he followed the lines of her body to her sex, teasing her overly sensitive nerves. She inhaled unevenly and rose on shaky hands and knees, thrusting her hips back. He pushed his briefs down and rubbed his hard length along her wetness, aching to be inside her so badly every muscle flexed. He wanted to feel all of her. His chest came down over her back, and he bit down on her shoulder, tasting the sweetness of the oil and the unique taste of *Sally*.

"Oh *God*, I love that," she panted out.

Her ass was cradled by his hips, rocking against his hard length. Desire mounted inside him, and he cupped her breasts, taking the tight peaks between his fingers and thumbs, and sealed his mouth over her neck. Her back arched, and a long, surrendering moan pierced his resolve.

"I don't want to sound like a prick," he ground out, "but I want to fuck you so badly right now—"

She looked over her shoulder, her hair covering half of her beautiful face, sultry eyes boring into him. "Then do it."

He sheathed his cock in record time. His heart pounded against his ribs as he grabbed her hips and drove into her so hard and deep, she cried out—and he saw stars.

Gage froze, fearing he hurt her.

"*More*," she demanded.

Hell yes.

He loved her harder, and she moved with him, meeting each thrust with a rock of her hips, taking and giving with equal fervor. Their bodies were slick with oil, covered with a sheen of perspiration. His pulse throbbed in his ears. Heat streaked down his spine. His arm swept around her waist, bringing them both up on their knees. His hands moved over her breasts, between her legs. He turned her face, feasted on her mouth.

"I need more of you, baby."

She turned over, his heart full to near bursting as she reached for him. Her softness conformed to the hard press of his body, and he held her gaze as he entered her. He traced her lips with his tongue and took her in a punishingly intense kiss, pulsing his hips with agonizing precision. Every thrust brought him closer to release, but he felt her sex tightening, sensed an orgasm on the rise, and slowed his pace even more, drawing out her pleasure. Her fingernails dug into his arms.

He wanted to make her so needy she could barely stand it, but when he gazed into her pleading eyes, emotions bubbled up inside him and teasing went out the window. He slanted his mouth over hers and loved her into the night with wild, heated passion.

CHAPTER SIXTEEN

SALLY STOOD AT the entrance to the gym watching Gage teach a group of little boys how to dribble a basketball. He was so big compared to the boys, and he treated them with gentle kindness and patience. Seeing him guiding them, cheering them on, and hearing his laughter mixed with their sweet giggles did funny things to Sally's stomach. She remembered the hurt in his voice when he'd told her about the child he'd had no say in losing, and she wished she could give that *Stacy* a piece of her mind. Gage would make a wonderful father, and he wanted children so badly. She'd always known that, but it had been a one-day type of thought, not something she'd given weight and credence to like she was now. But she wasn't getting any younger. Was she being selfish wanting to be with Gage, when a younger woman could give him lots of babies?

"He's something, isn't he?"

She startled at Danica's voice and smiled at her curly-haired, very pregnant friend. "He's really good with kids."

"Apparently he's good with a certain woman, too. Everyone says I'm glowing." Danica patted her stomach. "But you look like you've discovered the fountain of youth."

Sally couldn't suppress her smile. "I had forgotten how invigorating good sex could be." It was Thursday afternoon, and she'd been staying at Gage's house all week. They had yet to make it through an entire day and night without making love—in the shower, the bedroom, the living room, the kitchen. Tonight they planned to stay at her house, and she was a nervous wreck about it.

"And I want to thank you for not doing it in the supply closet again," Danica teased. "Oh! The baby's kicking." She grabbed Sally's hand and pressed it to her stomach.

Sally felt an elbow, or knee, or some other tiny baby part pushing against her hand. "I forgot how wonderful that feeling is."

"Not so wonderful at three in the morning when the baby's sitting on my bladder." Danica nodded toward the gym, where Gage was high-fiving with the boys as they said goodbye. "Speaking of babies, did you decide how to tell yours that you and Gage are together?"

"You mean that we're *married*?" She watched Gage put the balls away. He'd been her best friend, her rock, for so many years, and now that they'd moved past that, she couldn't imagine going back to *only* being friends for anything in the world. It was still a struggle in her mind, because she was knowingly putting her own hope for forever above Rusty's welfare.

"I'm trying not to overthink it anymore. It's not like I need Rusty's permission. I just want him to trust me, and I want to know I'm not going to screw him up, or mess up things between him and Gage." That was the hard part, because as much as she believed with her whole heart that she and Gage would be together forever, where her son was concerned, she couldn't afford a mistake.

Gage's powerful legs ate up the space between them.

Danica smiled at Gage as he came to Sally's side and slid an arm around her waist. "I think you found the fountain of youth, too."

"Yeah. It's called *Sally Tuft-Ryder.*"

She'd never tire of hearing him say that.

"Someone's eager to get this family started," Danica teased.

"Yes, I am, which reminds me. It's after hours," Gage pointed out. He leaned down for a kiss, and like a starving woman offered food, Sally kissed him back.

How could she be starved for him after only a few hours? This wasn't young love, or infatuation, both of which tended to include insatiable desires.

Because our love is bone-deep, the truest love of all.

So why am I worried about it falling apart?

A horrible thought knocked her for a loop. Could she be worried about losing *more* of her son to Gage? They were already so close.

No, she wasn't that selfish.

Was she?

Great. Now I'm grasping at straws to rationalize the over-worrying mother in me. It was time she shut those thoughts down once and for all.

"Mommy!" Chessie ran down the hall all bundled up in her pink coat and hat, her mop of dark curls billowing out around her adorable chubby cheeks.

Blake followed his daughter, carrying several large shopping bags. His dark eyes locked on his wife, and a guilty smile lifted his lips as he raised the bags.

"I see you and Daddy did some shopping." Danica's smile told Sally she didn't mind one bit.

Chessie slowed as she neared, hands outstretched. She flattened them against Danica's belly, her little eyes bright with excitement. “Hello, baby. I have lots of surprises for you.” She pressed a kiss to Danica’s belly and immediately launched into Gage’s arms. “Guess what, Aunt Sally and Uncle Gage!”

Gage scooped her up and kissed her cheek. “How’s my favorite girl?”

Blake kissed Danica and lifted his chin in greeting to Gage and Sally. Sally realized she had no idea if Danica had mentioned their marriage to him, but given the way he was looking at Gage, like he knew *all* his secrets, she had a feeling she had.

“I’m good! Me and Daddy bought lots of presents for the baby, including a tiny basketball and dolls, because Mommy said boys and girls can play with dolls and we don’t know if I’m going to have a baby brother or a sister.” Chessie pressed her hands to Gage’s face and kissed him smack on the lips, tugging on Sally’s heartstrings.

“That’s going to be one lucky baby.” Gage had a longing look in his eyes that could not be mistaken. This was what Gage wanted. His own family.

Chessie wiggled out of his arms and grabbed Danica’s hand. “We got you presents, too, Mommy.”

“Okay, sweet girl,” Blake said. “It’s time to take Mommy out to dinner before you let our secret out of the bag.”

“Secret?” Danica asked.

A knowing look passed between Blake and Gage. Blake flashed a cocky grin and said, “Seems secrets are going around these days. We’ll see you guys later.” He winked at Sally, confirming her thoughts.

After they headed for the exit, Gage wrapped Sally in his arms and kissed her again. “I have an office just waiting to be christened.”

“No. No way. Not on your life after what happened Monday," she said, secretly loving his desire to push her boundaries.

"I knew you'd say that, which is why I made other plans for us. Come on." He led her toward the lobby.

"Does it involve having sex in a public place?"

A dark look settled over his features. "Do you want it to?"

"*Want* and *willing* are two different things. We have a knack for getting caught, remember?"

"Ah, then there's still hope…"

And just like that, her mind tiptoed down a naughty path, contemplating his office, his truck, and just about every other place they passed as he drove through town.

GAGE PULLED OFF the mountain road and drove up the long driveway toward home. *Our home.* He couldn't help but think about it that way. They were going to Sally's house later that evening for the night, but in his heart he knew they belonged at his house. He stepped from the truck and came around to help her out. She was busy texting when he opened the door.

"Everything okay?" Gage asked.

"Mm-hm. Kaylie and Max want me to come over early a week from Saturday morning to set up for the baby shower."

He nuzzled against her neck, inhaling the familiar scent of her lavender shampoo. His whole bathroom smelled like her. Her perfume lingered in every room, and he loved it. "Not too early, I hope."

"Not *that* early." She tucked her phone into her pocket and turned toward him. She ran her fingers through his hair and he leaned into her loving touch.

"When you touch me like that my whole body exhales. It's like I've been running on overdrive all day, and your touch centers me and brings me home."

"What happens when I touch you like this?" She pressed her lips just below his jawline.

He took her hand and held it against his zipper so she could feel his rising erection. Her eyes flamed, and he pulled her to the edge of the seat and covered her lips with his. Heat coursed through him, and he intensified his efforts, fighting the urge to take her right there on the seat of the truck despite the freezing December temperatures.

He reluctantly broke their connection. "I have a surprise for you, babe."

"I like the surprise you were just giving me. I want to be eighty years old and still kissing you like that."

"We'll never stop." He brushed her hair away from her face with both hands and pressed his lips to hers again. "You and Rusty are my world, and that is never going to change." He helped her from the truck.

"I thought you made plans for us."

He draped an arm around her on the way up to the house. "I did."

He unlocked the kitchen door and followed her in. It took her a moment to notice the lights he'd secured to the sides of the kitchen table. He shrugged off his coat and hung it by the door.

"What are those lights for?"

"You," he answered simply. He helped her off with her coat and hung it beside his. Then he reached into the closet and lifted out an enormous bag of mosaic tiles and shook it.

"What *is* that?"

He took her hand and led her to the table. "This is your surprise."

He set the bag on the table, and she carefully unwound the ribbon he'd tied around the opening and peered inside. His heart was racing with anticipation. He had no idea if he'd bought the right supplies, although the salesperson he'd consulted had insisted that he'd purchased everything she'd need.

Her confused—and hopeful?—gaze caught his. She put one hand into the bag and filled it with tiles. "Gage," she said anxiously. "*Tesserae*. It's been so long."

"Tesserae?" He opened the closet and began putting the rest of the supplies he'd purchased on the table.

"That's what these pieces are called."

She watched him loading the table with every type of mosaic adhesive he'd been able to find, and several choices of materials for her to use as a base. She was silent for so long, he worried he'd misread the tears in her eyes.

When she finally reached up and caressed his cheek, a smile forming on her beautiful face, he exhaled.

"I can't believe you went to all this trouble."

"This wasn't trouble, bird. I want to help you do all the things that make you happy. I could see how badly you missed this even in the few minutes we spoke about it in Virginia. If your mom can't be here to share it with you, I can. I don't want to replace her, of course, but—"

She threw her arms around his neck and kissed him—*hard*. "Thank you. I haven't done this since I found out I was pregnant with Rusty."

He watched with delight as she sifted through the tiles and supplies. She stepped back from the table with an awed expression and took his hand, placing it over her rapidly beating heart.

Excitement shone in her eyes. "That used to happen every time I went into a studio with my mom. I can't believe all these years later I still feel the same thrill, only this time it's beating even harder, because of you."

SALLY HAD FORGOTTEN how wonderful it felt to create something unique and how inspiring true happiness could be. And more than that, she had forgotten what it was like to have someone supporting her dreams. Especially the dreams she hadn't even realized she still held on to. She and Gage worked side by side for hours, barely speaking as they pieced together tiny chunks of glass, stone, and ceramic, filling in the design she'd quickly sketched on a base. Their faces were so close, she heard his every breath. Their hands moved in tandem, fitting pieces together like puzzles with no interlocking confines, but somehow knowing exactly where each piece should lay and creating a gorgeous flow of colors. Why wouldn't she and Gage work effortlessly in sync? They'd known each other for years. They were a couple even before they'd officially become one. She knew that now with her whole heart, the way Gage always had.

Memories of creating mosaics with her mother flooded her. She'd looked forward to those stolen hours together. In a childhood that had seemed to fly by in a whirlwind of jetting from one luxurious location to another—with a father who was busy making business deals and her mother at his beck and call, attending fancy luncheons and dinners—those few stolen hours had been the glue that had held her relationship with her mother together. Maybe it had been the lack of time together that had allowed her to adjust to being away from her parents when they'd created the rift between them over her pregnancy. Her life had been a blur of responsibilities after Rusty was born, and even after she and her parents had made amends, they'd continued traveling. She'd never really had a home base until she'd married Dave. They'd built a home together, yet separate. They'd spent so many hours apart while he was building his business and she was going to school, and then they were chauffeuring Rusty around to school events, friends' houses, and sports practices. They'd been married decades, and somehow they'd never spent time together the way she and Gage had.

She realized she'd *never* had a relationship like this one before.

She swallowed hard and looked into the living room, where pictures of Gage's family were intermixed with photos of Sally and Rusty on the mantel. The pictures of her and Rusty had accumulated over the years, and she'd seen them so many times, she hadn't thought twice about them, until now.

She stole a glance at Gage, who was inspecting a chunk of bluish glass, and a wonderful sense of peace came over her. He'd been right there with her all along, the rock she'd needed, the friend who listened, and now, her sensual lover and the man who was helping her to return to the person she'd once been, only better.

He must have felt her staring, because he looked up and blew her a kiss. Then he placed the glass beside the stone she'd just set. They'd created this gorgeous piece of art together, and yes, it was just a mosaic, but it had become clear to her that they were meant to build a life together, too. As they set the last pieces in place, all of her worries about Rusty and what the future might hold disappeared.

She inhaled deeply, taking a step back from the table to admire their work. Gage's fingertips touched hers, and the adoration in his eyes embraced her. The answers she'd been seeking had been right there all along.

She placed her hand on his chest, remembering how he'd placed it there almost two weeks ago, and she realized she hadn't reached for her hair this time—but for him. He was her calming influence as much as he was the heat that stoked her fire.

"What do you think, bird? Do we make a great team?"

Team? They were so much more than a team. They were friends and lovers, confidants and sounding boards. They were *everything*, and more than anything, she wanted their relationship to remain as strong as they were today.

"The best team ever."

He hugged her, taking her in a warm and wonderful kiss. "I love you so much, Salbird. There are no words big enough to tell you just how it feels to build a life with you. Thank you for letting me be part of your world."

She couldn't form a response, could only kiss him again and again, anchoring herself to him.

He brushed his lips over hers and spoke just above a whisper. "Ready to go to your house for the night?"

My house? That house wasn't hers anymore.

That life wasn't hers anymore.

Everything had changed.

A lump rose in her throat, but this time, as she thought of the house where she'd lived for the majority of her life, it wasn't unhappiness causing her throat to thicken. She was on the cusp of ending a chapter of her life that she hadn't seen coming. And once she let out the words that were perched and ready to fly, they would open a door for the bountiful joy filling her up and nearly bubbling over.

"I think I've found my nest here with you," she said softly. "And if you'll have me, I don't ever want to leave it."

Chapter Seventeen

"IT'S OFFICIAL," SALLY announced to Kaylie and Max the following Saturday morning as they decorated Kaylie's chalet for Danica's baby shower. "We're telling Rusty about our relationship, and after he goes back to Harborside, I'm formally moving in with Gage."

Kaylie squealed and hugged her. "That is awesome!"

"Finally!" Max threw her arms around them both. "I swear you guys had the *longest* pre-dating courtship *ever*. Gage must be over the moon."

"Both of us are," Sally gushed. "I haven't stopped smiling since we made the final decision." Gage must have asked her fifty times since then if she was sure, and every time she answered, she was even more certain she'd made the right decision. When he realized she wasn't going to change her mind, he deemed the largest of the other three bedrooms Rusty's, which warmed her all over. He'd spent last weekend making their mosaic into an end table, which was now proudly displayed in their living room. He was also rearranging one of the guest bedrooms to make space for what he called Sally's *creative station*. He'd offered to set up a studio for her in the barn, but she didn't want to be that far away from him when the urge hit to work on a project.

"When are you telling Rusty?" Max asked. She handed Sally

one end of a streamer and walked to the other side of the table, twisting it as she went.

"When he comes home for the holidays. I hate to spring it on him when he's only home for a week, but I think it's best if he hears it in person."

Max secured the end of the streamer to the table, and Kaylie taped the middle, creating a scalloped pattern.

"He loves Gage," Kaylie said as she cut another length of streamer for the other side of the table. "But remember when he was sixteen? That poor boy carried so much anger and snuck off all the time. I'm not looking forward to those teenage years with Lexi and Trev."

"They're only in elementary school, like Adriana," Max pointed out. Her daughter was in second grade. "We have plenty of time to train them. And by *train* them, I mean scare the living bejeezus out of them about drinking and sex and everything else they can get into."

Sally laughed at their naïveté. "You think you can control a teenager with fear, but trust me. They think they're indestructible. And what's worse is that testing parents seems to be a rite of passage."

"Well, Adriana is like a saint, and a Daddy's girl. Dylan, on the other hand, is rascally as a monkey. That boy gets into everything. Poor Treat. He was such a good kid; he won't know what to do with him."

"Oh, please!" Kaylie waved a hand as they hung up the streamer. "Treat practically raised his five younger siblings. Think about *them* for a minute. Back then, Hugh was as into girls as he was cars, and you know python-in-his-pants Dane didn't keep that viper all to himself. I'm sure Treat will be one step ahead of your kids at all times." Both Hugh and Dane were now happily married and fathers to boot. Hugh was a professional race-car driver, and Dane was a shark researcher. They'd both been major players before falling in love with Brianna and Lacy.

The girls shared a giggle.

"Don't say that about Dane in front of Treat," Max warned. "It's no secret that Dane's the most well-endowed man to come out of Weston, Colorado, but my studly husband does *not* want to hear about it."

"Like I'd ever?" Kaylie said. "Hell, I'd never say that around my own drop-dead-gorgeous husband. Men and their penises. I swear you could tell a man you love him a hundred times a day, and he'd love you. But tell him he has a golden cock?" She spread her arms out to her sides and dropped down to one knee. "He'll worship you forever."

Sally wound a length of streamer around Max's waist, leaving a piece hanging down like a penis. She did the same to Kaylie, then herself.

Max put her hands on her hips and gyrated. "Come on, baby. Hang from the chandelier. I'm worth it."

Kaylie puffed out her chest and stroked the streamer. "Mine comes with *diamonds* and it tastes like ice cream. I swear it!"

They all doubled over in laughter. Max and Sally made a litany of bad penis jokes. They clung to each other, laughing so hard tears streamed down their cheeks.

A knock sounded at the door, and Kaylie said, "See? The girls are banging down my door already!" causing more fits of laughter.

Sally tried to catch her breath as Kaylie answered the door, but Max started swinging her streamer-penis, and Sally lost it again. She turned her back to try to regain control. A few seconds later a heavy hand landed on her shoulder, and she spun around, coming face-to-chest with Gage, who wore a dreadful, serious expression, turning her laughter into concern.

"What's wrong?" she asked.

"It's Rusty," Gage said solemnly, tightening his grip on her shoulder.

Fear shot through her.

"He's been arrested, and we need to go to Harborside."

"Arrested?" She tried to wrap her mind around the idea, but Rusty wasn't a troublemaking teenager anymore. He was responsible and sensible. Her heart hammered against her ribs as questions spilled out. "Why? What did he do? Is he okay?"

"He's fine. It sounds like it was a misunderstanding, but we have to leave now and get to Harborside. He's going in front of a judge at four o'clock and we have to be there to bail him out *if* they set bail."

Tears sprang to her eyes. "Bail?" She clutched his arm to stabilize her buckling knees. "What did he do? Does he need a lawyer? We need a lawyer, right? I don't know a lawyer in Massachusetts."

"I'm calling Treat." Max pulled out her phone. "I'm sure you can use his plane."

Arrested. Oh my God, Rusty.

Gage kissed her temple and said, "It's going to be okay. We'll get there and figure it out."

"Treat's alerting the pilot," Max informed them. "It's a three-and-a-half-hour flight to Boston, plus the drive time. He'll have a driver waiting to take you to Harborside. He said he knows an attorney, but you'll never make it by four o'clock."

Max held out the phone to them.

"I've got it, babe." Gage took it from Max and spoke to

Treat. "Thanks, Treat. I spoke to the clerk on my way over. She said if we're not there when they set bail he could be sent to prison until we arrive to post it. Think your attorney could show up and arrange for them to hold him locally? I don't want to deal with a bail bondsman or any of that if we can avoid it."

"Prison?" A sob broke from her chest. Max and Kaylie put their arms around her. "Rusty can't go to prison. *Gage...?*"

Gage pulled her from the girls' arms and into his own as he wrapped up his call with Treat. "Thank you. As much as I appreciate the offer of a driver, I think we need our own rental car. I don't want to have to rely on anyone else while we're there. Thanks, Treat. I owe you the world." He ended the call and handed the phone back to Max. "Thank you."

"Where's your purse and coat?" he asked Sally.

Kaylie handed Sally's purse to Gage and held up Sally's coat, helping her into it. "Go. Explain to her in the car, and call if you need us."

Gage was already moving toward the door. Once they were in the car, he headed for the highway. "Apparently Rusty borrowed his buddy's car to pick up something across town. One of the taillights was broken, and he got pulled over. They spotted a bag of pills on the floor in the backseat and nailed him for possession."

"Pills? That makes no sense. What kind of pills?"

Gage exhaled and squeezed her hand. "A few. OxyContin, Xanax, and ADD meds."

"OxyContin?" Her stomach sank. "I'm going to throttle him. He swore he wasn't into any of that stuff. Remember? I asked him about it last summer when we read that article about how kids were getting into heroin as a drug of choice. How could I have missed this? I know how. He's never home. This is all my fault."

"Baby, baby, baby," Gage said quickly. "He swears it wasn't his."

She pressed her lips together, fuming, wanting to believe her son and afraid to at the same time.

"There's more," Gage said. "I had to promise him I'd come alone."

"What?" *Move over drugs, because this new information is front and center.* "You promised my son you'd keep this from me?"

"Damn it, Sally. Does it look like I'm keeping it from you?" He ground his teeth together. "He was freaking out about you having enough to worry about with work and not wanting to bother you with something like this."

"Like *this*? He was *arrested*! If ever there was a time to tell his mother something, it's *now*. Why didn't *you* tell him that?"

"Do you really underestimate me that much?" He put two hands on the wheel, his biceps flexing with his tight grip. "Jesus, Sally. Give me some fucking credit. I tried to convince him, but he was adamant about not making you worry."

Tears welled in her eyes again. "I'm sorry. I'm just overwhelmed. I'm so confused. What if it *was* his? What if he's screwing up his life out there in Massachusetts and I'm letting him? I should have made him come home for the whole break. I never should have agreed to let him work this winter. I should have—" Angry sobs stole her voice.

Gage reached across the seat and took her hand. "He's twenty, Sal. He's a young man, and he makes good decisions. I think we should wait until we talk to him in person to get too upset."

"*Wait* to get upset?" She scoffed. "Like that's even an option? And why are you so calm? Even if the drugs aren't his, what kind of friends is he hanging out with? And how long will it take for peer pressure to drag him over to the dark side? His entire life will forever be shadowed by this arrest. Where did I go wrong? Do you think it's because his father is dead?"

Gage took the next exit and pulled over to the side of the road, giving Sally his full attention. He leaned across the console and embraced her. She was shaking all over, and even being in his arms didn't settle the fear running rampant inside her.

He drew back and wiped her tears. "Sally, he's *your* son. You taught him to make all the right choices. Even though I want to believe him—"

"I do, too! He's my son, but I'm not stupid enough to be one of those mothers who thinks 'not my kid.'"

"I know, Sal. If it's his, it doesn't mean he's throwing his life away. If it's his, then this arrest will probably shake him up enough to get on the right track."

"If the drugs are his, he's coming back to Colorado, living under *my* roof, with *my* rules, and straightening out his life."

They drove the rest of the way to the airport in silence. The long plane flight was just as tense. Sally could hardly believe they were flying to Massachusetts to bail her son out of jail. The stress made her feel sick to her stomach, and Gage hardly said two words.

It wasn't until they were driving into Harborside that Sally realized her mistake.

THEY MADE IT into town just in time to post bail before the cashier closed for the day. On the way back to the car, Sally's eyes were wide and worried, like a deer caught in the headlights.

"I never thought I'd be bailing out my son," she said solemnly. She pushed Gage's coat open and placed her hands on his chest. "I really want to reach for my hair right now."

"Always reach for me, bird." He covered her hands with his own, mentally working through how he'd handle things with Rusty when Rusty realized Gage had brought Sally against his wishes. The attorney told them that Rusty insisted the drugs belonged to his friend, although they'd been unable to reach the other kid. Until they heard the other kid's side of the story, Rusty was considered guilty. Gage fucking hated that, and he hoped to hell Rusty wasn't using his friend as a scapegoat, because that would only make things worse.

"I'm sorry for what I said about 'my house and my rules,'" Sally said apologetically. "I didn't mean to exclude you, or make you feel like you weren't going to be part of our lives. I just…It just came out."

Having let go of the sting of her words hours ago, he said, "Don't think twice about it. You're under a lot of pressure. Let's just get through this and make sure Rusty's okay."

She nodded, her eyes as sad as they were scared. "Thank you for being there for him, and for telling me even though he didn't want you to. I still can't believe he wanted to keep this from me, but I'll deal with him on that."

"I told you, I'll always be here for both of you."

They drove straight to the police station. Rusty came out of a room in the back, his dark blond hair hanging limply in front of his eyes. His face was weary and drawn. His shoulders were rounded forward. He was probably dead on his feet after a stressful, sleepless night. He lifted his chin with a surly expression and skulked out of the station with his mother on his heels.

Rusty spun around, his eyes hooking into Gage like fangs.

"What the hell, man? I *trusted* you. I asked you not to tell her."

"Don't yell at him for doing the right thing," Sally snapped. "*You* should have told me, Rusty, not Gage. What were you thinking trying to keep this from me?"

Rusty's eyes narrowed to angry slits, and his voice escalated. "What was *I* thinking? How can you even ask me that? I was thinking that I could trust *him* not to drag you into any of this mess. They weren't my pills, Mom. I'm not a druggie or a dealer. This was just a messed-up misunderstanding that you don't need to get all upset about."

Gage stepped between Rusty and Sally, looking Rusty directly in the eyes. "Rusty, take a breath. I get that you're pissed at me right now, but I'm not about to let you holler at your mother."

"Oh, *now* you're worried about my mother?" Rusty scoffed. "What the hell, Gage? Look how upset she is. That's on *you*, man. She doesn't need to worry about this shit on top of her job and everything else. You're supposed to be her *friend.* I was trying to protect her. Why aren't *you*?"

Gage gritted his teeth to keep from ripping into Rusty about the reason they were there in the first place. "I *am* protecting her, Rusty. I know you can't see that right now, but I care about you, and I care about your mother. I would never keep something this important from her. It wouldn't be good for either of you."

"What*ever.*" Rusty turned away.

"Rusty Michael Tuft!" Sally yelled. "Don't you dare blame Gage for your mistakes. Do you have any idea what it's like for me to hear secondhand that you were *arrested*? And do you realize the horrible position you put Gage in?"

"The position *I* put *him* in?" Rusty snapped. "Excuse me for thinking I could trust him." He scrubbed a hand down his face and paced.

"You *can* trust him," Sally insisted. "But what you asked of him was unfair. Rusty, you have to know that."

"How about the position *he* put *you* in?" Rusty challenged.

"Okay. Enough," Gage demanded. "I'm sure you're exhausted, Rusty, but that's no excuse to take it out on your mother. Why don't we go grab something to eat and talk about this rationally?"

Rusty stared him down, his jaw clenched tight. He shifted his gaze to his mother and said, "I'm sorry I got into this mess and that you got dragged into it." Grinding his teeth together, he turned to Gage. "Thanks for coming to bail me out, but I need to clear my head."

Sally stepped closer to her son, dwarfed by his size. She reached for him, stopping short, her expression torn. Gage could see her struggling between being the mother she wanted to be and letting her son be the young man he needed to be.

"You can tell me if they were your drugs," Sally said softly. "Don't make this any worse."

Rusty rolled his eyes. "Jesus, Mom. They're not. I promise, okay?"

She nodded, her eyes damp as she put her arms around Rusty and hugged him. Rusty stood rigid, his long arms hanging by his sides. Sally didn't move until Rusty reluctantly gave her a quick embrace and stepped back.

"Come on, we'll take you home." Gage unlocked the car.

"I'm going to walk," Rusty mumbled, heading for the sidewalk. "It's not far."

"Rusty," Sally called after him.

"It's okay, babe." Gage put a hand on her back. "Give him

time to decompress. He's been through a hell of a time."

"He shouldn't have treated you that way," she said.

"I broke his trust. He has reason to be pissed. We'll give him some breathing room, and then we can talk to him."

"He thought he was *protecting* me," Sally said as she settled into the car.

"It's ironic, don't you think? You're hiding our relationship from him for the same reason."

Chapter Eighteen

SALLY TRIED TO call Rusty twice after he left them to walk home, and when she didn't get a response, she texted him with the name of the hotel where they were staying, a few blocks from his apartment. She'd stayed up half the night trying to figure out how to handle the situation, and consequently, she'd ended up feeling sick for hours. As the sun peeked through the curtains, she cuddled up to Gage. He'd been her saving grace last night, calming her when she'd wanted to drive over to Rusty's and demand he talk this out. Gage was right. Rusty had probably gone straight to bed. When he was little he'd sleep so soundly she'd put her fingers under his nose to make sure he was breathing.

"How's the mama?" Gage asked in a groggy voice.

She rested her head on his chest, thinking about their talk, and Rusty, and their secret marriage. "Wishing I hadn't gotten so upset at him so fast."

"He wasn't exactly in a peaceful mood, babe. It was an emotionally charged day." He kissed her head. His hand snaked around her back, holding her closer. "How's your stomach? Feeling any better?"

"A little. I've been thinking about what you said."

"About?"

"About Rusty being practically a man. I keep seeing myself

as his protector, and I know he needs me to be on some level, but things have changed. I didn't understand why he was trying to protect me yesterday, but now I get it. After Dave died he began seeing me as his overwhelmed mother, and maybe I was back then. But I'm not now, and he needs to know that. He needs to understand that I'm strong and capable and that I can handle anything. Even him being arrested."

She lifted her face and looked at Gage. He'd been so patient with her, so willing to step back and do right by Rusty. Now she realized she was the one who needed to step back. "I need to stop thinking of him as a fragile fifteen-year-old who can't handle growing up. We need to tell him about us. All of it. Our marriage, moving in together. The whole shebang, for better or for worse. He deserves to know."

Relief washed over Gage's features. "We'll drive over and talk to him this morning. But he's probably still pretty pissed at me. You may need to give me and him some time to clear the air first."

"Of course." She rested her cheek on his chest again, absently drawing circles on his stomach. "I have to tell you something that isn't easy to admit."

"Bird, you can tell me anything."

"It hurt knowing Rusty called you instead of me. I was a little jealous, and that was a weird feeling to have as his mother. I hate thinking that when he finds out we waited almost three weeks to tell him about us, he could be even more hurt. I think it was a mistake to wait."

Gage pulled her up beside him on the pillow and turned, giving her his full attention. "It wasn't a mistake, babe. You were being careful, and that's never a mistake."

"I'm not so sure." She rolled over, untangling Gage's shirt

from around her waist. They'd left town so fast they hadn't stopped to pack a bag. She'd slept in the shirt Gage had worn yesterday. She grabbed her phone from the bedside table and checked her messages.

"Three texts from Danica, Kaylie, and Max, and none from Rusty."

"He's probably still sleeping. We'll pick up breakfast and head over after we shower."

She sent a quick text to the girls and set her phone on the table again. Feeling queasy, she scooted to the edge of the bed and sat up. "I'm going to use the bathroom. Would you mind calling the front desk to see if they have toothbrushes and toothpaste? A comb or a brush would be great, too." She pushed to her feet, and Gage's shirt tumbled down her thighs.

Sally leaned against the bathroom sink, waiting for her nervous stomach to settle, and studied her face in the mirror, feeling ten years older than she had yesterday. How did parents get through these types of situations? What if Rusty was lying? She hated to think that way, but how could she be sure until she sat down and looked into her boy's eyes when he wasn't flaming mad at Gage?

Should he be punished for putting Gage in that position in the first place? Punish a twenty-year-old? Was he well within his rights as a young man to ask his confidant to keep his secret in order to protect his mother? She closed her eyes against hot tears, feeling completely overwhelmed.

She leaned forward and stared at her face in the mirror. "Stop crying, or your boy is never going to see you as strong and capable."

She straightened her spine, drew her shoulders back, and yanked a towel from the rack. Wiping her tears, frustrated that keeping secrets had made her emotionally edgy, she told herself they'd get through this.

After using the bathroom and washing her face, she drew in a few deep breaths, readying herself to face the day, no matter what it brought.

"Gage?" she said as she left the bathroom. He was answering the door, shirtless and sexy in a pair of low-slung jeans. She touched the edge of her—*his*—shirt where it hit her thighs, smiling to herself. She loved wearing his shirts. "Hopefully that's toothbrushes."

"Rusty," Gage said in a tight voice.

"Hey, I was looking for my mom's room, but they didn't have her listed at the desk."

Sally's stomach lurched, sending bile into her throat. "Rusty—"

Rusty peered over Gage's shoulder. "Mom?"

She grabbed her jeans and scrambled to put them on.

"What the fu—" Rusty shouldered past Gage. If looks could kill, she'd be dead and buried. "I'm out of here."

He stormed out the door, and Gage grabbed his arm. "Rusty, wait."

"Fuck you." He twisted out of Gage's grip and disappeared from view.

Gage started after him, but Sally bolted out to stop him. "Hold on. Let me talk to him first." She took off down the walkway, the frigid morning air stinging her face, cold concrete burning her bare feet as she ran after her son. "Rusty! Wait!"

He descended the steps at a fast clip, but there was no faster runner than a mother in fear of losing her son. She caught up to him in the parking lot and grabbed his arm. He spun around with fire in his eyes.

"Wait—" She bent over at the knees, her stomach churning, dizzily trying to catch her breath. "We need to talk." She was shaking from cold, and her stomach lurched again. She turned away just as she threw up, barely missing his sneakers.

"Mom! Are you okay?" His voice was filled with concern. He took off his coat and put it around her shoulders.

She held up a hand, afraid to speak for fear of puking again. She took a few steps away from the mess and sank down to her heels.

"Mom, I'm sorry. Are you sick? Is that why you were in the room with Gage?"

She shook her head, afraid of sending him into a fit of anger, but all this stress was tearing her up. The truth came weakly. "No."

She pushed to her feet, dizzily grabbing his arm to steady herself, and looked into her son's confused eyes. "I'm not sick, honey. This is just stress or something I ate."

"Bird," Gage called as he ran across the parking lot. He handed Rusty his coat and wrapped Sally's around her. He set her boots down beside her and held her as she stepped into them. "Are you okay?"

She nodded, though she was anything but okay. Her stomach felt like the ocean after a storm, unsure if it would rise up again or calm. But it was the worry in her son's eyes that was breaking her heart.

"You need to sit down." Gage guided her toward a bench in the grass.

"Rusty—"

He came to her side. "I'm here. I'm sorry. I didn't mean to make you sick."

"You didn't make me sick," she said, lowering herself to the bench, flanked by the two of them.

Rusty leaned his elbows on his knees, rubbing his hands together.

Gage kept a hand on Sally's back. "You sure you're okay? Want me to get you some water?"

"No. I think all this secret keeping is eating away at my stomach." She sat back, knowing she'd brought this on herself. It was no wonder Rusty thought he should keep his arrest a secret. He was his mother's son after all.

"Rusty, we have something to tell you." She reached for her son's hand, and he reluctantly allowed her to hold it.

"I think it's pretty clear, Mom. You and Gage are hooking up." The dark stare he pinned on Gage and the way he squeezed her hand told her he was not okay with it.

"No, honey. We're not hooking up."

His brow wrinkled, a softer look rising in his eyes.

She drew in a deep breath and sat up straighter, taking Gage's hand in hers. "We're married."

Rusty's eyes widened. "Married? As in, *married*?"

"Yes," she said. "It was an accident, but it's not anymore."

"An accident? How do you *accidentally* get married?" He pulled his hand from her grip.

"It turns out what happens in Vegas doesn't stay in Vegas," Gage said with an air of let's-lighten-the-mood, but Rusty's jaw was tight, his eyes stern. He looked as annoyed as ever. "Rusty, nothing will change. I love your mother, and I love you."

"No shit," Rusty snapped. "Everyone in the fucking town knows you love her, but this changes everything."

Oh God, here we go. "That's enough, Rusty. You don't need to get nasty. This is hard for all of us."

"So...*what*? You got drunk and ended up married?" Rusty

pushed to his feet and paced. "You were in Vegas three *weeks* ago."

"I know, and I'm sorry." Sally stood, swaying on her feet, still mildly dizzy. Gage's arm came around her waist, and she was thankful for the support—both physical and emotional.

"After all you've been through, your mother wanted to be sure about us before we told you," Gage explained.

"This explains a *lot*." Rusty pushed a hand through his hair, staring at the ground. He stopped pacing and lifted a challenging gaze at Gage. "What else have you told her?"

"Rusty." Sally stepped forward. "I know you trust Gage—"

"Trust*ed*," he said icily.

"Rusty," Gage said, "even if I weren't in a relationship with your mother, I would have had to tell her about your arrest. That's not like a bad grade or a car. Nothing has changed between you and me," he insisted. "You and your mom have both been, and remain, my priorities."

"Wait," Sally said, wondering what else he was keeping from her about her son. "A bad grade?"

"It was just an example," Gage reassured her.

"Who are you kidding?" Rusty snapped. "*Everything* has changed. The two people I trusted most in this world have been keeping the biggest secret of all from me. How can that possibly *not* change things?"

Sally felt him slipping away, just like she had after Dave died, and she realized that she hadn't even begun to touch the hurt she'd caused. She was doing what his father did to him all over again, springing a secret relationship on him. She sank down to the bench in shock.

"Sally?" Gage knelt beside her.

"Mom?"

She looked at them both with tears in her eyes. "He's right. This changes everything. How could I be so stupid?"

"Baby…?" Gage took her hand with imploring eyes.

"We're Dave all over again," she said flatly. "After Dave died, we found out that he had been secretly seeing Chase and his mother, building a relationship with them before he revealed the truth to us. He thought he was protecting us, and it tore me and Rusty to pieces." Tears streamed down her cheeks, and she turned to Rusty, hoping with all her heart that she hadn't ruined their relationship beyond repair.

"We were doing the same thing, building a relationship to make sure it was solid before telling you. I thought it was the *only* smart choice. Gage wanted to tell you right away. But my biggest worry was that if things didn't work out with me and Gage that you would lose him as your confidant. He promised me that would never happen, but I needed to know in my heart that I wasn't risking your relationship with him for my own happiness. And on top of that, I was so afraid of losing your trust, I didn't realize I was putting you in a position where I couldn't help but lose it."

Rusty clenched his jaw.

She pushed to her feet again, her gaze moving between the two men who owned her heart. "I love you both so much. Rusty, this was my mistake, not Gage's. The only thing he did to break your trust was to tell me about the arrest, and honestly, if he hadn't, and I found out, it would have ruined the relationship you have with him anyway. And Gage…" She swiped at her tears, but more followed. "I did this to us, and I'm so sorry."

"Babe." He gathered her in his arms. "You did what you thought was right for Rusty."

"Jesus," Rusty ground out.

Sally pushed from Gage's arms. "I'm sorry. I know that's probably hard for you to see."

Rusty rolled his eyes. "Obviously he makes you happy." He stared at Gage and motioned to Sally. "And clearly you've been in love with her for years."

"Yes." The unwavering love in Gage's voice calmed and worried Sally at once. She hoped it didn't set Rusty off again.

"Fuck." Rusty sank down to the bench and covered his face with both hands. His long legs stretched out before him and his arms fell heavily to his sides, his gaze moving between the two of them. "This is fucking weird."

"Can you please stop saying that word?" Sally asked. "I know it's weird. It was weird for me, too." She slid an arm around Gage's back. "But then I realized it was only weird because I'd fallen in love with my best friend."

"This makes you my stepfather," Rusty said uneasily as he pushed a hand through his hair. His bangs fell right back down in front of his eyes.

Gage sat next to Rusty, bringing Sally down beside him. "You're a man, Rusty. Legally, yeah, it gives me that title, but I don't want to replace your father. Hell, I don't want our relationship to change at all, although I can see how it has to, in some ways. This is a lot for all of us to adjust to."

"You think?" Rusty scoffed, but a hint of a smile followed, giving Sally hope that they could eventually move past this. "So, what now?"

Sally and Gage exchanged an uneasy look, and she read his silent question. *Do we go for it and tell him about the house?*

"Whatever it is, just spit it out," Rusty said. "There's not much you can do to top this."

"We could get arrested," Sally said with a smile.

Rusty scowled. "That sucked, and as soon as my friend is back from his cruise with his parents, he'll clear it up."

"I was just trying to take the edge off." She guessed they'd be dodging sharp edges for a while, and that was okay, as long as it didn't sever any ties. "Honey, it's about the house. I'll keep it as long as you want me to, but I'm going to be moving in with Gage."

"Dad's house?" Rusty asked solemnly.

"I'm sorry. It feels wrong to try to start over there."

Rusty looked at Gage for a long moment, as if he was trying to envision him in their house, and sighed heavily. "I guess that makes sense. When are you moving?"

Sally looked at Gage. They'd agreed she wouldn't move until after the holidays so Rusty could spend one last Christmas with her in their house. "After the holidays, when you go back to school."

He nodded sullenly. "But don't sell it yet."

"We won't."

"As your mom said, we'll hang on to it as long as you want us to. There's no rush," Gage reassured him. "And I want you to know that you'll always have your own room at our house. And by *our* house, I mean yours, mine, and your mom's."

Sally watched Rusty with worry, hoping he wouldn't lash out again.

Rusty held Gage's gaze, squared his shoulders, and nodded curtly.

It was such a manly affirmation, it took Sally by surprise. She'd watched as her son's world was turned upside down and he'd struggled through and found his footing. Her boy had grown up right before her eyes. He was no longer a kid on the cusp of manhood watching his friendship unravel through broken trust and breached confidence. He was a young man staking claim as such in his new reality.

And Sally knew in her heart, no matter what else came his way, he would be okay. *They* would be okay.

Chapter Nineteen

"YOU SAID YOU wanted to travel," Gage called out to Sally from the bedroom in Allure as he changed his clothes. By the time they'd left Harborside, things with Rusty were mildly comfortable, but Gage knew the underlying tension would probably last a while.

"Bailing my kid out of jail in Massachusetts in the winter wasn't my destination of choice," she said when he joined her in the living room. "But at least now he knows the truth."

Her phone vibrated with a call, and Gage picked it up off their new mosaic table and handed it to her. "It's Rusty."

She put the phone to her ear with a tentative expression. "Hi, honey." She paused, listening, her eyes widening along with her smile. "That's great news. Hold on." She lowered the phone and told Gage that the police had reached his friend, who'd admitted the pills were his. "The attorney told him he'd probably get the charges dropped."

"Thank God," Gage said.

She lifted the phone, listening again. "Thanks, honey. I love you." She handed the phone to Gage. "He wants to talk to you."

Surprised, Gage put it to his ear. "Hey, buddy."

"Hey. I need a favor."

"Sure."

"I want to surprise Mom and come down next weekend so she can move before the holidays. I mean, I assume you want her to move in sooner?"

"Are you sure?" Gage wanted to do a fist pump, but he had to choose his words carefully so as not to clue Sally in to Rusty's surprise. "You know why that was the plan, right?"

"So I could spend the holiday in my dad's house, I assume. My father's been gone a long time, and I'm glad Mom is finally moving on. She doesn't need to drag her ass on the move because of me."

"Man, I really appreciate that, Rusty."

"I figure I owe her after the whole arrest thing. Think you can keep it a secret so I can surprise her, or does that break some sort of marriage code?"

Gage chuckled, relieved that Rusty was reaching out to him again. "I think I can manage that."

"Thanks. If I come in Friday, can you pick me up, or should I call someone else?"

He watched his beautiful wife scrolling through the Internet on her laptop, blissfully unaware of her son's plans. He wished he could tell her just to see the thrill in her eyes when she realized how big a step Rusty was taking for her, but this was one secret he would keep. "Text me the details. I can handle it."

"Thanks, and, Gage?"

"Yeah?"

"Is Mom right there?"

"Mm-hm."

"Can you put me on speaker?"

"Sure." He pressed the speaker button, and Rusty's voice came through the phone. "Hey, Mom?"

Sally startled and turned. "Yeah? Hi, honey."

"I just wanted to say congratulations to you both. That kind of got lost in our conversation. I know I didn't act like it, but I'm glad you two are finally together."

Sally came to Gage's side. "Thank you. I'm sorry we sprang it on you like that. But honestly, we kind of sprang it on ourselves, too."

"Just for the record," Rusty said with a teasing tone, "next time I do something stupid, I'm totally holding your drunken marriage over your head."

Gage hugged Sally, all of them laughing.

They talked for a few more minutes, and after they ended the call, Gage tipped up Sally's chin and gazed into her relieved eyes. "I told you everything would be okay."

"Shut up and kiss me, Mr. Know-It-All." She went up on her toes, and he met her halfway in a series of slow, drugging kisses.

"You know what we have to do now?" he said in his most seductive voice.

She slid her hands into his back pockets. "I can think of a lot of things I want to do right now."

"Slow down, Salbird." He pulled his phone from his pocket and sent a group text to his family. *Family Skype. Urgent.* "We have a few things to take care of first."

He took her hand and led her out the front door and into the cold, dark night. He drew in a deep breath and hollered, "I married Sally Tuft!"

Sally's laughter filled the air, and he pulled her into his arms. He gazed into her smiling eyes and said, "You're my beautiful wife, and I'm never, *ever*, going to let you go."

He lowered his mouth to hers, holding her shivering body tight against him, and kissed her until she stopped shivering and melted against him.

"That wasn't a rooftop," she teased.

"If we didn't have a foot of snow, I'd be on the roof. Come on. We have a couple more things to take care of."

Back inside the warm house, he set the laptop on the coffee table in front of the couch and navigated to Skype. He pulled Sally down beside him, unable to stop smiling. "Smile pretty, sweetheart."

"Who are we Skyping?"

"My family. Do you want to try to reach your parents?"

Her expression turned serious, and she shook her head. "No. They're not very good with technology. I'll call them later."

"Do you want to call them first?" he offered.

"No. Let's call your family before you burst."

He chuckled, wishing her parents were more involved in her and Rusty's lives. He hoped to help facilitate a mending of those relationships, but it didn't have to start today. He began the group Skype call, and one by one his family members' faces appeared on the screen, each looking concerned. His mother, Andrea, sat at his father's desk, and his father peered over her shoulder. Jake must have been outside, because he was bundled up in a parka, and his phone bobbed up and down, giving them glimpses of snow-covered trees. Duke, Cash, and Blue appeared one after the other.

"What's going on?" Duke asked.

"Hi, Sally. Gage," his father said. "What's wrong?"

"What's up?" Blue asked.

They spoke in such quick succession that Gage didn't have a chance to respond. Jake smirked smugly, as if he had one up on everyone. He did, but there was so much more to tell.

"Nothing is wrong," Gage said as Trish signed on.

She was sitting on a couch with her husband, Boone, holding their cat. "Hi, you guys. What's going on?"

Sally looked nervous, and like everyone else, she wore an expectant expression. Gage had waited so long for this moment, and now that the time had come, he didn't know how to share their news. Simply saying "We're married" seemed too insignificant for what he felt.

"Gage…?" his father urged.

"Sorry," Gage said. "I'm a little nervous."

"That's a first," Jake chimed in, making Blue laugh.

"Just spit it out," Cash said. "Whatever it is, I'm sure we've heard worse."

"But you probably haven't heard better news." Gage put his arm around Sally, and gazed into her eyes. Heat pulsed between them, and he didn't care that everyone could probably see it, because in that moment, even with his family staring on, Sally was all that existed. His *wife*.

"Gage," Sally whispered, urging him on.

He leaned in and kissed her. "I love you, Sally Tuft-Ryder."

There was a beat of silence. Sally's gaze widened with surprise, then warmed with love, claiming his rapt attention.

"Did you just say…?" Trish's voice trailed off.

"Oh my gosh!" his mother exclaimed.

"The son of a bitch did it!" Cash whooped. "You two got married?"

Duke's deep laughter drowned out Blue's and Jake's cheers.

"Gage!" Trish chimed in. "Are you two married? We missed the wedding?"

Sally's eyes glistened with joy. Gage's response came in a hard press of his lips to hers, as his family called out their congratulations, laughing when he kept going back for more kisses. Once he'd taken his fill, he hauled Sally even closer and answered all of his family's questions, stealing kisses in between. By the time they ended the call, his mother and Trish were crying, and excited about planning a special celebratory dinner when the family came out for Christmas.

"Are you happy now?" Sally asked.

He touched his forehead to hers, his own eyes wet with happy tears. "There's just one more thing I need to do. Wait here." He disappeared into the bedroom, and when he came out, he turned off the lights.

"I like where this is headed," Sally said as he lit candles on the mantel.

"I hope so," he said under his breath. "In keeping with the king and queen of all things cheesy..." He turned on George Michael's "I Want Your Sex," and turned his back to Sally, swaying his hips to the high-pitched eighties beat.

"Oh my God!" She squealed and began clapping to the beat.

Gage spun around, unbuttoning his shirt as George Michael sang about things you guessed and things you knew. He pushed his shirt off his shoulders, gyrating his hips, and Sally's jaw dropped open. When the chorus rang out, he swung his shirt over his head, strutting toward her. He dragged the material over her arms and breasts, causing her cheeks to ripen with embarrassment—spurring him on.

OHMYGOD! YOU'RE REALLY stripping! The words played like a mantra in Sally's head as Gage dropped his shirt in her lap, mouthing lyrics about wanting her sex and her love. He unbuttoned his jeans and dragged the zipper down slowly and seductively. She reached for him and he shook his head as he sang, stepping just out of reach and driving her out of her mind. He turned around again, giving her a view of his perfect, beautiful ass, covered in denim. His hips swayed as he pulled his jeans down and stepped out of them. The music hit a high note and he turned dramatically, wearing only the pair of black tuxedo briefs with a white strip of material stretched tight over his cock and a bow tie at the top. She wanted to rip the bow tie off with her teeth.

Sally howled with laughter.

He held up two fingers and pointed to his eyes as he sang about looking in his eyes—but her gaze dropped right back down to that enticing bulge beneath the bow tie. *Yummy.*

He moved across the floor doing pelvic thrusts. His powerful thighs tested the elasticity of those fancy briefs. He belonged onstage, with his boyish charisma and the way he glided across the floor—all sex and lust, a wicked look in his eyes. He straddled her legs and leaned forward, making her fall back against the cushions. He sang to the beat, about dirty thoughts and pornography, and how he loved her so much it hurt.

He brushed his lips over hers, and when she tried to capture the kiss, he pushed to his feet, pulling her up with him, singing about how it was time she had sex with him.

God, yes! She was *so* ready.

Gage danced around her, rubbing against her hip and dragging his hands all over her body. His touch sent shocks of heat prickling beneath her skin. Her nipples pebbled, her breathing hitched, and she couldn't take her eyes off him. Her husband had moves! And a package that was eager to be set free! Liquid heat spread through her and her hips swayed without thought.

He hooked his thumbs into the hips of his briefs, thrusting to the beat as he inched them down. She covered her face, laughing.

"It feels weird to be fully dressed as you strip!"

Strip for me!

He pulled her hands down and planted one leg on either side of her thigh, rubbing his hard length against her.

Embarrassed and turned on at once, she couldn't stop smiling.

As the chorus rang out, he hooked his thumbs in his briefs again. Every thrust took them lower. *Oh Lord.* She felt herself go damp and didn't think, only reacted to the heat building inside her as she pulled her sweater over her head and threw it to the ground. When his briefs hit the floor, exposing every inch of his arousal, it was all she could do to stare. She was giddy and turned on, laughing and fumbling with the clasp on her bra.

"Get over here, *wife*," he growled, and swept her into his arms, kissing her deeply as he carried her into the bedroom, replacing her giddiness with white-hot desire.

CHAPTER TWENTY

"KNOCK, KNOCK," DANICA said as she walked into Sally's office Friday evening carrying a plate of pink and blue bootie-shaped cookies that one of the parents of a child who took dance lessons at the center had brought in earlier in the day. "Last chance to claim a cookie before I take these home to Chessie and Blake."

"No, thanks. You've been trying to pawn them off on everyone all day. Are they that bad?" Sally had been bummed about missing Danica's baby shower, but she was glad she and Gage had cleared the air with Rusty. And from the sounds of it, the baby shower had been a grand success and Danica had had a wonderful time.

"Are you kidding?" Danica set the tray on the desk and took a bite out of a cookie. "I'm pawning them off because I can't stop eating them. You love cookies. What's up?"

Sally set the contract she was reading down beside the tray. "My stomach's been off lately. We have so much going on, with Rusty and Gage's family coming next week for the holidays and moving my stuff to Gage's right after Rusty goes back to Harborside. I just need a few days when we're not hot off the heels of an arrest or turning Rusty's world upside down. Then I'm sure my stomach will calm down and I'll eat all the cookies I can find."

"Hopefully after the holidays everything will settle down. Are you sure you're not preggers?" Danica patted her belly. "My baby could use a playmate."

Sally laughed. "Treat and Max are giving you that. Besides, it would be impossible. We've never had sex without protection." She casually glanced at the calendar, trying to remember when her last period was.

"Then it's probably just stress. Although, pregnancy would be way more fun." She waggled her brows. "The best part of pregnancy is no condoms, no pills, just doing it when the feeling hits."

Sally loved the thought of making love with Gage without worrying about birth control. They'd talked about her going back on the pill so they didn't have to think about condoms, but Gage was anxious to have a family. It seemed silly to start the pill only to go off it again when they were ready to start trying.

Danica took another bite of her cookie. "Mm. These are way too good. I should throw them out. They'll never make it home."

"Want me to toss them?" Sally reached for the tray.

Danica covered it with her hands with a fierce look in her eyes. "Are you crazy? When else can I chow down on delicious cookies without worrying about my figure?" She picked up the tray and headed for the door. "It's late. Are you leaving soon?"

"I'm waiting for Gage. We're going to pick out our Christmas tree tonight, but he had an errand to run, and I was on a conference call with Haylie. She's going to be a great administrator. We definitely made the right choice. She's already met with Sable and her band, organized catering, and designed invitations for the grand opening even though it's weeks away.

And she's got ads in the local papers for the open positions."

"I had no doubt that you'd hire the best person for the job. I'll see you tomorrow morning." Danica waved and disappeared down the hall.

Sally organized her desk, unable to believe Christmas was less than a week away.

"Hey, beautiful." Gage walked through the door. His hair and shoulders were covered with snowflakes.

She came around the desk and into his arms, greeted with a warm press of his lips. His nose was ice cold against her cheek. "You're freezing."

"Not anymore." He brushed his lips over hers before taking her in a long, hot, toe-curling kiss. "Ready to pick out our tree?"

"When you kiss me like that, the only thing I want to do is kiss you more."

"That can be arranged." His lips met hers as soft as a caress, a tease of a kiss.

His tongue traced the bow of her upper lip, sending her senses reeling. She went up on her toes, her arms circling his neck as she pulled him down, and he kissed her, rough and demanding. She curled her fingers in his hair, holding on tight. When their mouths finally parted, she was barely breathing, and he was looking at her like she was his whole world.

"I want to engrave that look into my mind for five—*ten*—years down the line," she said anxiously. "So I remember when life gets in the way of these moments."

"I waited a lifetime to find you and years to be with you. *Nothing* will ever get in the way of these moments. I promise you that, bird. When we're old and gray, I'll still be copping feels and looking at you just like this." His mouth descended upon hers again, sealing his promise with another steamy kiss.

THE LAST THING Gage wanted to do was stop kissing Sally, but after a series of desperate kisses, he forced himself to break away. She clung to his coat, breathless and so sexy, he had to have one more taste. He kissed her roughly and lifted her onto the desk, stepping between her legs so they were as close as they could be.

"We have to pick out our tree," he said as he kissed his way down her neck.

"*Tree*," she repeated.

He sealed his mouth over her neck, stroking it with his tongue and earning a string of wanton sounds.

"Baby," he ground out. "We have to go."

"Why? It's just a tree." She gazed up at him with a seductive and somehow innocent look.

He was *this close* to making a bad decision, but he glanced out the window and saw the snow was coming down harder, kicking his rational mind into gear.

"But it's our first Christmas tree, and the snow's really coming down." He framed her face with his hands and pressed his lips to hers. "We also promised Danica we wouldn't do this in the office."

"In the storeroom," she corrected him.

He chuckled. "I promise we'll pick this up where we left off. But if we don't get our tree now, we'll be stuck here all night." He couldn't resist taking one more kiss, and tore away with a groan. "I want to make love to you in our bed, baby, not on the desk."

She sassily arched a brow and pushed her finger into the waist of his jeans. "You don't want to fool around on my desk and talk dirty to me?"

He ground his teeth together, knowing they had to get out of there. "Fuck, birdie. I want to do so much more than talk dirty to you. I want to take you on the desk, on the floor, on the couch." He clutched her hips, pulling her tighter against him. "I want to tug down these pants and devour you until you come on my mouth. I want to make you so wet and needy, it's all you can do to remember how to breathe."

"I want that" flew from her lips.

"*Christ*, you're going to be the death of me." He crushed his mouth to hers. His cock throbbed to get in on the action, but they'd spent enough time indulging their needs. They really had to leave. "We gotta go, baby."

She pushed off the desk and to her feet.

"Okay, *hubby*. With our luck, Danica would have forgotten something and come back and caught us again anyway."

He adjusted himself in his jeans and she giggled.

"I offered to take care of that for you."

"Trust me. I already regret not taking you up on it," he said as they headed for the lobby. Sometimes being a responsible adult sucked.

It was dark outside, save for misty showers of light coming from the streetlamps on either end of the parking lot. Gage held Sally close, kissing her as they crossed the lot toward his truck.

"You weren't kidding," she said. "We'll probably get several inches of snow tonight. Maybe we should wait to pick out our tree."

"We'll see," Gage said.

The passenger door to his truck opened, and Rusty stepped

out. Sally slowed, squinting into the darkness.

"Who is that? *Rusty*?" She looked up at Gage, eyes wide, then back at her son, who was closing the distance between them. "Oh my gosh! Rusty!"

She ran into Rusty's open arms, like a scene from a movie when a long-lost son returns from war. Only Rusty hadn't been at war, even if it had felt that way for a while.

"Hi, Mom." Rusty smiled as Sally touched his cheeks, his shoulders, his chest, as if she couldn't believe it was really him.

"I thought you were working to earn extra money until next week."

Rusty shrugged and glanced at Gage. They'd talked on the way back from the airport about how Rusty felt about Gage and Sally's relationship. It turned out that what Rusty had feared most was losing his ability to confide in Gage. He said he'd finally found a man he trusted, and Gage reassured him that he'd navigate this new relationship with that in mind. There were apologies on both sides and manly hugs that put it all behind them.

"I was," Rusty said. "But I figured you might need help moving."

"But we're not moving until after Christmas," Sally reminded him.

"If we're going to do this family thing, we should do it right." Rusty lifted his chin in Gage's direction. "We're part of Gage's family now, too. That's where we need to wake up on Christmas morning."

"Oh, Rusty." She threw her arms around his neck, tears streaming down her cheeks.

Rusty gave her a quick hug and laughed. "It's not like it's a big deal."

Sally stepped back, wiping her eyes. "It's a big deal. A *very* big deal. Thank you." She turned to Gage. Snowflakes covered her shoulders, hair, and wet her cheeks. "You kept this a secret from me?"

"Some secrets are meant to be kept." Gage took her hand. "This is the second time I've caught you crying in this exact spot. Do you remember the first?"

She pressed her lips together. "How could I ever forget?"

He dropped to one knee, took the black velvet box from his pocket, and opened it so Sally could see the beautiful cushion-cut canary diamond engagement ring he'd had made for her. The canary diamond was surrounded by two carats of white diamonds.

Sally covered her gaping mouth.

"My sweet Salbird, you know I have adored you, and loved Rusty, for what feels like forever. I have fallen even deeper in love with you with every passing minute these last few weeks. I know we're already married, but you were a little shnockered when you accepted my first proposal."

He rose to his feet and gazed into her gorgeous eyes. "Will you take me as your husband and let me love you and Rusty for the rest of our lives?"

She nodded, crying and smiling. "Yes!" She looked at Rusty as Gage slid the ring onto her finger. "Did you know?"

"The goof asked my permission," Rusty said, which only made Sally cry harder.

Gage swept Sally into his arms, twirling her around as the snow fell.

Sally's eyes were wet with tears and filled with joy as she said, "What took you so long?"

His heart nearly stopped at the words she'd said to him

when he'd proposed in Vegas. "You remembered?"

"I remember, Gage. I remember it all now, and I'll never forget a second of it again."

LATER THAT EVENING, after the three of them picked out and decorated their Christmas tree, including their ornament from Lovers' Lodge, Gage went outside to bring in an armful of wood. He caught sight of Sally and Rusty through the guest-room-turned-mosaic-studio window, and his heart filled with love.

They were a family now. *His* family.

He looked up at the hazy gray sky, no longer feeling like he needed to shout it from the rooftops. The people who mattered most were right there in *their* house.

Chapter Twenty-One

GAGE WOKE UP to the sounds of howling winds Saturday morning. Sally was draped across his chest, the ring on her left hand a reminder of their magical night. They'd stayed up late with Rusty watching *A Christmas Story*. And even though Rusty had borrowed Gage's truck so he could stay at the other house one last night, Gage's house felt settled, and more like a home, despite having a big day of moving ahead of them.

Sally snuggled closer. Her thigh moved over his, and all her sweet softness pressed against him, arousing the sleeping giant between his legs.

"Why are you awake?" she asked sleepily.

"Just woke up." He kissed her cheek and moved over her. "Good morning, beautiful bird." Perched on his forearms, he nuzzled against her neck.

"Feels like your eager eagle is searching for a nest."

He chuckled. "We have a big"—he pressed his lips to hers—"important day ahead of us. How do you want to do it?"

"I'm not a sexpert, but I'm pretty sure we can do it just like this." Her hips rose off the bed.

He nipped at her lower lip. "I mean the move. Do you want some time alone with Rusty at the house?"

"*Oh*. You want me to think clearly with you lying naked on top of me? Not happening."

He kissed his way down her neck, pushing her arms up above her head. "Try to concentrate." He swirled his tongue around her nipple, bringing it to a tight nub. Then he took it between his teeth, tugging ever so gently, until she bowed off the bed.

"*Oh God—*"

He lowered his mouth over the peak and sucked it against the roof of his mouth, rocking his hips and rubbing his cock against her wetness. He released her breast and said, "The *move*, bird. Do you want some time alone with Rusty?"

"No," came out in a hot whisper.

He blazed a path south, tasting every luscious inch as he went. Her knees drew up, and he pushed his hands beneath her bottom, lifting her sex to his mouth. She rocked and moaned, urging him on.

"Watch me love you, baby."

She trapped her lower lip between her teeth and her eyes fluttered open, her gaze locking on him. Damn, that was a fucking turn-on. The heat of her gaze seared into him as he placed openmouthed kisses along her inner thighs and around her swollen, wet lips. She fisted her hands in the sheets, and he did it again, coming torturously close to the promised land. She writhed and whimpered.

Holding her gaze, he said, "Tell me what you want, baby."

"Lick me…*there*."

He dragged his tongue around her clit and reached for her hand. She squeezed his fingers as he teased her sensitive nerves.

"Lower," she pleaded.

He brought her finger to his mouth, swirling his tongue around it.

"That's so hot," she said breathlessly.

"Not nearly as hot as this." He placed her hand between her legs. Her eyes widened, and he covered her hand with his, moving it how he knew she liked it. "Touch yourself for me, baby. You're so sexy. Let me watch you."

She closed her eyes, and he said, "Eyes open, bird. I want to see the love in them." He knew he was pushing her past her comfort zone, but he also sensed she wanted to be pushed.

Her eyes opened and she met his gaze as she touched herself. He lowered his mouth to her sex, licking and loving her into a frenzy of desire. When he pushed his fingers inside her, she moaned, and her hand stilled.

"Keep going, baby. Don't stop. Help me get you there."

She moved her hand, biting her lower lip, and looking sexy as hell. Her eyes were dark and sultry, and her gorgeous breasts moved with her efforts as she played his seductive game. He stroked the spot that tore a long, guttural moan from her lungs, and she clutched the sheet. He sucked her clit between his teeth as she rode his hand, and a stream of sinful sounds poured from her lips.

"Oh *God*, *Gage*. Don't stop. Right there. *Oooh*."

As she came down from the peak, he guided her legs onto his shoulders and feasted on her, taking her right up to the peak again. She was right there with him, bucking against his mouth, pulling his hair. There was no slowing down as he teased and pleased, until she collapsed to the mattress, gasping for air, a sated smile on her lips.

Gage sheathed his hard length and she reached for him. *That's my girl, always ready for more.*

"I love you, bird," he said against her neck as their bodies came together.

Heat spread like wildfire, burning through his veins, rushing from his core all the way to his fingertips. He captured Sally's mouth in a ravenous kiss. She tasted heavenly, and felt even better, cradled beneath him. Their bodies moved in sweet harmony. But it wasn't enough. Would anything ever be? Cradling her in his arms, he shifted positions and lay beneath her, feeling greedy and needing to see *all* of her. She straddled his hips, her long blond hair sweeping over her breasts. A coy smile reached all the way up to her eyes.

"Ride 'em, cowboy," she said playfully.

She used his shoulders for balance as she rode him, her hair curtaining their faces. He rose and took her breast in his mouth, sucking so hard she cried out. When he pulled away, she grabbed his head, guiding it to her other breast, which he lavished with the same fierce love. He moved his hand between her legs, taking her higher. Her breathing hitched and her eyes slammed closed. She gasped in sweet agony as her climax claimed her. The feel and sight of her coming sent him soaring after her.

"Love you, *bird*—" he ground out, surrendering to his own powerful release.

When the last aftershock rippled through their bodies, she collapsed against him, and they rolled onto their sides. She snuggled in close, murmuring lovingly into his chest.

"Thank you," she whispered.

"I think I should be thanking you."

She tipped her chin up and laughed. The sweet melody cut straight to his heart. "Not for the sex, you nut. For believing everything would work out when I was so worried."

He pressed his lips to hers. "We have yet to master keeping our hands off each other while we're at work."

"We will." She giggled. "*After* we cross my desk off our

naughty to-do list."

"We have a naughty to-do list?"

"After last night we do…"

SALLY STOOD IN the doorway of Rusty's childhood bedroom watching him empty his desk drawers. Gage was in the kitchen, packing dishes and pots and pans for Rusty to use at his apartment, and a few odds and ends Sally had wanted. The rest would go to Goodwill, along with the furniture. Sally had long ago gotten rid of Dave's things, save for a few small items she'd saved for Rusty.

Rusty pulled open another drawer and began sifting through the contents. She remembered when they'd bought him the wooden desk when he was twelve. *Mom, I need a desk more than I need a dresser.* It hadn't made sense to her, since he'd refused to do homework anywhere but in front of the television. But he'd been so adamant, she'd caved, and they'd bought the desk. It wasn't until two weeks later, when she'd noticed that he'd set up the desk just as his father's was set up in the den, that she'd realized he was connecting with Dave—over a desk.

Was he thinking of his father now?

She walked in and put a hand on his shoulder. "You doing okay?"

"Yeah. Just going through all this crap." He glanced up with a casual half smile that reminded her of Dave. "I had no idea I'd kept so much junk." He tossed a handful of papers into the trash. "Look what I found in my closet."

He crossed the room and reached into another box, withdrawing a stack of pictures. "Remember these?"

She sat on the bed, looking through the photographs. "How could I forget? They were taken on your thirteenth birthday." Her heart ached at the sight of Dave and Rusty beaming into the camera, holding ski poles in front of the slopes. Their cheeks were pink, and their hair poked out from beneath their hats. The look of sheer excitement in their eyes brought her smile.

"Aspen," Rusty said. "That was a great trip." He went back to his desk and opened another drawer. "I shouldn't have been such a dick when I was a teenager. I don't know how you and Dad put up with me."

Sally looked up from the pictures. "You weren't a *dick*, and I don't like that word. You were a typical moody teenager."

"Then all teenagers are dicks."

She turned back to the pictures, flipping through a few of Rusty and Dave. They were so happy that day. All of them. She uncovered the last picture, revealing a photograph of her and Dave. Her breath caught in her throat. Dave was looking at her adoringly. She pressed the photograph to her chest, tears slipping down her cheeks, and closed her eyes against a thread of guilt tightening like a noose around her neck.

She wiped her eyes. "Sorry."

"You okay?"

"Yes." She handed him the pictures. "Those are nice, honey. Do you want me to put them in an album for you?"

"Nah. I'll throw them in my desk at Gage's." He set them in the box and exhaled a long sigh. "Shouldn't this feel different? *Worse* or something? You cried when you saw the pictures, but I didn't feel that. I mean, I miss Dad like crazy sometimes, but I feel like I moved out two years ago. And I feel guilty for *not* feeling guilty about it. Shouldn't I feel like I'm turning my back on him or something?"

"No, honey. You did move out two years ago, and you said goodbye to your father over the years. I think that's normal." She patted the mattress beside her and he sat down. "Did I ever tell you about when I found out I was pregnant with you?"

"Just that I was an accident."

"A blessing," she corrected, and he scoffed. "Okay, an accidental blessing. Rusty, I got pregnant before your dad and I were married. I probably should have told you that a long time ago, but I didn't want you thinking it was a good idea to get some girl pregnant."

A cocky grin spread across his handsome face. "That would *never* have even entered my mind. Kids are nowhere near my radar screen."

"Good." She shook her head. "You're not mad that I didn't tell you?"

"Why do I care? You also got drunk and married Gage. It kind of makes you human instead of the perfect mom you always seemed like."

"Hardly perfect. Your grandparents had a really hard time with it, and they didn't talk to me for a long time after I married your dad. I remember when I moved out. I never looked back, and even though my parents were still alive, I felt abandoned. But I had Dave, and I had you on the way, and I didn't miss them like people thought I should have. I think certain events move us forward and make it easier to close the doors that we leave behind. Maybe it's self-preservation, or maybe it's just time really does heal all wounds."

She brushed his hair from his forehead, and he moved out of her reach, the way kids did when their mothers were being overly touchy.

"You don't need to feel guilty for moving on with your life.

Your father would have wanted that for you. And you aren't leaving his memory behind by moving out." She pressed her hand to his chest, over his heart. "He lives on in here, and that's something that has taken me a while to come to grips with, too. I think, or *hope*, it's normal. But I guess that doesn't matter so much. It's *our* normal."

"Hey, I never claimed to be normal," he teased. "Now please get out of my room so I can get rid of all the dirty magazines I've got hidden under my mattress."

"Really, Rusty?"

He rolled his eyes. "Do you think I'd buy magazines when I can get it for free online?"

She covered her ears, laughing as she headed down the hall. "I don't need to know this about you."

Rusty and Gage left a little while later to pick up more boxes, and Sally packed up her things from the bedroom. Her stomach growled, but she felt too queasy to eat. Hopefully after the move things would settle down.

When she finished with her closet, she went into the bathroom and began emptying the cabinet beneath the sink. She was a bit of a hoarder when it came to toiletries. She stacked up extra rolls of toilet paper, boxes of toothpaste, two unopened toothbrushes, and a half-empty box of Q-Tips. The supply of junk was endless. She found a pack of bobby pins that she couldn't remember buying, and a handful of hairclips went directly into the trash. They looked like they were from the nineties, and probably were. She reached behind the annoyingly centered pipes and grabbed three slim boxes. Pregnancy tests. Holy cow, those had to be ten years old.

She sat on the tile floor thinking back to when she and Dave had thought she was pregnant. He'd freaked out. He definitely hadn't wanted more children, though she would have liked more. He had been glad when Rusty began having a social life, which allowed her and Dave to have more time together and also freed up Dave to do more of what he loved most—skiing.

She eyed the boxes again. Why on earth would she have needed so many? She glanced into the cabinet and spied two more pregnancy tests beneath a box of tampons and remembered she'd bought them in bulk. She made a mental note to never let a bathroom vanity turn into the Bermuda Triangle again, and looked over the boxes. Danica's voice sailed into her mind. *Are you sure you're not preggers?* Okay, she might have been ignoring the fact that she was almost a week late, but her periods had never been all that regular and her life had been a roller coaster lately.

She opened one of the boxes and shook out the contents. What could it hurt to take a test? Her pulse spiked with the possibility, though rationally she knew there was no chance of her being pregnant. She and Gage had never had sex without protection. She tore open the packaging, pulled down her jeans, and sat on the toilet, willing herself to pee.

Did she want to be pregnant? Her heart felt full with the thought of how much joy a baby would bring Gage, but was she ready to dive back into diapers and three a.m. feedings? Colic and…*sweet baby giggles*? She loved those giggles.

She set the test on the counter, checked the time on her phone, and went back to cleaning out the cabinet from hell, her mind whizzing with uncertainty. *One* minute later she was staring at the stick, her heart slamming against her ribs as two blue lines formed right before her eyes. Her jaw dropped open, and she didn't know if she should laugh or cry. She picked up another box and tore it open.

Fifteen minutes later she sat crying on the bathroom floor, surrounded by five empty boxes, four positive pregnancy tests and one negative.

"Mom?" Rusty called from the bedroom. "Gage went to pick up lunch. I put the boxes—"

She dove across the floor, scrambling to gather the evidence.

"What are you…?"

She turned, clutching the pregnancy paraphernalia to her chest. She wiped her eyes, and several boxes tumbled from her grip.

"You're crying." Rusty picked up one of the tests, and understanding rose in his eyes. He sank down to his butt beside her.

"These are old tests," she said quickly. "I'm not sure they work."

"Mom, is this why you're crying?" He set the test on the floor, his gaze skirting over the others as she pushed them all away.

There was no lying, no covering up or waiting to talk to Gage. Could she make Rusty's life any harder? Fresh tears burned down her cheeks. "I can't be pregnant. We've been careful. Not that you want to know that about your mother, but…" She shrugged. "I'm old enough to be a grandmother."

"Bite your tongue," he said with a smile.

"Well, I *am*. You're fully capable of making babies."

"Apparently so are you." He draped an arm over her shoulders.

It felt safe and comfortable in a way that it probably shouldn't. He was her child. She should be comforting *him*.

"Mom, what's wrong? Don't you want kids with Gage?"

"Yes! But we're not even settled yet, and it's been a long

time since I've had a baby to deal with. What if I'm not as patient anymore? And what about you? God, how could this happen?"

"Well," he said with a sly grin. "You see, when two people love each other—"

She elbowed him and he laughed. "You know what I mean. Rusty, I keep messing up your life, throwing drunken weddings at you and moving out of the house."

"Do you really believe that?" His gaze turned serious. "You're an amazing mother. You're patient and you're loving. And most importantly, you've put off being happy for years *because* of me."

"I've been happy."

He shook his head. "No. You're happy with Gage, Mom. You've been *managing* without him for a long time. Everyone who has ever seen you two together knows how much you love him. And he loves you so much. Man, after the talk we had in the truck on the way home from the airport, all I can say is that I hope I'm lucky enough someday to love someone the way he loves you."

She wiped her tears, in awe over her son's adult attitude. She'd expected to be reamed for having gotten pregnant. "You really have no bad feelings about any of this?" She picked up a pregnancy test. "What about this? Becoming a big brother at twenty?"

"Well, I'll probably be twenty-one by the time the little guy is born, but no, I don't have any hard feelings. I'll be the little dude's cool older brother and teach him all the things he needs to know."

"You realize it could be a girl."

"And I'll protect her with my life." He paused, and in that

moment, his serious expression made him look five years older. "Mom, you don't need to feel guilty for moving on with your life, either. I'm happy for you and Gage."

Hearing her own words given back to her with such care brought more tears. *Damn pregnancy hormones.*

"Bird?" Gage appeared in the bathroom doorway. "What's going on?"

Before Sally could respond, Rusty said, "You're going to be a dad...*Dad.*"

"I'M...*WHAT*?" GAGE took in the mess strewn across the bathroom floor, spotting pregnancy tests among the chaos of toiletries. A smile tugged at his lips as Sally and Rusty rose to their feet. "You're *pregnant*?"

Sally shrugged, laughing and crying at once. She was doing a lot of that lately, and this explained it all.

"Baby!" He lifted her off her feet and kissed her. "We're going to have a baby!" He searched her eyes, making sure she was okay with the news. His answer came in the form of a radiant, joyful smile.

She nodded, tears sliding down her cheeks. "We are."

Tears filled his eyes as he spun her around. He stopped midtwirl and set her on her feet. "Sorry, bird. That's probably not good for the baby, right?"

"It's fine," she said.

Gage's mind spun. He was elated over the news, and when he turned to Rusty, Rusty's words came back to him. "You called me *Dad.*"

Rusty shoved his hands deep in the pockets of his jeans and

looked sheepishly down at the floor. "Yeah. That was weird, dude."

"Right?" Gage laughed under his breath. "*Weird.*"

"Sorry, man, but you're Gage to me."

Gage pulled Rusty into a manly embrace, patting him on the back. "It's cool. I'd rather be Gage than 'that asshole.' Come on, let's go celebrate. I brought lunch, and we have some shouting from the rooftops to do."

"Huh?" Rusty arched a brow.

"You'll get used to it," Sally said. "In fact, you'll probably grow to love it."

CHAPTER TWENTY-TWO

"I'M GOING TO be a father," Gage said for the umpteenth time since his family had arrived Christmas morning. They'd called their family members and told them the incredible news the day after they'd found out—after purchasing new pregnancy tests and verifying the results. Gage stood beside the fireplace with his father and his brothers, Duke and Jake, and Trish's husband, Boone. "Sally doesn't know this yet, but I've already stuffed the hall closet with two kid's baseball gloves—one brown and one pink—a set of kids' skis, and the designs to a treehouse for the backyard. Not that I'm excited or anything." Gage glanced into the kitchen, where his beautiful wife had been cooking all day with his mother and the other women. The house smelled like cinnamon and mulled cider with a touch of bourbon, turkey, and cookies all wrapped up in the arms of love. Sally looked gorgeous in the red empire-waist dress they'd bought in Virginia. Gage swore the sweetheart neckline looked fuller since they'd bought it, but Sally insisted it was wishful thinking. He couldn't wait to see her body change as their baby grew. They'd tried to figure out how she ended up pregnant, and as they pieced together their wedding night, they remembered making love more than once, but neither of them remembered opening more than one condom. It was destiny, Gage had told her, but Sally had liked Danica's answer better.

That she'd needed the alcohol to take what she'd wanted for so long. Like he'd said, alcohol or not, it was all meant to be. *Destiny*. His beautiful bird had come home to nest, and he couldn't be happier.

His father draped an arm over his shoulder, bringing his mind back to their conversation. "Well, son, I think I know where you got that from. Your mother doesn't think I know this, but she's got a cabinet full of baby clothes—pink and blue—toys, and all sorts of things, just waiting for her new grandbaby."

"She's got another baby to buy for," Duke reminded him.

"Your mother's got another cabinet full of stuff for yours and Gabby's baby," his father said. "And she's ready to purchase gifts for another grandchild. But it appears Blue hasn't gotten the memo yet."

Blue looked up from the couch where he sat beside Cash, each bouncing one of the twins on their lap. "Nothing like a little pressure. How about Boone and Trish?"

Boone splayed his hands with a mischievous expression. Tattoos snaked out from his rolled-up sleeves. "You never know."

"Better you than us," Jake chimed in. "Right, Addy?" he called into the kitchen.

Addy blew him a kiss. Lizzie set a tray of cookies on the counter, and Trish snagged one, passing it from hand to hand like a hot potato. The girls laughed, and Sally's laughter rose above the rest, calling Gage's attention. *Man, that laugh.*

Rusty came in from outdoors and kissed his mother's cheek before stealing a cookie. After the initial shock of the marriage had worn off, Rusty had surprised them with his maturity. He'd offered to help paint the extra bedroom and set up the nursery.

He'd even given them a onesie that said *Made in Vegas.* Gage looked forward to spending more time with Rusty as their family blended together.

Gage turned his attention to the man who had taught him about strength, love, and loyalty, feeling thankful. In a world where so many couples ended in divorce and families fell apart with the change of the wind, his father had been a pillar of strength. And today, when Gage needed him most of all, he was right there by his side. He hoped to be as good a father and role model as Ned had been for him.

"Hey, Dad, thanks for standing by me."

Ned pushed his wire-framed glasses up the bridge of his nose. His goatee was flecked with gray, but the mischief in his eyes made him look ten years younger. "That's what fathers are for, son. You'll see."

"Now I understand why Dad got so pissed at us when we used to sneak out," Cash said. "I'd go out of my mind if I woke up at two in the morning and one of these guys was missing."

"You've got double trouble on your hands, buddy." Gage patted his shoulder as he made his way toward his beautiful wife.

"Don't worry, Gage," Rusty said as he came out of the kitchen. "I'll keep my little brother or sister in line."

"Little Rusty's all grown up," Jake teased.

Rusty scoffed and faked a punch to Jake's gut. Gage chuckled. Sally looked up from the vegetables she was chopping and handed the knife to Trish. She moved gracefully across the floor and into Gage's arm.

"Merry Christmas, my beautiful bird."

"Merry Christmas."

He kissed her tenderly. "Our nest is very full tonight." He

nibbled on her neck the way he knew drove her mad.

"I wish my parents could have made it back to celebrate with us."

"Me too, babe."

She put her arms around him. Her parents had been excited about their marriage and baby, which had surprised Sally. But it hadn't surprised Gage, because they'd given up their daughter once, and anyone who had lost this incredible woman surely wouldn't want a repeat performance.

Gage slid his hand down her hip, giving her butt a gentle squeeze. "How much time do we have until dinner?"

Sally's cheeks pinked up, and she lowered her voice. "Not enough time for *that*, especially with your entire family here."

SALLY'S STOMACH FLIPPED and dipped as Gage tried relentlessly to seduce her, nipping at her lips, whispering sweet thoughts into her ears, and brushing his cheek over hers. She was so used to seeing him in casual clothes that when he'd dressed that morning in his dark slacks and a white button-down, he'd actually taken her breath away. And now, as his family mingled around them, the look in his eyes caused the same lapse of lung power.

"Two minutes, baby. Give me two minutes to make you feel good. You know I can do it," he said in an enticing voice. "Seeing you in this dress is driving me crazy."

"Could have fooled me. You and your brothers spent most of the day outdoors."

"Be glad I kept them out of your hair. You know how riled up they can get."

He slicked his tongue around the shell of her ear. "Come make out with me, baby. I'll make it up to you."

She clutched his shirt as he placed openmouthed kisses along the base of her neck, wreaking havoc with her mind. "It won't be enough. I'll need *you.*"

"That can be arranged," he said heatedly.

He winked and headed for the bedroom, leaving her alone to ponder his offer. Her finger would lose circulation if she twirled her hair any tighter around it. Maybe no one would notice if they were gone for just a few minutes. She glanced furtively around the room. Everyone seemed content. With her heart pounding out a thrilling beat, she slipped into the bedroom.

"Gage?" she whispered.

He hauled her into the bathroom and locked the door behind her with a rapacious look in his eyes. "I knew you'd come. Now let your man make you *really* come."

He backed her up against the door, his hungry eyes pinning her in place as he gathered the hem of her dress and lifted it up. He dropped to his knees and pulled her panties down.

"Gage, we shouldn't—" She tangled her hands in his hair as he did that magical thing with his tongue that made her toes curl. "*Ohmygod*—we *should.* We definitely should if you can be *fast.*"

His talented fingers took her right up to the edge, and just as she was about to come, he bolted to his feet and dropped his pants, burying himself to the hilt. *Nothing* compared to making love with him without anything between them. Pregnancy rocked. Sensations exploded inside her chest like fireworks. She wound her arms around his neck and he lifted her up, using the wall for leverage.

"Gage, you in there?" Jake's voice came through the bathroom door.

"Ohmygod!" Sally whispered.

Gage put his finger over her lips, silencing her. "I'll be another minute or two."

Sally tried to push from his arms, meeting the halting look in his eyes with an are-you-freaking-crazy glare.

"The girls are looking for Sally," Jake said.

He chuckled, and she glared at him again. "Check the guest bathroom."

Jake was quiet for a second, and then he said, "While I pretend to do that, how about you two hurry up. *Jesus,* what is it about Ryders and bathrooms?"

Gage ground his teeth together, slowly thrusting, and driving Sally mad despite their embarrassing situation. They listened to Jake leave the room, and Sally finally breathed.

"I can't believe I let you convince me to do this!"

"Baby," he said in that sexy, loving voice that broke down her defenses. "He kept our other secret. He won't tell a soul. Let me knock this off my naughty bucket list. Do you know how many Christmases I've dreamed of doing this with you?"

"About as many times as I have."

She surrendered to the fierce domination of his lips. Their bodies took over, creating that perfect harmony, which carried them to the peak of passion.

CHAPTER TWENTY-THREE

TRUE TO GAGE'S word, Jake didn't say a word to anyone about their bathroom tryst. But that didn't stop Sally from imagining that everyone knew why she'd come out of the bathroom freshly washed up and grinning like the well-fucked wife she was.

Dinner passed with lots of laughter. Coco and Seth were so cute, she spent most of the evening watching them, imagining how cute her and Gage's baby would be.

After dinner, the guys cleared the table and the girls washed the dishes. Blue and Jake started wrestling in the living room and Duke and Gage hauled them, and the rest of the guys, outside to chop wood, which seemed silly to Sally, considering they were all decked out for the holiday. *Boys will be boys.*

Siena and Andrea, Gage's mother, went to change the twins' diapers, and Gabby wasn't feeling well, so Lizzie took her outside for some fresh air, leaving Trish and Sally alone in the kitchen.

"Your dress is really spectacular." Trish ran her fingers down the crinkled chiffon skirt. "I'd wear something like that to the Oscars."

"Your brother insisted on buying it for me in Virginia. You and Boone are definitely going to win. You can borrow the dress if you'd like."

"If I still fit in it." Trish put her hand over her stomach. "We're not telling anyone yet, but Boone and I are trying to get pregnant."

Sally gasped. "Oh, Trish! That's wonderful."

"I'm a little scared," she admitted. "I know I'll be stressed about the Oscars. That's not good for the baby, right?"

"Babies are pretty resilient. Besides, if you're like me, you'll be so in love with the idea of having Boone's baby, nothing else will matter. I feel like my stress has gone way down, even though it should be through the roof."

"*Baby bliss*," Trish said. "That's what Gabby calls it. She said nothing can stress her out anymore, because she's too happy about their baby."

"She's right. Although I could do without having to pee every few minutes. I swear this baby's only as big as a penny and it's already affecting me that way. Can you excuse me for a sec?" Sally went to use the bathroom, and when she came out, the house was too quiet.

She walked out of her room and found Rusty standing in front of the tree. He looked so grown up in the white dress shirt and slacks he'd insisted on wearing. *I'm not a kid anymore, Mom. I can dress up.*

"How's it going, honey?"

Rusty smiled. "I was wondering where you were. We have to go." He put her black wool shawl over her shoulders and offered her his arm.

"Go where?" She held on to his arm as he led her to the door.

"You'll see."

"Rusty..." They went outside and followed the lighted path down toward the barn. "Is that where everyone disappeared to?

The barn?"

Rusty pushed open the barn doors, and Sally clung to his arm, afraid her legs would give out. The big wooden barn had been transformed into a wedding wonderland. White lights and greenery hung beautifully from the rafters. The posts were draped with white silk and bound with more twinkling lights. A red carpet ran down the center, separating two rows of chairs, which were decorated with red and white roses and pink and blue ribbons. At the other end of the red carpet, Gage stood beside his father, looking handsome and so very proud beneath a wedding canopy like the one he'd constructed in Oak Falls, it drew more happy tears. Treat flanked his other side. She'd forgotten Treat was ordained.

Her eyes swept over the room, catching on a table that she hadn't noticed behind Rusty. On it was a five-tiered wedding cake decorated with red roses and imprinted with the pictures they'd taken over the last few weeks—in the gym in Virginia, while they were skiing, in their honeymoon suite. Emotions bubbled up inside her.

"Happy wedding day, Mom. Would it be okay if I gave you away?" Rusty handed her a tissue.

"Yes." She wiped her eyes and tried to regain control of her emotions as the song "A Thousand Years" by Christina Perri rang out and her son led her down the aisle.

Every seat was filled. Danica, Blake, and Chessie sat with Kaylie, Chaz, and their twins. Max held little Dylan on her lap, and her daughter, Adriana, looked beautiful decked out in a pretty pink dress beside her. Tears filled Sally's eyes as they swept over Gage's family, and—*Ohmygosh*. A rush of emotions swamped her as her parents came into focus sitting beside Gage's mother. Her parents' smiles brought a flood of tears she didn't even try to stop.

She had no idea how she made it down the aisle, but when Rusty kissed her cheek like the man he'd become and said, "I love you, Mom. And I'm happy for you," she forced herself to stand tall and blink away her tears.

Gage mouthed the words to the song as Treat said what she was sure was a lovely ceremony, but she couldn't hear past her thundering heart, couldn't see anything but her beautiful husband who was promising her forever. When he slipped the wedding ring on her finger, she realized she didn't have a ring for him.

His father handed her a gold man's ring. "It belonged to Gage's grandfather."

Fresh tears spilled from her eyes. She was trembling as she put the ring on Gage's finger. Then she was in his arms, and his lips were on hers, her happy heart drowning out everything else, as Treat pronounced them man and wife, and their friends and family cheered.

They cried and laughed, and when Gage set her on her feet and said, "I love you, my precious bird, and I will love you until my very last breath," she thanked the heavens above that what happened in Vegas didn't stay in Vegas.

EPILOGUE

IT SEEMED LIKE the whole town of Oak Falls showed up for the opening of the new youth center. It was a beautiful spring morning, and people spilled over from the lawn to the sidewalks. Haylie had hired the rest of the staff, and they were gathered at the front of the crowd. Sin stood tall and protective beside the group. They'd put together a great team, and Gage was excited for what they could do for the community. Sable's band played their own original upbeat country songs on a makeshift stage in the grass, where Brindle and two other girls danced with Justus, Trace, and another beefy guy. Gage's eyes found his beautiful wife as she gathered Danica and Blake's new bundle of joy, Harrison, in her arms. The adorable dark-haired baby was named for Blake's father. Sally's lily-white hair had gotten thicker with her pregnancy, falling loose and sexy over her shoulders. Her eyes caught the morning sunlight as she cradled the baby. Her pretty peach dress gathered just above her baby bump, swishing in the gentle breeze around her legs. Her breasts and cheeks had gotten fuller, and she looked radiant. Her gaze drifted to Gage, and a smile lifted her lips. His pulse amped up, the way it always did when she caught his attention.

She dropped one hand to her round belly and mouthed, *I love you.*

He blew her a kiss, unable to believe it had been less than

two months since they'd returned from their two-week honeymoon in Anguilla, where they'd taken long romantic walks on the white sandy beaches and spent their evenings beneath the stars making plans for their future and falling deeper in love. So many wonderful things had happened lately. Blue and Lizzie's wedding had been beautiful, and they had loved the mosaic tray Sally had made for them. Trish and Boone had won Oscars for the movie they'd starred in together, and now they were going to have a baby of their own. Gage woke up every morning half expecting to find out it was all a dream.

Marilynn Montgomery, Sable and Brindle's mother, came to his side. "I need you to open a youth center every three months. Think you can handle that? I can't believe you got all six of my seven children in one place at the same time. My oldest, Grace, is a playwright in New York City and couldn't be here." She pointed to two girls standing a few feet away. "At least Pepper made it back. That's her over there with her sister Morgyn. Pepper's a scientist, and you know how they are—all work all the time. I need to find a way to get Grace and Pepper back home for good. You don't have a few single brothers hanging out, do you? I miss my girls something awful."

"Sorry. I was the last single Ryder." Although in his heart he hadn't been single for several years. He'd been Sally's from the very start of their friendship.

"Well, that's good, I guess." She motioned toward the handsome man heading toward them with a halo of women surrounding him. All the world knew about Axsel Montgomery, one of the hottest musicians around. "Axsel is our only boy."

"The rock star." Gage wondered if he knew Boone. Somewhere in the back of his mind he wondered if he and Sally had a son, would he be into sports or would he find his own path?

"Yes. Why do these young women think they can turn a gay man straight?" She laughed softly. "Thank you for unknowingly bringing my family together. You've done great things for this community, and you've hired a strong staff. Sinny and Haylie are good people."

Sinny. He'd have to give him a hard time about that one. "Thank you. We can't wait to see how things turn out."

His attention returned to his wife. It never strayed far. She handed Danica the baby and headed his way with a thoughtful expression. It took all of his willpower not to step away from the lovely Mrs. Montgomery and go to his wife. But after she'd come out early with Sable and Brindle and had helped them set up, he didn't want to be rude.

"Is this your first child?" she asked.

Gage's chest swelled with pride. "It's our first, but we have a twenty-year-old boy, my stepson, who cannot wait to meet his baby brother or sister." He and Sally had also talked about trying to have more children relatively quickly. He was thrilled that Rusty seemed to be okay with that, too.

"There's nothing like siblings to bring a family closer together. Speaking of family…"

A pretty brunette walking a golden retriever waved Marilynn over.

"That's my daughter Amber. I'd better go see what trouble they're cooking up for tonight. Best of luck with your baby." Marilynn crossed the grassy lawn, stopping to chat with Sally. She embraced her, touched her belly, then went to join her children.

Sally headed his way with a seductive glimmer in her eyes. Her queasiness had dissipated and was replaced with sexual hunger. *Pregnancy hormones*, she'd told him. *Another reason to have more kids.*

He reached for her, gathering her close. "How's my beautiful bird?"

"Ready to go back to the hotel."

"Tired?"

She pressed a kiss to his lips and whispered, "Not even a little."

Meet the Montgomerys!

Welcome to Oak Falls, Virginia, home to horse farms, midnight rodeos, bookstores, coffee shops, and quaint restaurants where you're greeted like family and treated like treasured guests. Buckle up for a wild ride. Like any Southern girls worth their salt, the sweet-talking, sharp-tongued Montgomery sisters can take men to their knees with one seductive glance or a single sugarcoated sentence.

Please enjoy this sneak peek of the first book in The Montgomerys series, EMBRACING HER HEART

In EMBRACING HER HEART…

Leaving New York City and returning to her hometown to teach a three-week screenplay writing class seems like just the break Grace Montgomery needs. Until her sisters wake her at four thirty in the morning to watch the hottest guys in town train wild horses and she realizes that escaping her sisters' drama-filled lives was a lot easier from hundreds of miles away. To make matters worse, she spots the one man she never wanted to see again—ruggedly handsome Reed Cross.

Reed was one of Michigan's leading historical preservation experts, but on the heels of catching his fiancée in bed with his business partner, his uncle suffers a heart attack. Reed cuts all ties and returns home to Oak Falls to run his uncle's business. A chance encounter with Grace, his first love, brings back memories he's spent years trying to escape.

Grace is bound and determined not to fall under Reed's spell again—and Reed wants more than another taste of the woman he's never forgotten. When a midnight party brings them together, passion ignites and old wounds are opened. Grace sets down the ground rules for the next three weeks. No touching, no kissing, and if she has it her way, no breathing, because every breath he takes steals her ability to think. But Reed has other ideas…

Chapter One

"Ouch!"

Brindle? Grace blinked awake at the sound of whispers in the dark room. It took her a moment to remember she was in her childhood bedroom at her parents' home in Virginia, and not in her Manhattan loft. She narrowed her eyes, trying to decipher which of her five sisters were intent on waking her up at…She shifted her eyes to the clock. *Four thirty in the morning?*

"Shh. You're such a klutz."

Sable. Of course. Who else would think it was okay to wake her up at this hour besides Brindle, her youngest and most rebellious sister, and Sable, the night owl?

"I tripped over a suitcase," Brindle whispered. Something *thunk*ed. "Oh shit!" She tumbled onto the bed in a fit of laughter, bringing Sable down with her—right on top of Grace, who let out an "*Oomph!*" as her cat, Clayton, leapt off the bed and tore out of the room.

"Shh! You'll wake Mom and Dad," Sable whispered.

"What are you doing?" Grace tried to keep a straight face, but her sisters' laughter was contagious. She covered her mouth as laughter bubbled out. The last thing she needed was to be awake at this hour after a grueling twelve-hour workday and a painfully long drive, but her sisters were excited about Grace coming home, and if Grace were honest with herself, despite the mounds of scripts she had to get through during her visit, she was excited to see them, too. She hadn't been home since Christmas, and it was already May.

"Get up." Brindle tugged her up from the bed and felt around on the floor. "We're going out, just like old times." She threw the slacks and blouse Grace had worn home the night before in Grace's face. "Get dressed."

"I'm not going—"

"Shut up and take this off." Sable pulled Grace's silk nighty over her head despite Grace's struggles to stop her. She knew it was a futile effort. What Sable wanted, Sable got. Even though she was a year younger than Grace, she'd always been the pushiest of them all.

Grace reluctantly stepped into her slacks. "Where are we going?" She reached for her hairbrush as Brindle grabbed her hand and tugged her out the bedroom door. "Wait! My shoes!"'

"We'll grab Mom's boots from by the door," Sable said, flanking her other side as they hurried down the stairwell tripping over each other.

"I'm *not* wearing cowgirl boots." Grace had worked hard to shake the country-bumpkin habits that were as deeply ingrained as her love for her sisters. Habits like hair twirling, saying *y'all*, and wearing cutoffs and cowgirl boots, the hallmarks of her youth. She stood on the sprawling front porch with her hands on her hips, staring down at her sisters, who were waiting for her to put on her mother's boots.

"Step into them or I swear I'll make you climb that hill barefoot, and you know that's not fun," Sable said.

"God! You two are royal pains in the ass." Grace shoved her feet in the boots. *They're only boots. They don't erase all of my hard work.* Oak Falls might be where her roots had sprouted, but they'd since spread far and wide, and she was never—*ever*—going to be that small-town girl again. Boots or not.

The moon illuminated the path before them as they crossed the grass toward the familiar hill. Grace groaned. They were taking her to *Hottie Hill. Great.* She wondered why she hadn't tossed them out of her bedroom and locked the door instead of going along with their crazy *like-old-times* plan. Three weeks at home would be both a blessing and a curse. Grace loved her sisters, but she imagined three weeks of Sable playing her guitar until all hours of the night and her other younger sisters popping in and out with their dogs and drama, all while their mother carefully threw out queries about their dating lives and their father tried not to growl at their responses.

Brindle strutted up the steep hill in her cowgirl boots and barely there sundress, expertly avoiding the dips and ruts in the grass, while Grace hurried behind her, trying to keep up.

Sable reached the peak of the hill first and turned on her cowgirl-booted heels, placed her hands on her hips, and grinning like a fool, she whispered, "Hurry up! You'll miss it!"

It was one thing to deal with family drama from afar, when all it took was a quick excuse to get off the phone, but *three weeks*? Grace couldn't even blame her decision on being drunk at the time she'd made the plans, since she had been stone-cold sober when her sister Amber had asked her to help bolster her bookstore's presence by hosting a week-long playwriting course. *You made it, Gracie! You're such an inspiration to everyone here*, Amber had pleaded. *Besides, Brindle is leaving soon for Paris, and it's the last time we'll all be together for months. It'll be like old times*. How could she say no to Amber, the sweetest of them all?

Grace slipped on the hill and caught herself seconds before she face-planted in the grass. "Damn it! This is the last thing I want to be doing right now." She should be sleeping. She had a pile of scripts to read through tomorrow for her next production.

"Shh," Brindle chided as she reached for Grace's hand.

Sable ran down the hill annoyingly fast, holding her black cowgirl hat in place atop her long dark hair with one hand and reached for Grace with the other. "Get up, you big baby."

"I can't believe you dragged my ass out of bed for this. What are we? Twelve?" Grace asked in her own harsh whisper.

"Twelve-year-olds don't sneak out to watch the hottest men in Oak Falls break in horses," Brindle said as they reached the top of the hill.

"Liar. We've been doing it since you were twelve," Sable reminded her.

"I can't believe *they're* still doing this at this ungodly hour." *They* were the Jericho brothers, and they'd been breaking in horses before dawn since they were teens. They claimed it was the only time they had before the heat of the day hit, but Grace thought it had more to do with it feeling more exciting doing it before the break of day.

The Jericho brothers were the hottest guys around Oak Falls. Well, at least since Reed Cross left town after high school graduation. Grace tried to tamp down thoughts of the guy who had taken her virginity and turned her heart inside out. The man she'd turned away in pursuit of her production career—and the person she'd compared every single man to ever since. She refused to let herself go down memory lane. She was living her dream, producing plays in New York City, just as she'd always dreamed, and she wasn't going to let anything dampen that joy.

"I'm exhausted," Grace complained as they reached the peak of the hill overlooking the Jerichos' corral.

"It's not like I haven't seen these guys a million times," she pleaded. "Besides, Brindle, you've slept with Trace more times than you can probably count. Why are we even—"

"Shh!" Brindle and Sable said in unison as they pulled Grace down to her knees.

She followed their gazes to the illuminated corral below where the four Jericho brothers, Trace, Justus, Shane, and Jeb, and a handful of other shirtless, jeans-clad guys were milling about. They were always shirtless, because what men weren't when they were proving they were the manliest of the group?

"Trace and I are over," Brindle whispered. "For real this time." Brindle and Trace had had an on-again-off-again relationship forever. They were a hopeless case of rebellious guy and rebellious girl, up for anything risky. Two people who didn't have a chance in hell of ever settling down but seemed to fill a need in each other's lives—or at least in their beds.

Grace and her sisters had spent many hours as teenagers lying on this same hill when they should have been sleeping, watching the Jericho brothers and other local guys break wild horses or rope cattle. Their sister Amber had come with them only twice, because they'd forced her to. As the most reserved of the sisters, Amber had been more embarrassed than turned on by the shirtless cock-and-bull show, and the girls had stopped dragging her along. Grace wished Sable and Brindle had let her sleep this morning. Maybe she should start acting shy.

She laughed to herself. Shy? Right. She'd blazed a path in a man's world, in New York City. There was no room for *shy* in her repertoire. And there was no room for this nonsense anymore, either. She pushed up onto her knees. "Brindle, maybe at twenty-four this is still fun, but I'm twenty-nine. I'm so far past this it's not even funny."

"God, Grace! You've turned into a workaholic ice queen,"

Sable whispered as she yanked Grace back down to her stomach. "And I, your very loving sister, who feels the need to keep you young, aim to fix that. Starting *now.*"

Grace rolled her eyes. "Ice queen? Just because I've grown up and don't find this type of thing fun anymore?" As she said the words the men below walked out of the corral.

"*Ice queen* because you think you're too good for—" Sable swallowed her words as Trace and Justus pushed open the enormous wooden barn doors and a wild horse blasted into the corral with a shirtless man on its back.

Their eyes snapped to the show below. They'd seen the Jericho brothers break horses for years, but it wasn't a Jericho on the back of this horse for its first ride.

"Damn," Brindle said in a husky voice.

"Holy shit, that's hot. See, Gracie? Totally worth it."

Grace squinted into the night, feeling a tug of familiarity in the arch of the rider's shoulders as the horse bucked him forward and back, his thick arms holding tightly to the reins. His longish, thick dark hair and the square set of his chin sent a shudder of recognition through her.

Sable sucked in a breath. "Ouch! You're digging your nails into me." She pried Grace's fingers off her forearm.

"Is that…?" Grace choked on the anger and arousal warring inside her. She'd recognize him anywhere, even after all these years of seeing him only in her dreams. She wanted to run down the hill and fall into Reed's arms. To feel his hard chest, smell his masculine scent, and hear his gruff voice telling her he wanted her again—and she wanted to pummel him in equal measure. She'd tried to forget him, and she really, truly thought she had. She hated herself for the instant attraction she couldn't deny.

She pushed to her feet, unable to make sense of seeing Reed

Cross in Oak Falls, with the guys who once hated the sight of him. The forbidden lover she'd risked everything to have—and then cast aside. What the hell was he doing here? The last she'd heard, he'd moved to somewhere in the Midwest after high school. Not that she'd asked after him over the years.

"Reed..." His name rolled off her tongue too easily, making her even angrier at herself. She stumbled backward as her sisters rose beside her, reaching for her. Grace took off running the way they'd come, chased by memories she wanted to escape.

"Gracie, wait!" Sable shouted after her.

With the familiar scents of the hills and livestock, and her sisters' hushed whispers filling her senses, she couldn't stop memories of Reed from flooding her mind and heating her blood.

"You didn't think to warn me?" Grace spun on her heels, tears of anger and hurt burning her eyes.

"I knew you wouldn't come," Sable said.

"Damn right I wouldn't." She started down the hill again.

"Wait, Grace." Brindle grabbed her hand and tried to slow her down, but Grace kept going, dragging her sister with her. "*What* is going on? Why are you so mad?"

Grace slowed, realizing in that moment that Sable had kept her secret for all those years. That was something she hadn't expected. Then again, she hadn't expected to have a visceral, titillating reaction to seeing Reed again, either. Hell, she hadn't expected to ever see him again. Period.

They'd been careful never to be seen together, and of course she'd never seen him anywhere near the Jericho brothers unless it was on the football field. Small-town rivalries weren't taken lightly back then, but she'd snuck over to Meadowside with Sable late one evening when Reed had told her he'd be roping cattle with a group of friends. The men's deep voices carried in the night air, bringing with them memories of Reed's young, muscular body and the fierce determination in his dark eyes as he'd swung the lasso over his head and expertly roped cattle while his buddies had whooped and hollered.

"I thought you were over him," Sable accused.

"I am," Grace huffed. She reached up and touched her lips, remembering the taste of their stolen sensual kisses—spearmint and teenage lust mixed into one delicious kiss after another. Kisses that had never failed to leave her lips tingling and her body thrumming with desire.

Now she couldn't stop thinking of him. This was bad. Very, very bad. She never should have allowed her sisters to drag her out here and unearth memories she'd rather forget.

"Over *who*?" Brindle demanded. Her eyes darted between Sable and Grace.

"Then what's the problem?" Sable snapped, ignoring Brindle, which was good, because Grace didn't need to explain her decade-old secret to her youngest sister—*or to think about it again, damn it.*

Sable grabbed Grace's arm, stopping her in her tracks.

Grace's heart slammed against her chest as they stared each other down. She'd thought she was over Reed Cross. She *was* over him. Sable knew how hard it had been for her to break up with Reed all those years ago. The last thing she needed was to have him waved in front of her face again. She'd put him out of her mind.

Mostly.

Sure, it was Reed's face she conjured up on lonely nights. It was his lopsided grin and easy laugh she recalled to pull her through the toughest of productions. But that was *her* secret. Grace hadn't ever needed anything from anyone in life. And she'd never *needed* anything from Reed. And he'd hated that. Fought her on it even. When he'd wanted to come clean, to tell the world about them, all she'd wanted was to follow her dreams and produce plays in New York City. She didn't want to fight with her friends about dating a guy from a rival town when she'd be leaving for college soon. But even after all these years his words haunted her. *I'm not going to be your dirty little secret.*

She should have stuck to weekend visits home, as she had for the past several years. Weekend visits were safe. Fast. Brindle never would have dragged her out if she'd be facing a long drive home in twenty-four hours. Tomorrow she'd tell her parents she had to go home after the weekend. She couldn't do this. Especially now that she knew Reed Cross was back in town. She still felt the sting of his betrayal after they'd broken up, when he'd left town—and her—behind.

Brindle threw her arms up toward the sky. "Will someone *please* tell me what the problem is? Why are you storming off? And why are you mad at Sable? It was *me* who wanted to come out and see Trace tonight. Not her! I thought it would be fun, like old times. We'd laugh and joke and talk about how sexy he was."

"Grace." Sable's tone softened, her eyes imploring her for forgiveness Grace couldn't give.

"There's no problem, Brin," Grace managed, holding Sable's gaze. "I just..." *I'm confused and angry by my stupid body's reaction to a man I don't need in my life.* "I need to sleep. I have a lot on my mind and I'm exhausted."

To continue reading, please buy

EMBRACING HER LOVE

Fall in love with Blake and Danica

Please enjoy this introduction to Blake and Danica's love story, SISTERS IN LOVE, the very first book in the Love in Bloom big-family romance collection—and the story that started the Love in Bloom sensation, which has been enjoyed by more than 3 million readers.

Chapter One

THE LINE IN the café went all the way to the door. Danica Snow wished she hadn't taken her sister Kaylie's phone call before getting her morning coffee. Living in an overcrowded tourist town could be a major inconvenience, but Danica loved that she could walk from her condo to her office, see a movie, have dinner, or even stop at a bookstore without ever sitting in a car. Every minute counted when you lived in Allure, Colorado, host to an odd mix of hippie and yuppie tourists in equal numbers. The ski slopes brought them in the winter, while art shows drew them in the summer. There was never a break. Every suit and Rasta child in town was standing right in front of her, waiting for their coffee or latte, and the guy ahead of her had shoulders so wide she couldn't easily see around him. Danica tapped the toe of her efficient and comfortable Nine West heels, growing more impatient by the second.

What on earth was taking so long? In seven minutes they'd served only one person. The tables were pushed so close to the people standing in line that she couldn't step to the side to see. She was gridlocked. Danica leaned to the right and peered around the massive shoulder ahead of her just as the owner of that shoulder turned to look out the door. *Whack!* He elbowed her right in the nose, knocking Danica's head back.

Her hand flew to her bloody nose. "Ow! Geez!" She ducked

in pain, covering her face and talking through her hands. "I think you broke my nose." Each word sent pain across her nose and below her eyes.

"I'm so sorry. Let me get you a napkin," a deep, worried voice said.

Two patrons rushed over and shoved napkins in her direction.

"Are you okay?" an older woman asked.

Tears sprang from the corners of Danica's closed eyes. *Damn it.* Her entire day would now run late and she probably looked like a red-nosed, crying idiot. "This hurts so bad. Weren't you looking where—" Danica flipped her unruly, brown hair from her face and opened her eyes. Her venom-filled glare locked on the man who had elbowed her—the most beautiful specimen of a human being she had ever seen. *Oh shit.* "I'm…What…?" *Come on, girl. Get it together. He's probably an egomaniac.*

"I'm so sorry." His voice was rich and smooth, laden with concern.

A thin blonde grabbed his arm and shoved a napkin into his hand. "Give this to her," she said, blinking her eyelashes in a come-hither way.

The man held the woman's hand a beat too long. "Thanks," he said. His eyes trailed down the blonde's blouse.

Really? I'm bleeding over here.

He turned toward Danica and handed her the napkin. His eyes were green and yellow, like field grass. His eyebrows drew together in a serious gaze, and Danica thought that maybe she'd been too quick to judge—until he stole a glance at the blonde as she walked out of the café.

Asshole. She felt the heat of anger spread up her chest and neck, along her cheeks, to the ridge of her high cheekbones. She snagged the napkin from his hand and wiped her throbbing nose. "It's okay. I'm fine," she lied. She could smell the minty freshness of his breath, and she wondered what it might taste like. Danica was not one to swoon—that was Kaylie's job. *Get a grip.*

"Can I at least buy you a coffee?" He ran his hand through his thick, dark hair.

Yes! "No, thank you. It's okay." She had been a therapist long enough to know what kind of guy eyes another girl while she was tending to a bloody nose that he had caused. Danica fumbled for her purse, which she'd dropped when she was hit. She lowered her eyes to avoid looking into his. "I'm fine, really. Just look behind you next time." Not for the first time, Danica wished she had Kaylie's flirting skills and her ability to look past his wandering eyes. She would have had him buying her coffee, a Danish, and breakfast the next morning.

Danica was so confused, she wasn't even sure what she wanted. She chanced another glance up at him. He was looking at her features so intently that she felt as though he were drinking her in, memorizing her. His eyes trailed slowly from hers, lowered to her nose, to her lips, and then settled on the beauty mark that she'd been self-conscious of her entire life. She felt like a Cindy Crawford wannabe. Danica pursed her lips. "Are you done?" she asked.

He blinked with the innocence of a young boy, clueless to her annoyance, which was in stark contrast to his confident, manly presence. He stood almost a foot taller than Danica's impressive five foot seven stature. His chest muscles bulged beneath his way-too-small shirt, dark curls poking through the neckline. *He probably bought it that way on purpose.* She glanced down and tried not to notice his muscular thighs straining against his stonewashed denim jeans. Danica swallowed hard. All the air suddenly left her lungs. He was touching her shoulder, squinting, evaluating her face.

"I'm sorry. I was just making sure it didn't look broken, which it doesn't. I'm sure it's painful."

She couldn't think past the heat of his hand, the breadth of it engulfing her shoulder. "It's okay," she managed, hating herself for being lost in his touch when he was clearly someone who ate women for breakfast. She checked her watch. She had three minutes to get her coffee and get back to her office before her next client showed up. *Belinda. She'd love this guy.*

The line progressed, and Adonis waved as he left the café. Danica reached into her purse to pay for her French vanilla coffee and found herself taking a last glance at him as he passed the front window.

The young barista pushed Danica's money away. "No need, hon. Blake paid for yours." She smiled, lifting her eyebrows.

"He did?" *Blake.*

"Yeah, he's really sweet." The barista leaned over the cash register. "Even if he is a player."

Aha! I knew it. Danica thrust her shoulders back, feeling smart for resisting temptation.

MORE BOOKS BY MELISSA

LOVE IN BLOOM SERIES

SNOW SISTERS

Sisters in Love

Sisters in Bloom

Sisters in White

THE BRADENS at Weston

Lovers at Heart

Destined for Love

Friendship on Fire

Sea of Love

Bursting with Love

Hearts at Play

THE BRADENS at Trusty

Taken by Love

Fated for Love

Romancing My Love

Flirting with Love

Dreaming of Love

Crashing into Love

THE BRADENS at Peaceful Harbor

Healed by Love

Surrender My Love

River of Love

Crushing on Love

Whisper of Love

Thrill of Love

THE BRADEN NOVELLAS

Promise My Love

Our New Love

Daring Her Love
Story of Love

THE REMINGTONS
Game of Love
Stroke of Love
Flames of Love
Slope of Love
Read, Write, Love
Touched by Love

SEASIDE SUMMERS
Seaside Dreams
Seaside Hearts
Seaside Sunsets
Seaside Secrets
Seaside Nights
Seaside Embrace
Seaside Lovers
Seaside Whispers

BAYSIDE SUMMERS
Bayside Desires
Bayside Passions

THE RYDERS
Seized by Love
Claimed by Love
Chased by Love
Rescued by Love

SEXY STANDALONE ROMANCE
Tru Blue
Truly, Madly, Whiskey

THE MONTGOMERYS

Embracing Her Heart
Our Wicked Hearts
Wild, Crazy, Heart
Sweet, Sexy, Heart

BILLIONAIRES AFTER DARK SERIES

WILD BOYS AFTER DARK

Logan
Heath
Jackson
Cooper

BAD BOYS AFTER DARK

Mick
Dylan
Carson
Brett

HARBORSIDE NIGHTS SERIES

Includes characters from the Love in Bloom series

Catching Cassidy
Discovering Delilah
Tempting Tristan

More Books by Melissa

Chasing Amanda (mystery/suspense)
Come Back to Me (mystery/suspense)
Have No Shame (historical fiction/romance)
Love, Lies & Mystery (3-book bundle)
Megan's Way (literary fiction)
Traces of Kara (psychological thriller)
Where Petals Fall (suspense)

Acknowledgments

I have waited years to write Gage and Sally's love story. Sally had such an emotional ride in Sisters in Love, and Gage has always been there for her. It was a joy to finally give them their happily ever after. As with all Love in Bloom couples, Gage and Sally's story is not over. You'll see updates in future Love in Bloom novels. Visit my website for a complete list of Love in Bloom subseries.
www.MelissaFoster.com/LIB

I'd like to thank you, my loyal readers, for taking the Love in Bloom big-family romance collection into your hearts. It brings me so much happiness to continue writing stories about the characters we've enjoyed—our extended "family"—and to know how eager you are for each upcoming story. Please continue to send me emails and private messages on Facebook. I love hearing from you. And if you haven't joined my fan club yet, please do! I share my writing process, sneak peeks, and more.
facebook.com/groups/MelissaFosterFans

The best way to stay abreast of Love in Bloom releases (and receive a free short story) is to sign up for my monthly newsletter.
www.MelissaFoster.com/Newsletter

Follow me on Facebook for fun chats and giveaways. I always try to keep fans abreast of what's going on in our fictional boyfriends' worlds.
facebook.com/MelissaFosterAuthor

Thank you to my awesome editorial team: Kristen Weber and Penina Lopez, and my meticulous proofreaders: Juliette Hill, Marlene Engel, Lynn Mullan, Elaini Caruso, and Justinn Harrison. And last but never least, a huge thank-you to my family for their patience, support, and inspiration.

MEET MELISSA

www.MelissaFoster.com

Melissa Foster is a *New York Times* and *USA Today* bestselling and award-winning author. Her books have been recommended by *USA Today's* book blog, *Hagerstown* magazine, *The Patriot*, and several other print venues. Melissa has painted and donated several murals to the Hospital for Sick Children in Washington, DC.

Visit Melissa on her website or chat with her on social media. Melissa enjoys discussing her books with book clubs and reader groups and welcomes an invitation to your event.

Melissa's books are available through most online retailers in paperback and digital formats.

CPSIA information can be obtained
at www.ICGtesting.com
Printed in the USA
LVOW03s2119080218
565821LV00001B/166/P